Praise fo   **g author**

"An entertaining read."
—*Publishers Weekly*

* * *

"A wonderful, thoughtful book full of vivid characters
and a place—Inside—that is by turns alien,
and heartbreakingly familiar."
—Rachel Caine, *New York Times* bestselling author of
The Morganville Vampires series

* * *

"Snyder has constructed a work that I see as
the beginning to a new and fantastic series."
—*yaReads.com*

* * *

"The world Snyder invented is fun to discover....
I enjoyed reading the book thoroughly."
—*Book Love Affair*

* * *

"Trella and her world in *Inside Out* make for an entertaining,
fast-paced read."
—*The Book Smugglers*

Also by *New York Times* bestselling author Maria V. Snyder

from
Harlequin Teen

Inside series

INSIDE OUT

from
MIRA BOOKS

Study series

POISON STUDY
MAGIC STUDY
FIRE STUDY

Glass series

STORM GLASS
SEA GLASS
SPY GLASS

MARIA V. SNYDER

OUTSIDE IN

HARLEQUIN® TEEN

HARLEQUIN®
TEEN

ISBN-13: 978-0-373-21011-4

OUTSIDE IN

Copyright © 2011 by Maria V. Snyder

Recycling programs for this product may not exist in your area.

This is a work of fiction. Names, characters, places and incidents are either the product of the author's imagination or are used fictitiously, and any resemblance to actual persons, living or dead, business establishments, events or locales is entirely coincidental.

This edition published by arrangement with Harlequin Books S.A.

For questions and comments about the quality of this book please contact us at Customer_eCare@Harlequin.ca.

® and TM are trademarks of the publisher. Trademarks indicated with ® are registered in the United States Patent and Trademark Office, the Canadian Trade Marks Office and in other countries.

www.HarlequinTEEN.com

Printed in U.S.A.

To Mary-Theresa Hussey,
for her editorial excellence and extreme patience.
Thanks for the help, encouragement and smiley faces!

INTRODUCTION

MY WORLD CHANGED IN A HEARTBEAT. THAT'S HOW it felt to me. As if one second ago, I was Trella the lower level scrub, cleaning the air and water ducts of Inside, and now I am Trella the victorious leader of the Force of Sheep rebellion. Yes the name sounds ridiculous, and I still can't believe we named a major life changing event after livestock—or actually a stuffed animal—but it made sense at the time.

Why? Because I once thought my fellow scrubs were sheep, passive and content with the status quo. I was wrong and learned if you put enough sheep together you have a herd—a force to be reckoned with. A force that turned our world upside down and inside out.

Of course, it really didn't change in a second. It took six weeks, which in Inside time is six hundred hours (one hundred hours per week). But if I compared it to how long we've been living here in Inside—147,019 weeks—it's a mere four thousandths of a percent. And here's the kicker, we have another 852,981 weeks to go before we reach our destination. Mind-boggling!

Where are we going? Good question. According to Logan, our computer expert, our metal cube-shaped world is traveling through Outer Space. And since Outer Space is incredibly huge, it will take us a total of a million weeks to get to a planet where we can go Outside and live. We're not sure what exactly Outside is since many of Inside's computer records have been deleted.

According to our remaining records, another so-called "rebellion" happened around week 132,076 when Admiral Trava reported saboteurs had tried to destroy the computer systems with magnets, erasing all the historical files. But Logan says it's bogus and he suspects the Trava family deleted those files so they could rule the people of Inside.

Before that first rebellion, Inside was ruled by a Committee comprised of all the nine families, but the Trava family didn't want to share. Since they were in charge of security, they had the weapons and they took control. Each family had been responsible for the different systems that keep us all alive. Air, water, hydroponics, shepherds, recycling, the infirmary, the power plant, and the kitchen. Yeah that's a lot, but when you're living in a big metal cube in the middle of Outer Space, you need every one.

The Travas separated the people into uppers and lowers (a.k.a. scrubs), and kept us confined to our levels (uppers on levels three & four, scrubs on levels one & two). They sowed the seeds of distrust and created the Population Control Police (a.k.a. Pop Cops) to make sure we all followed the rules. Their propaganda worked. The scrubs, including me, thought the uppers were living in big apartments with big families and cushy jobs, while we lived in overcrowded barracks with no privacy and were forced to clean and maintain the systems (after all, rust and dust are the twin evils of Inside).

It worked. The scrubs hated the uppers and the uppers hated us.

Now back to our rebellion. It started with an upper named

Domotor. His first attempt at overthrowing the Travas failed, but he discovered the location of Gateway—the mythical Gateway to Outside—and saved the info on disks.

This is where I come in. Domotor hid his disks in an air duct above his rooms on level three. Later, Domotor recruited me to retrieve his disks and I did. This one event set off a whole heap of trouble for me. And my best and only friend Cog was arrested for covering for me.

Now I'm not going to detail everything that happened. If you want to know all about it, you can go to your computer and read through this file: ISBN-978-0-373-21006-0.

But I will summarize. I discovered the uppers didn't have it any better than scrubs, and I met one I really liked named Riley. He helped me, along with Logan and a few others, to find Gateway. Unfortunately when Cog and I opened it, we learned Outside was really Outer Space, a big black freezing nothing that sucked my friend out. Cog's very last act was saving my life.

So much for freedom in Outside. But the others didn't let the disappointment stop them. Riley, Logan and a few uppers—the rest of the Force of Sheep—still wanted to re-store power to all the families. And we did. The Travas were arrested and a temporary Committee was formed.

Even with this new Committee, I knew it wasn't going to be easy to change our ways. And with four levels, Inside was still too small for our population.

I had a hard time sitting through meetings, so I escaped to explore the ducts every so often. Without having to worry about the Pop Cops, I could really search places I had only briefly passed.

And guess what? I discovered that Inside wasn't just four levels high. There was a vast space above level four. Plenty of room for many more levels. We could spread out!

After this breakthrough, I thought Inside was done with trouble.

Too bad, I thought wrong.

MY FINGERS ACHED AS MY LEG MUSCLES TREMBLED.
Beads of sweat snaked down the skin on my back, leaving an itchy trail. I clung to the almost sheer metal wall and breathed in deep. When my heart slowed to a more normal rhythm, I relaxed my right hand's grip and stretched for the next hand hold—a short piece of pipe. Then I repeated the motion with my left, climbing another meter higher.

Far below, spots of daylight illuminated the half completed construction on level ten. Distant voices floated on the stale dusty air. I had passed the last of the bluelights. Nothing but blackness remained above me.

I cocked my head, sweeping the flashlight's beam across the wall in search of another pipe to grab. Logan had designed a special helmet equipped with a light to keep my hands free.

"Trella?" Riley's voice startled me.

I lost my grip. Falling, I cursed my own stupidity for not switching my earring/receiver off.

"I know you can hear me," he said with an annoyed tone. "Where are you?"

Getting one hell of a rope burn, I grabbed my safety line

and squeezed to slow my fall. After what felt like a thousand weeks, I reached the end of the rope and jerked hard, biting my tongue. I swung, tasting blood and lamenting the slip. That had been the highest point I or anyone else had attained. Ever.

Riley grunted in frustration. "Trella, you can go exploring later. You're late for the Committee meeting. They're waiting for you."

He wasn't the only one frustrated. For the last twelve weeks, I'd been promised time to go exploring the Expanse. All my previous forays had lasted about an hour before I'd been summoned to another important meeting. This time, I had been determined to ignore everyone, only to forget about the receiver.

I had hoped to reach the ceiling of the Expanse, but the effort needed to re-scale the wall would be too much for my tired muscles. Resigning myself to yet another delay, I stopped my swing by dragging my hand along the wall.

The construction workers wanted to build a ladder up the side of the Expanse, install daylights and find the ceiling. But the Committee insisted they first finish the six new levels for the citizens of Inside to spread out. I agreed, yet my curiosity would not be satisfied until I knew the height of the Expanse.

Pressing the top button on my shirt, I said to Riley, "Tell the Committee I'll be there in an hour. They can start without me. They don't need me there to quibble over every minor detail."

"You're right," Riley said. "They need you when they quibble over the insignificant details, the worthless details and the waste-of-everyone's time details."

While understandable, his sarcasm was too harsh for someone as even-tempered as Riley. "What happened?"

"I can't get a work crew to fix the faulty wiring in level five. It's a mess, but they're too busy with level six. We've lived in those four levels for the last one hundred and forty-seven thousand plus weeks, it won't kill us to wait a few more."

Overcrowding in the bottom two levels had been insufferable, but now that the uppers and lowers were united, there should be more room. Except the uppers wouldn't consider any plans for the scrubs to move into their levels. They insisted it would be a wasted effort since the new levels would be ready soon.

"I'll see what I can do," I said. I transferred my weight back onto the wall and unclipped the rope from my safety harness. Climbing down two meters to the roof of level ten, I glanced up. Next time, I would need a longer rope.

By then, level six would probably be finished. I walked over to the access stairs. It was so nice not to squeeze between levels. But before I reached them, the construction foreman called my name.

I waited for him to join me and smiled in recognition of the burly man. "Hi Hank, how's it going?"

"Lousy," Hank said. He had buzzed his gray hair to a stubble on his head. Holding a wipe board in one hand, he tapped the board with a marker. "I've a list of repairs for levels one to four, but no one will do them. And I'm losing construction people every hour."

"Losing how?"

"They take a break and never come back." My alarm must have shown on my face, because Hank rushed to assure me. "It's not like that. They're angry the uppers aren't doing any of the work. My crews are being difficult, showing up late, leaving early or not coming at all."

A passive resistance. Wonderful. "Why won't anyone fix the repairs?"

"Same reason. The uppers aren't doing their share."

I suppressed a sigh. The Pop Cops had threatened the uppers with exile in the lower levels in order to scare them into cooperating. They had thought life below would be nothing but hard physical labor. Since they had run all the systems in Inside, their jobs involved sitting in front of a computer, and telling the scrubs what to do. Changing their perception of the scrubs was still ongoing, and I believed would be one of the hardest tasks. But not impossible.

"Okay, Hank. I'll tell the Committee."

He looked doubtful. "That Committee can only agree on one thing."

"What's that?"

"To disagree."

I laughed, but Hank didn't. "Oh, come on. It's not that bad. We don't have Pop Cops anymore."

"Maybe we should."

Hank's words followed me as I descended to level three. He had to be joking. No one…well, no scrub—and Hank had been one for maintenance—would ever wish for the return of the Pop Cops. I dismissed his comment as being melodramatic and hurried to my room.

Since it had only been twelve weeks since the rebellion, I still slept in the extra room in the infirmary in Sector B3. It had been designated for the Doctor's intern, but, so far, no one could handle the job. I wouldn't mind—a place of my own was a luxury I've never had—except I shared the suite's washroom and kitchen with Doctor Lamont. Also known as Kiana Garrard. Or as I liked to call her, the Traitor.

Unfortunately, I remained in the minority. The Committee

had reviewed her actions during the rebellion. They decided she had been duped by Lieutenant Commander Karla Trava and her betrayal had minor consequences. Of course, the two infirmaries full of wounded from the revolt had nothing to do with their ruling. And the limited number of doctors hadn't been a consideration, either. Yeah, right and I was Queen of Inside.

The Traitor tended to a few patients in the main room of the infirmary. Which consisted of two rows of beds lined up along each side. Curtains hung from U-shaped tracks in the ceiling for privacy and a narrow path cut through the middle. A high counter full of medical supplies covered half the back wall. Next to the counter was another door that led to the Traitor's office, the exam room and the surgery. Beyond them was the apartment.

Without looking at her, I hurried past the beds, aiming for the far door.

"Trella," she called.

I paused, but kept my back to her.

"I have a surgery scheduled for hour sixty. I'll need your assistance."

"What happened to Catie?"

"She passed out when one of the construction crew came in with a bloody gash on his forehead that exposed the bone."

Closing my eyes, I suppressed the accusation that she purposely tried to gross out the people I found to help her. Yet another item for my long to-do list—find the Traitor an intern. "I'm busy. You'll have to find someone else to help." I glanced at the clock. Hour fifty-five.

"I can't train them in five hours, Trella. You have experience and an iron stomach. Plus…"

I waited.

In a softer voice she said, "Plus you're good. You have a

natural talent that shouldn't be wasted. You must have inherited that from me."

Whirling around, I confronted her. "Now you decide Karla wasn't lying. Does thinking I'm your daughter help you with the guilt over betraying us? Am I supposed to feel special that you risked all we had worked for and *died* for because of motherly love?"

She stepped back in surprise, clutching a tray to her chest as if it were a shield. Her long hair—the same color as mine—had been braided into a single plait that hung to her waist.

I hadn't meant to be so nasty, but since the rebellion, she had never once acknowledged the possibility of our relationship, insisting it had been another one of Karla's twisted tricks. I agreed. Riley, though, had speculated that if she believed I was her offspring, then the enormity of what she had done would have overwhelmed her. He had tried to explain it, to help me see it from her point of view.

But a traitor was a traitor in my mind. No need to waste time justifying her actions. I had enough to do.

Despite my personal feelings, we did need her doctoring skills. "What about Doctor Sanchia?"

"Busy with his own patients and the scrub...the caretakers in the lower levels..." She hesitated.

A ripple of unease lapped against my stomach. "They refused?"

She met my gaze. "Not in so many words. They just won't answer my requests, and when I go down there, they ignore me or give me the runaround until I give up and leave."

Dark circles, new wrinkles and streaks of white hair aged her. She appeared older—closer to fifty centiweeks than forty.

"How critical is the surgery at hour sixty? Can it be delayed?" I asked.

"It's Emek's appendix. If I don't remove it soon, it will burst and kill him."

"All right, I'll help you. For *Emek's* sake." I headed to my room. My thoughts returned to the Committee. They would need to investigate why the lower care workers were ignoring requests for help.

My palms stung as I washed up. I had forgotten about the rope burns. Grabbing a tube of antiseptic, I rubbed it on the abrasions. Abrasions? I needed to find another place to sleep before I started spouting medical lingo like a pro.

Riley's father had offered to move from their apartment, but it was too soon for us to go that next step. Since the rebellion, Riley and I had little to no time to get to know each other better. I touched my silver sheep pendant—a gift from Riley. Perhaps I could live in our storeroom and spend more alone time with Riley. Only a few members of the Force of Sheep knew of its existence. Which made staying there even more appealing.

The Committee met in the large conference room next to Inside's main Control Room, both within Quadrant G4. I had argued for the new levels to be built in a different configuration than the existing levels without success.

With so many changes happening so fast, the Committee thought a new design would just confuse everyone. So level five resembled levels one through four—a three by three grid, like a Tic Tac Toe board. The four corners were labeled Quadrants and the middle sections were Sectors. Starting from the top row on the left, the first Quadrant was A, then Sector B and Quadrant C. The middle was Sectors D, E and F and the last row had Quadrant G, Sector H and Quadrant I. Just add the level number and any idiot could find a location.

I arrived at the meeting two hours late. Slipping into an empty seat beside Jacy, I glanced around the long oval table. The Committee had been comprised of one representative from each of the nine upper families and one leader from each scrub area like hydroponics and waste-water. Eighteen in all. Since an even number could cause problems when members voted, a nineteenth spokesperson had been added.

Despite repeated requests that I become the nineteenth member, I refused, preferring to be a part of the Committee as a consultant only. Less responsibility. Riley had been asked next, but he'd quipped that the Committee didn't need both him and his father and he'd claimed that he would be more useful as support personnel.

They finally elected Jacy.

After my initial surprise at his appointment, and, when I thought it through, it made sense. He had taken over the organization and leadership of the rebellion when I had been captured by the Pop Cops. Plus he was well connected through his network of people in the lower levels.

I leaned close to him. "What did I miss?"

"They're trying to decide which group can move into level five."

"Group?" That was new.

"Once all six new levels are completed, the Committee thinks the nine families can share five levels and the scrubs, broken into groups by areas, can live in the other five."

"That won't work."

"I know and you know, but try and explain it to those eighteen." He swept his hand out. "They're still thinking in terms of uppers and lowers."

Which reminded me. "Are you aware of the labor strike?"

Jacy stared at me with a guarded expression. "Yep."

"How do we get the workers back?"

"By having the uppers get their hands dirty for once."

And Jacy just proved he also thought in terms of uppers and lowers. If I was being honest, I did as well. That was the problem. But I couldn't figure out a solution.

Why should I? I'd done my part and found Gateway, led the rebellion and discovered the Expanse. The multiple scars on my arms, legs and torso from Pop Cop Commander Vinco's knife proved I had sacrificed for the citizens of Inside.

I had also lost my closest friend, Cogon. He had acted more like a brother, and I missed him so much my insides felt rusted and brittle. Cog would have loved organizing the construction crews. He'd have insisted on perfection before moving on to another level.

Slouching in my chair, I let the Committee's voices roll over me. They didn't need me. The Committee would take us to the next stage.

After listening to the sixth scrub area representative list the reasons they should be the first to move into level five, I willed the clock to move faster. These meetings were a waste of my time. I could be spending these hours with Riley. The session went on and on. Assisting the Traitor with surgery grew more appealing with each minute. I lasted until hour fifty-nine.

"I'm outta here. I'm helping the…Doctor Lamont," I whispered to Jacy.

"Will you be back before the vote?" he asked.

"Why? Nothing I say changes their minds." Frustration and weariness welled, but I swallowed them down.

"You've given up, Trell. That's not like you."

"Sitting in endless meetings for twelve weeks isn't like me either. I'm a big picture girl." I tried a smile, but Jacy kept his frown. I made a sudden liberating decision. "Tell the Committee I'm resigning as a consultant and going back to what I do best."

Shock, anger and censure warred on Jacy's face. His lips moved for a moment before he spoke. "And what do you do best?"

"Explore. We have no idea how high up the Expanse's ceiling is. What if I find another hatch at the top? There could be another Expanse filled with supplies. That's just as important as arguing over who gets to move into the new levels first."

I left before he could respond. For the first time since the rebellion, I strode through the bland white corridors of Inside feeling light as air. I couldn't wait to tell Riley!

My good mood dissipated once I arrived at the infirmary and spotted Emek's colorless face. Grimacing with pain, he clutched his sheets in tight fists. He wouldn't respond to my questions. His skin felt cold and clammy. The Traitor wasn't in the main room so I raced to the back.

She prepped for surgery. "You're early."

"Emek looks bad. When's the last time you checked on him?"

Pushing by me, she ran to him. I caught up to her as she probed the skin below Emek's waist with her fingers. He screamed.

"His appendix has burst." She kicked off the brakes on the bed. "Move!"

I helped her roll him into surgery and we transferred him to the operating table. Then she issued rapid-fire orders. The experience, which usually passed by in a blur of blood and frantic activity, slowed this time. Even with the emergency, I anticipated her needs a few times and handed her instruments without being asked. Despite my resistance, I was learning.

As she worked to save Emek's life, I no longer viewed her

as the Traitor, but as Doctor Lamont. According to Doctor Sanchia, Lamont was the best diagnostician in our world and a skilled surgeon as well. More reasons she was here and not locked in the crowded holding cells with the Travas.

After sewing up Emek's incision, Lamont told me to dress the wound as she adjusted the anesthesia. It didn't take us long to finish. I wheeled him into the recovery room, which also served as the examination room.

Once the new levels were completed, the infirmaries on levels two and three would be combined into one large medical facility, spanning two grids. This had been an easy decision for the Committee. A shame they all weren't.

Keeping an eye on his vital signs, I stayed with Emek until he stabilized. When he roused, we moved him to a regular bed in the main room. I ensured he was comfortable, helped him sip a glass of ginger water, then tucked him under a blanket as he drifted off to sleep.

I turned and met Lamont's measuring gaze. She had watched me, but instead of commenting on my nurturing instincts, she checked Emek, nodded and returned to the operating room to clean up. Knowing the importance of a sterile area, I helped. We worked in silence, but the tension between us wasn't quite as thick. When the surfaces gleamed and the place smelled of antiseptic, I tossed the dirty rags into a special medical bag and sent it down the laundry chute.

"You did well," she said. "Thank you."

I grunted a reply, heading to my room. The rush from the emergency surgery fizzled and exhaustion soaked into my bones.

"There's a package on your bed from Logan," Lamont said as I pushed open the door.

Good thing she had mentioned Logan's name. Because if I hadn't known he brought it here, I would have assumed it was from Lamont. Then I would have carried it to Lamont's office and smashed the thing to little pieces. Instead, I set the vampire box on the table. The device had been used by the Pop Cops to test the scrubs for illegal drugs and pregnancy by taking blood samples. It could also settle the issue of my birth mother, determining if Lamont was indeed my parent. It had been Logan's idea to use the box.

I stretched out on the bed. Staring at the ceiling, I wondered why Logan sent it now. He knew I had no desire to prove the relationship. Lamont hadn't acknowledged me— that was proof enough. Guess I would need to visit Logan and ask him.

Eventually I drifted to sleep. Floating in a sea of blackness and surrounded by nothing, I strained to reach solid ground. But my body thinned. My arms turned translucent. My legs disappeared. I dissolved into a void.

Sound and touch returned with a vengeance. A roar woke me. The noise rattled the floor and my bed lurched so hard it tossed me across the narrow room. I slammed into the wall along with the table. The vampire box clipped my forehead as it shattered against the sheet metal.

Loose items spun around and knocked into me as if the contents of my room had been stuffed into one of the huge laundry dryers and turned on.

The bluelight died, plunging me into darkness. Then it all stopped. I ended up sprawled in a heap on the floor amid a pile of debris. Dazed and confused, I stayed still, trying to clear my head.

Then the silence hit me. As familiar as the beat of my own heart, the Hum had always rumbled throughout Inside. A comforting constant noise noticed more on a subconscious level than noted on a conscious level.

The Hum meant the power plant was doing its job, producing electricity and heat, keeping us alive.

Silence meant the opposite. Until that moment, I hadn't known true terror.

2

IN THE BLACKNESS OF MY ROOM, I UNTANGLED FROM
the heap and stood. A wave of dizziness hit, spinning me back
onto the ground. Pressing my fingers to my temple, I touched
a tender spot covered with a sticky wetness—blood. I probably had a concussion.

Unable to trust my legs, I crawled, shoving aside debris
as I moved toward the door. Or so I hoped. In the darkness,
direction was hard to determine.

My hand touched a round dome, and I picked up my exploring helmet with a cry of triumph. Funny how the small
things become important in an emergency. I donned the
helmet, toggling on the light.

I faced the wrong way and the room was a mess—no surprise. A thick glass splinter jutted from my right forearm—a
surprise since it didn't hurt. Of course once I stared at the
blood welling from the wound, pain shot up my arm. Basic
first aid instructions that I'd learned when I lived in the care
facility replayed in my mind. I left the glass in place.

The crushed innards of the vampire box crunched be-
neath me as I reached the door. Despite my refusal to use the

box, the damn thing had still gotten my blood via the glass shard.

I stumbled through the door and illuminated another disaster area. The sitting room appeared as if a giant had upended all the furniture. I checked Lamont's bedroom. It mirrored mine, but at least she wasn't trapped under debris.

The sudden understanding that whatever had shaken Inside most likely caused major injuries and maybe death, cleared the confused fog from my mind in a microsecond. Energized, I wove through the carnage of the apartment. Ignoring the disaster area that used to be her office and exam room, I reached the patient area.

I swept the light around the broken beds. Emek waved a bloody hand from underneath a pile. Digging through the debris, I uncovered him.

"What happened?" he asked.

"No idea. Are you injured?"

"I woke up on the floor."

"Any pain?"

"Don't think so."

I righted a bed, returned the mattress and helped Emek lie down. A groan sounded across the room. I followed it to the other patient. She had a gash on her cheek, but I couldn't find any other injuries.

"Is Doctor Lamont all right?" she asked.

"I haven't seen her," I said.

"She was right here before…"

What to call it? The Big Shake? Then the thought of Lamont being one of the casualties sent panic, fear and… grief?…shooting through my heart. It triggered another horrible possibility—Riley. He could be hurt or worse.

My first impulse was to run to his apartment and check on him, but he could be anywhere. The ten-hour shifts had ceased after the rebellion and no other schedule had replaced it yet. Once I settled my out-of-control pulse, I decided to stay here. Riley knew my location. He would come to me. If he could.

I searched the infirmary and found Lamont unconscious and bleeding from a nasty gouge on her head. Something like relief flowed through me, but, if asked, I would deny the feeling. After I hefted her into a bed and bandaged her wound, I worked to get ready for the inevitable arrival of the injured.

As I rushed to clean up, redlights came on. I skidded to a stop. Redlights? That was new. And creepy. I'd never seen it before or even heard stories from the old-timers. In Inside, bluelights stayed on for sleeping or in temporarily unoccupied areas. Daylights brightened occupied rooms and work places. Darkness stayed in places like the Gap between levels, and closed rooms. In the Expanse, there had been a couple rows of bluelights in the Expanse, marking the walls.

I switched off my light and removed the helmet. The eerie red glow gave enough illumination to see, which meant I had little to no time before my "guests" showed up.

At first, they trickled in, coming in pairs or by themselves, seeking medical treatment. The trickle transformed into a stream then a deluge. I recruited those who had carried friends. We divided the injured into three groups—bad, really bad and dire. The first two groups were taken next door to Quad A3—a common area. The last stayed in the main infirmary.

Then the emergencies arrived. Panicked, I flipped the switch that called Doctor Sanchia even though I knew he would be swamped with his own problems up on level four. I tore through the piles on the floor under the supply cabinets, searching for smelling salts to wake Lamont.

When I found them, I broke the package open and waved it under her nose.

She jerked away, but opened her eyes. "Trella? What—"

Her eyes cleared as I rushed to explain. By the time I finished, she was on her feet and issuing orders. Every able-bodied person was pressed into service. She took one look at the glass shard in my arm and yanked it out.

"Wrap it for now. We'll deal with it later," she said.

The hours blurred together. It seemed complete and utter chaos was but a moment away, yet somehow Lamont kept us on track. I sewed stitches until my fingers turned numb. Set bones until my arms ached. The bandage around my forearm dripped blood, but I had no idea if it was mine or not.

At one point a mechanical voice boomed. Everyone froze for a second as an announcement played. "Citizens of Inside, please do not panic."

Too late.

"All life support systems are fully operational," it continued. "Please remain at your posts. Those off-duty, please remain in your barracks and apartments. Anyone with medical experience is asked to report to the infirmaries on levels four, three and two. More information will be relayed when available."

We all stared at each other for a moment. Who was speaking, the computer or one of the Committee members? Before the rebellion, only the Travas had made announcements. However, nothing like this had happened when the Travas held power.

Just like the redlights, the mechanical voice was probably an automatic safety measure. After another minute of stunned silence, activity resumed and I gave up keeping track of anything.

But all through the frantic hours, bits and pieces of what

had happen started to emerge. From half caught conversations and comments, I learned the power plant had caused the Big Shake. The plant occupied Quadrant C on all four levels. And the most severely injured were from Sectors B, F and a few from E. All shared a wall with Quad C. Which explained why the infirmary—Sector B3—had been in such disarray.

At some point, the daylights returned, which meant we had power again. Eventually, the flow of patients eased and dribbled. I filled a tray with glasses of water and handed them out. A numb exhaustion had soaked into me, muting my emotions and slowing my reactions.

For the first time since the…accident, I saw faces. Before I had focused on the injuries. But now I searched for those I recognized.

Half of me was relieved not to see Riley among them, but the other half was terrified that his lifeless body was in the pile on level one, waiting to be fed to Chomper. Other horrible scenarios danced through my tired mind. His body hadn't been discovered yet. He clung to life in level four's infirmary. He was trapped, pinned under a heavy piece of machinery.

I reached for another glass, but my tray was empty. Staring at the ripple pattern on the metal, I tried to remember what I should do as I swayed. Strong hands grabbed my shoulders from behind and guided me to my room. The bed had been cleared and the hands encouraged me to lie down.

My weak protests were ignored. Unable to resist, I collapsed onto the mattress and through a slit in my heavy eyelids, I saw Doctor Lamont. She pulled a blanket over me. And the touch of her lips on my forehead was my last memory.

Familiar voices woke me. They argued. I tried to produce the energy to care, failed and rolled over to return to sleep.

But my mind wouldn't cooperate. It mulled and tugged until it plucked the proper memory from the depths, exposing it in a series of images. The Big Shake. The injured. Beds filled with people. Blood everywhere.

I lurched to my feet and ran from my room. My sudden exit surprised the two people on the other side of my door. Not caring I almost knocked Lamont down, I flung myself into Riley's arms.

He squeezed me as I clung to him. Questions poured from my mouth. "Are you all right? Where have you been? What happened?"

"I'm fine. I've been helping Doctor Sanchia. Logan—"

I pulled back. "Is he…" The word stuck in my throat.

"He'll be all right." Riley swept my sleep-tousled hair from my eyes. "He looks better than you." He rubbed his thumb lightly over the cut on my forehead. "This needs a few stitches. Want me to sew you up?"

I studied his face and realized he was half serious. "Doctor Sanchia let you suture wounds?"

"He didn't have much choice. We were swamped with people." Riley feigned nonchalance, waving a hand dismissively. "It's just a needle and thread. I've repaired rips in Sheepy before so I was more than qualified." Humor sparked in his blue eyes.

My mouth formed an automatic smile whenever I thought of Sheepy and his mother. The stuffed animal family had a special place in my heart. "I hope Sheepy and Mama Sheepy weren't damaged."

"They're fine. I checked on them before coming here. I do have my priorities straight," he teased.

I swatted him on the shoulder and he winced. Yanking his collar down, I exposed a fist-sized purple bruise.

He peeled my fingers from his shirt. "It's okay. No broken bones."

"How did you get hurt?" I asked.

"I was inspecting the wiring on level five with Logan and the floor just heaved, tossing us across the room. He hit his head, but it's a minor concussion."

"Heaved?"

"An explosion happened in the power plant and we stood directly above it," he said.

"Does anyone know what set it off?"

"No. That's for another week." He straightened his shirt and smoothed his black hair. Since the rebellion, Riley had let it grow. It smelled of shampoo. "Right now attending to the wounded and finding missing people is the main concern."

"Have you slept?"

He nodded to the couch. "I arrived just after you went to bed. I didn't want to wake you, so I showered and slept here. I've been helping Doctor Lamont."

Which reminded me. I stepped away from him, glancing around, but Lamont had left. "I should…"

Riley stared at me in horror. Not my face, but my clothes. Dried blood stained almost all the white fabric, which had stiffened.

"Relax, it's not mine."

He pointed to a wet patch on my forearm. "And that?"

"Just a cut. I need to shower and—"

Unwinding the tattered bandage, he exposed the gash. I hissed in pain when he touched it.

"Come on." He grabbed my hand and pulled me from the apartment.

Patients recovering from their injuries lay on the floor in Lamont's office and in the exam room. Only a thin walkway remained free. At the examination table, Lamont finished with a young girl. The girl's mother, who hovered nearby, swept the girl into her arms and carried her out.

"Since you refused to get some rest, you might as well do Trella next," Riley said to Lamont.

He had been more forgiving of her betrayal. Which didn't make sense to me. His mother had been recycled when he was little because of her. Well, not directly. But with Lamont spying for the Pop Cops, the Force of Ten had failed. The consequences had been high. My father—if Karla Trava had been telling the truth about me—Riley's mother and two others had been recycled.

Lamont claimed she had spied to protect her daughter, Sadie, which would be me if Karla's word could be trusted. Except Karla said she recycled Sadie along with Lamont's husband afterward. The lesson that should have been learned—don't trust Karla or her word.

Yet when the rebels were on the verge of winning, Karla told Lamont her daughter had really been living in the lower levels as a scrub. Once again Karla threatened to harm Sadie unless Lamont helped Karla stop the rebellion.

How could such an intelligent woman fall for the same trick twice? When Karla had pointed to me as the long lost Sadie, Lamont had refused to believe her. It had been too coincidental. And I agreed.

"Sit up on the table," Lamont said to me.

I stared at her. Deep lines of exhaustion etched her pale face. She moved as if she'd shatter at any harsh sound.

"You're in no condition. Go to bed before you do more harm than good." I snapped my mouth shut before I said "again." As a doctor, she might be one of the best, but as a decent, reliable person, she failed.

"But your arm—"

"I can do it."

"One handed?"

"Riley will help. We'll keep an eye on everyone for you. If there's an emergency, we'll wake you." I gave Riley a significant look.

Understanding my hint, he released my hand and led Lamont back to her bedroom.

I sorted supplies. Since the majority of the injuries from the accident had been cuts, we were low on sutures. I would need to restock them.

"Why did she listen to you and not me?" Riley asked when he returned.

I shrugged. "She thinks I'd be a good doctor."

"Like her?"

"Don't start." I almost growled at him.

He kept pestering me to test my blood. I couldn't make him understand that the result wouldn't change my opinion of her.

"We're running out of supplies. Has anyone opened all the crates found in the Expanse?" I asked.

"Not yet."

"Somebody should go through the crates and inventory them."

"Good idea, you should bring it up at the next Committee meeting. Oh, wait." He smacked his head as if remembering something. "Since it's a good idea, it will be promptly ignored."

"They have a ton of decisions to make. Just give them time to sort everything out."

"You're defending them?" Riley cupped my cheek. "Are you feeling ill? Headache? Fever?"

I swatted his hand away. "I'm serious."

"And this change in opinion is due to…"

"I realized they have a tough job and I shouldn't be

so critical. Especially since I'm no longer a part of the Committee."

He gaped at me. "What did you just say?"

"I resigned. They don't need me. I'm going to explore, and now I'll have time to go through those crates."

"I think that's a bad idea."

"What? Inventorying the crates or exploring?"

"Resigning."

"Why? I'll have more time for...Sheepy. I'm sure he misses me."

"Sheepy can wait. You're the voice of reason. You've seen both sides."

"They don't listen to me. I'm too young."

"You led the rebellion."

"And almost all the people who were involved are on the Committee—Domotor, Hana, Takia, Breana, Jacy and your father. If you really think about it, I started it, but Jacy, Anne-Jade, Logan and the rest finished the rebellion. This is the same thing. The Committee has it covered. I'm just in the way."

Rilcy tried to argue, but I didn't want to dwell on how useless I was in those meetings. I handed him the antiseptic and pointed to the gash on my arm. He grumbled, but helped to clean and then suture the cut. Although a bit awkward, he didn't balk when it was time to pierce my skin with the needle. That part tended to unnerve potential interns. I shouldn't be surprised. He had assisted Lamont with surgery in our storeroom when a Pop Cop had knifed me. Maybe he should be the one to train with Lamont.

When he finished tying the last stitch, I examined his handiwork. Yet another scar on my arm. Between Vinco's knife and my various injuries, I resembled one of those striped tigers listed in the computer files. A wild animal we had left behind. Why we left, I'd no idea, but I was sure Logan's efforts to find the original files for Inside would be successful. Then we would know everything.

After Riley and I finished checking on all the patients, I showered and changed into clean clothes. Since I no longer traveled through the air ducts and pipes, I wore the comfortable light green V-neck shirt and pants Lamont and the other caretakers wore. Yes, I realized the irony, but since I was only 1.6 meters tall, only a few uniform types fit me—unless I wanted to wear the student jumpers. And I wasn't about to go around Inside wearing my air scrubbing uniform or the surgery whites—a special white fabric worn during an operation that allowed the blood stains and other fluids to be easily bleached clean.

After my shower, I returned to the infirmary and organized the mess left by the Big Shake. Riley went to search for his father. Their rooms were located in Sector E4, cattycornered to the power plant, but he wasn't too worried.

"He didn't come to the infirmary on level four," Riley had said. "I doubt he's hurt, but I want to make sure."

As I worked, people stopped by to look for loved ones and to visit the injured. Everyone seemed dazed, and I wondered how long it would take them to recover.

Hana Mineko arrived to record the names of the injured. She carried a portable computer—one of Logan's new devices. Not only a member of the Force of Sheep, she had also been involved with Domotor's first effort to regain control of Inside from the Trava family. Now she was a member of the Committee.

Her black curly hair, usually fixed in an intricate knot, hung in messy clumps. Dirt smudged her cheek and scratches marked her petite nose.

When she finished, I asked her how bad it was.

Pressing a few buttons on her computer, she said, "So far, I've listed five hundred and three..." Hana glanced at my forehead. "Make that five hundred and four injured and sixty-six to be recycled."

My heart lurched and I put a hand to my chest. "That many are going to Chomper? Are you sure? The blast wasn't that strong."

"The number is unfortunately accurate and bound to increase slightly. It could have been worse," Hana said. "The explosion happened between levels four and three. The hardest hit areas were Sectors F3 and F4, which houses apartments for the uppers. If the blast had been in the lower two levels, the scrub barracks in Sectors F2 and F1 would have been in the line of fire, and thousands would now be waiting for Chomper." She swept a hand, gesturing to the far wall of the infirmary. "Another piece of luck, the energy went south. If it had gone west, this place would have been torn to bits. You and Doctor Lamont would be waiting for Chomper. And if it had blown to the east or north..."

Horrified, I stared at her. "Was it strong enough?"

"To punch a hole to Outside?"

A disaster that would cause the end of our world. "Yes."

"We don't know yet. Maintenance is looking into it."

At the start of week 147,020, another announcement played. It had been thirty hours since the accident—looking at how much we've done in the meantime, thirty hours seemed an impossibly short time. The mechanical voice—which I had been correct in assuming was the computer's automatic safety system—informed us maintenance had bypassed the damaged sections of the power plant and operations have resumed.

Once again electricity and heat were being generated and we would be up to full capacity in a matter of hours.

A new voice, sounding like Hana, requested helpers to assist with cleanup in Sector B4. One of the water storage tanks had ruptured. I imagined rust growing on the walls and floor of B4, spreading like a disease.

During the week, the infirmary emptied as people healed. About mid-week, I finally had a few hours to myself. I decided to inspect the damaged areas, starting with Sector F3.

In the back of my mind, I knew the force of the blast had been significant. But to see a huge jagged hole, crinkled metal and scorch marks was a whole other experience. A number of apartments had been destroyed. Wires hung to the floor and water dripped and pooled. The ceiling had been peeled back, exposing the Gap between levels three and four.

Using the buckled metal wall, I climbed up into the Gap. At this location, I could stand, but normally I would have to crouch in the one and a half meter space. The damage to level four resembled level three, except the floor had been ripped apart instead of the ceiling. The water pipes and air conduits that criss-crossed this space looked like broken toys.

Climbing higher, I found Logan in the plant's main Control Room on level four. He pounded on a keyboard, muttering and cursing to himself. A white bandage covered his left temple and eyebrow. Dark purple and red bruises colored his left cheek.

"How bad is it?" I asked him.

He jerked. "Where the hell did you come from?"

It took me a moment to respond. Riley had said Logan looked better than me, but I'd slept since the explosion. Logan's haggard oval face and bloodshot eyes told me it had been a long time since he'd rested.

"Where else would I come from? Outer space?"

He grunted and his focus returned to the computer screen.

"I'm fine. Thank you for your concern. However you look like Chomper's been chewing on you. When's the last time you've eaten?"

"No idea. What time is it now?" Logan cursed and slammed his fist down.

I pulled his chair away from the console.

"Hey!" He braced his feet, trying to scoot back.

"No." I swiveled him to face me. Nose to nose, I gave him my best scowl. "You need food and sleep."

"But—"

"Inside has power and heat."

"But—"

"Whatever you're working on will still be there when you return."

"But—"

"You can't think straight without rest."

He clutched the chair arms as if I had threatened to pick him up and carry him to the cafeteria. No need. I would roll his chair if I had to.

His words rushed out in a panicked burst. "But this is important!"

I straightened and crossed my arms. Keeping a stern expression, I said, "This had better be good."

Logan's wild gaze flicked to the door and back to me. "Promise to say nothing?"

"I can't."

"For now. Just for now. Until I confirm it."

"Logan, you're starting to worry me."

"Promise to keep quiet for now?"

"Okay, okay. Now spill."

Once again he checked the door. He pointed to the top button on his shirt. "Is your microphone off?"

"Yes." I almost screamed the word at him.

"The power plant wasn't the only system to be damaged by the explosion."

"All the systems were affected by the electrical outage. Why is this a secret?"

He rubbed a hand over his face. "We didn't even know this system existed until ten weeks ago."

"Oh. An *Outer Space* system?"

"Yep. And not a minor one like Gateway. This one is called the Transmission. In simple terms, it takes a portion of the energy produced by the power plant and transmits it to Outer Space, pushing us toward our destination. With me so far?"

"Yeah. It's moving us through Outer Space."

"Right. Except the explosion wrecked it. Without the Transmission operating, we can't go faster or slow down or maneuver."

"And why is that so upsetting?"

He raked his fingers through his brown hair. "Outer Space isn't empty. There are massive objects called Planets, huge projectiles with names like Asteroids and Comets, and dense balls of burning gas named Suns. If we don't crash into one of them, all these things exert a force that can either slow us down, push us off course or trap us. In other words, we're dead in the water."

3

"ARE WE IN ANY IMMEDIATE DANGER?" I ASKED Logan.

"I don't think so."

"Think?"

"Sorry, some well-meaning scrub interrupted me before I could finish my calculations," he teased, but his humor didn't linger.

"Can we fix the Transmission?"

"I don't know. The maintenance scrubs didn't perform the routine cleaning and upkeep on it. I've a terrible feeling the Travas had been in charge."

Not good. Since Inside had a limited number of holding cells, most of the Trava family had been confined to their quarters in Sector D4.

"Can I go back to work now?" Logan asked.

"You can finish your calculations," I said.

"You're not going to leave, are you?"

"Nope."

I stood behind him as his fingers flew over the keyboard.

After twenty minutes Logan whistled in relief, relaxing back against his chair.

"Good news?" I asked.

"We're not about to crash into anything in the next four weeks." He turned and met my gaze.

"But?"

"We might be on a collision course."

"Might?"

Logan gestured weakly to the computer. "I need to search through the data..."

"Not now. You need to eat and sleep." I cut off his squawk of protest as I yanked him from his chair. Marching him down to the upper's cafeteria in Quad G3, I stayed with him while he ate. Then I escorted him to his little suite next to Inside's main Control Room. The small cluster of rooms had been used by the Captain so he would be nearby in case of an emergency.

We didn't have a new Captain yet, but Logan came close. With his technical knowledge and familiarity with the computer systems, he had his fingers on the pulse of our world.

Since the rebellion, the uppers kept doing their jobs, monitoring the life-support systems. I realized the scrubs hadn't. They didn't want to clean and perform the mindless tasks anymore. I didn't blame them, but those tasks were vital to our existence. How could we convince them?

I tucked Logan into bed. "Don't leave until you've had a few hours of sleep. Do you understand?"

He gave me a tired salute. "Yes, sir."

As I headed to the infirmary, I mulled over the problem of dividing up the work. No brilliant idea sprung to mind. I wondered how the people had done it before the Travas took control and separated us into uppers and lowers. Logan had discovered hidden files about the history of our world. Perhaps our ancestors had found a perfect balance. They must have had a system worked out. Once this crisis was over, perhaps Logan could cull this information from those files and show it to the Committee.

I stretched as far as I could, groping for the next hand-hold. It remained just out of my reach. Resting my sweaty forehead against the cool metal, I let the disappointment roll through me. At least I had gone an additional five meters higher than my previous climb. I would have to find another path to reach the top.

Sliding down the rope, I returned to the half-completed roof of level ten. Work on the new levels had ceased until the power plant repairs were finished. I was used to the sounds of construction and the bright daylights, so the Expanse felt desolate. I walked the perimeter of the completed section, shining my light over the metal wall, looking for another potential route to the Expanse's ceiling.

Hank had suggested I use magnets to climb. A great idea, except I needed a way to hold on to the magnets, and they couldn't be too strong or I wouldn't be able to move them as I climbed. He offered to build me a set, but I couldn't ask him now. Hank was one of the few who volunteered to help clean up the mess from the explosion and to repair the damage. Even though it'd been over a week, the work progressed at a slow pace.

When I found a promising place to climb, I marked the spot with paint. My shift started at hour ten and I needed to change. I hurried back to my room. Riley waited for me in the sitting area. He sat on the couch, but didn't look relaxed as he rolled my earring/receiver between his finger and thumb.

"Forget something?" he asked.

"No. I left it here." Wrong answer. I braced for the lecture.

"Out exploring without it?"

"It's distracting." I pointed to the transmitter pinned on my collar. "I can still call for help. And I have my pendant." The necklace Riley had given me always hung around my neck. If I squeezed the little metal sheep, it would broadcast a signal, reporting my location.

"What if I or Logan needed *your* help?" He studied my expression. "Didn't think of that, did you?"

"I'll take it with me next time. Okay?" I held my hand out for the earring.

Riley dropped it into my palm. "Promise?"

I swallowed my retort. Riley's overprotectiveness grated on my nerves at times. For more weeks than I could count, I had climbed all over Inside without any way to signal for help and without any trouble either. Cogon had warned me of the danger, but I had ignored him. Good thing, too. Without my knowledge of the ducts and my ability to travel through them, our rebellion wouldn't have succeeded.

"I promise," I said, rushing past him.

"Where are you going?" he asked.

"To change. I'm late." I closed my door on his reply and switched the drab gray overalls the recycling workers wore for my skin-tight climbing clothes.

When I returned to the sitting area, Riley blocked my exit. "Late for what?"

I gestured to the ceiling. "My shift. I'm helping to repair the ductwork between levels three and four."

His shoulders drooped. "Oh. I thought we could—"

"I'm done at hour sixteen. I'll meet up with you later." I slipped around him and waved.

"It's always later, Trella."

I rounded on him. "This is important."

"And so is exploring and the Committee meetings before that, and—"

"I quit the Committee to spend more time with you. I wasn't counting on an explosion. But I'll remember to factor that in for the future." I mimed writing on my palm. "Riley first, emergencies second. Got it." I saluted him, rushed from the room and almost plowed into Lamont.

She said, "Trella, I need—"

"Find someone else," I said. "I can only do so much."

My anger cooled as I reported for work. I regretted my nasty comment to Riley. He had been putting in long hours, too. One of a few. The same handful of faces kept volunteering. Each time, they looked more and more exhausted.

During my shift, we fixed airshaft number fifteen. A small accomplishment, but that didn't stop us from cheering.

After I organized the tools for the next group, I found Logan and his sister, Anne-Jade, arguing in the corridor near the power plant.

"...force them. I'm not a Pop Cop," Anne-Jade said. Her dainty nose was identical to Logan's as well as the light-brown color of her long hair. It hung past her shoulders in a shiny cascade.

The family resemblance was unmistakable, and I wondered if they were fraternal twins. They've always known they were related—a rarity among the scrubs—perhaps they knew who their parents were.

I hung back and waited for them to notice me.

"We need more people. I don't care how you get them," Logan said.

Anne-Jade fiddled with her belt buckle. She wore a modified Pop Cop uniform. The silver stripes down the sleeves and pants had been removed as well as any rank insignia. Her weapon belt held a stunner only, and the symbol representing Inside—a cube with the capital letter I on the front side—had been stitched onto her right collar.

After the rebellion, Anne-Jade had volunteered to organize a security force comprised of both uppers and lowers.

"What about the Trava family? They're not doing anything but taking up space. And we could *force* them to help," she said.

"No." I jumped into their conversation. "They can't be trusted."

"To do what?" she asked. But she didn't let me answer. "We have all the weapons and lock codes. I can post guards. It won't be hard to do."

By the thoughtful hum emanating from Logan's throat, I knew he mulled over her suggestion. Between the two of them, Anne-Jade had all the common sense. As Tech Nos, they had needed to hide their activities from the Pop Cops. When they had built their illegal technology, she disguised their gadgets as everyday items. Those devices had played a critical role in winning the rebellion.

Sensing her brother's agreement, Anne-Jade added, "And we can inject tracers in them. So even if they climb into the pipes to escape, we can track them."

"Tracers?" I asked.

She grinned. "Tiny little bugs that are injected under the skin. They emit a signal we can pick up."

"What's to stop them from cutting it out?" I asked.

"They won't know it's there. We'll use vampire boxes, but instead of taking blood samples, we'll inject the tracer. They won't know the difference. At least the civilian and lower ranked Travas won't suspect anything." An impish spark lit her greenish-brown eyes.

"Why not the upper ranks?" Deemed too dangerous, this group had been incarcerated in the holding cells.

"Because it was their idea," she said. "I found notes on the project in Commander Vinco's office. Although his tracer was twice the size of ours."

Logan corrected his sister. "It was four times the size, Humongous. The scrubs would have panicked, thinking the lump on their arms was a tumor."

I marveled over their skills. "How do you make your devices so small?"

"When I was experimenting with a circuit board, I—"

"You can tell her later, Logan," Anne-Jade interrupted. "I need to know if you want me to schedule the Travas for repairs."

"Do you have enough tracers?" he asked.

"Enough for a small group. Once we know if they'll work, I can make more."

"Then go ahead. Keep me informed."

Logan's grown-up, decisive tone surprised me. He usually deferred to her opinion.

As Anne-Jade turned to leave, I said, "Wait a minute. Shouldn't you get permission from the Committee first?"

"No," Logan said. "They put me in charge of the repairs. And time is critical."

Using Travas to rush the repairs didn't sit well with me. Perhaps the Committee could entice people to help by offering them first choice of the living space in the new levels. It was a good idea, which meant it would be ignored along with all my other ideas. Riley had called me the voice of reason, but the Committee remained deaf to me.

I returned to the infirmary, slipped past Lamont who was preoccupied with a patient and took a long hot shower. Half expecting Riley to be waiting in the sitting room when I finished, I felt a pang of disappointment over the empty couch. After donning my comfortable green shirt and pants, and weaving my wet hair into a single braid, I debated between food, sleep and Riley.

Riley won. I switched on my button microphone and turned it to Riley's frequency. "Hi Riley. Where are you?" I asked.

No response. I tried reaching him two more times before giving up. He must be asleep. I heated a bowl of soup. The kitchen was another reason I stayed in Lamont's suite. So nice not to fight the crowds in the cafeteria.

Unfortunately my enjoyment ended when Lamont entered. I tried to ignore her, but she sat next to me and clanged her plate on the table.

I glanced up, catching her staring at me. "What?"

She didn't flinch. Her frank appraisal sent warning signals. Ever since the explosion, Lamont's confidence had grown. Not as a doctor, she had never hesitated when working, but in her interactions with me. Before, her guilt made her uncertain around me, which it should. She was a traitor after all. Her actions during the rebellion had almost gotten me and my cohorts sent to Chomper.

"What?" I asked again.

"If you plan to keep living here, you have to help me in

the infirmary. If you don't want to work for me, then you need to move back into the barracks."

I gaped at her.

"The extra room is supposed to be for an intern," she said. "Off-hour emergencies are harder to respond to if I have to wait for my assistant to come from another level or Sector." She leaned forward and her voice softened. "I've been thinking about Karla's claims about you."

Snorting in disgust, I stood.

Lamont jumped to her feet and blocked my path. "You're not running from me. Not this time. Sit down or I'll—"

"What? Strap me to a gurney again?"

"If that's what I have to do to get you to listen to me, then I will."

A hard determination settled on her face as if her skin had turned to metal. The woman was serious. She seemed to have two separate personalities, Kiana and Doctor Lamont. I was facing the Doctor right now.

"You can't. Not when—"

She brandished a syringe and a "try me" stance.

I stepped back, bumping into wall. Damn. "Where did…" She had planned this little chat.

"Sit down."

If she knocked me out, I could have her arrested for assault. But would Anne-Jade's new Inside Security Force (ISF) even charge her? Probably not. Especially not since she proved to be invaluable after the explosion.

Unwilling to make this easy for her, I crossed my arms, sat and glowered. "I'm listening."

"Good." Lamont remained on her feet with her weapon pointed toward me. "For the last 1,430 weeks my heart has ached for my daughter and husband. And yes, I betrayed all of you just for the slim chance to hold Sadie in my arms again. Karla knew my weakness. And she had the comb I had hidden in Sadie's diaper. It was wrong, and stupid, and I regret it. But I can't change the past. All I can do is atone for my mistakes. Karla might not have lied about you. Why would she send a hundred-and-two-week-old to Chomper? I'd like you to take a blood test."

I surged to my feet. "No blood test."

"It would settle the question once and for all. And if you're Sadie, you can stay here."

"But if I'm just plain old Trella, I need to leave?"

"No. You're still welcome to be my intern and stay."

"I'm not interested in being your intern or your daughter." As I brushed past her, I braced for the needle's prick. Would she stoop to knocking me out and testing my blood? Not yet. Unharmed, I hurried into my room and stopped. I wore my pendant, earring and transmitter. Besides my tool belt and moccasins, there was nothing here I needed.

Changing back into my air scrub uniform, I buckled my belt, secured my mocs to a loop, climbed up to the air vent, opened the cover and entered the air ducts. I wasn't about to give Lamont another chance to trap me. After securing the vent, I followed the familiar twists and turns, deciding which way to go.

The abandoned controller's room in Quad C1 remained empty. Domotor had hidden in there during the rebellion, but it was next to the power plant and the heat and dirt made it less than ideal. However, it did have a small kitchen and bathroom.

Despite the amenities of the controller's room, I headed toward the storeroom on level four. The place where I first met Riley. It had a comfortable couch—all I needed. I'd eat in the uppers dining room in Quad G3, and use the scrub washrooms on level two. It'd be just like old times. Well, without the constant fear, which was a bonus.

And just like the past, I'd have to use the air ducts to get to the storeroom. Since the room was located deep within Sector D4, I couldn't use the hallways. I wanted the room to remain forgotten by all but a few people, and Sector D4 was patrolled by the ISF to keep the Travas in their quarters.

When I reached the room, I peered through the vents. The bluelights were on, and I couldn't spot any signs of recent activity. Opening the vent, I swung down and dropped onto the couch. Dust puffed and I sneezed. The daylights snapped on, triggered by my motion. Riley hadn't disconnected the motion sensor and I wondered if my entrance would signal him.

By the film of dust on all the furniture, I knew Riley hadn't been here since the rebellion. I tried to contact him again. No response. Perhaps he was still mad at me.

I cleaned the room as best as I could. Finally exhausted, I switched back to bluelights, dumped my tool belt in a corner, curled up on the couch and fell asleep.

The sudden brightness of the daylights woke me. I stared at my surroundings for a few seconds in confusion until I remembered my location. According to the clock, it was hour twenty-five of week 147,021. Riley leaned on the door to the hallway, but his posture was far from relaxed. His black hair hung in his eyes, obscuring half of his expression.

I sat up and pulled my legs in close, making room for him to sit down.

He didn't move. "What are you doing here?"

"Lamont kicked me out. It was either this, the pipes or the barracks."

"Dad and I have a couch." His flat tone held no emotion.

I sensed I trod on thin metal. One wrong word and it would buckle underneath me. "Last I heard, your brother had claimed it."

"Blake moved back to the barracks weeks ago. He couldn't stand the quiet."

Which made sense. Growing up in the lower two levels, we had been assaulted by the constant noise of the other scrubs. For most of the scrubs, the clamor soothed and comforted. For me, the racket grated and drove me into the pipes, seeking privacy and distance from the noise.

"I tried to contact you a couple times," I said in my defense.

"I know."

Not good. "Riley, I'm sorry for getting angry. I'll skip my next shift and we'll spend time together."

His muscles relaxed just a bit. Progress.

"Why did Doctor Lamont kick you out?" he asked.

"She gave me an ultimatum." I told him about the argument.

As I talked, he moved away from the door and closer to me. "I'm surprised she didn't tell you to leave sooner."

"Why?"

"You're nasty to her at every opportunity. And I suspect the only reason you stayed there is to make her suffer for her actions during the rebellion. Her guilt was probably why she put up with you as long as she did."

I wanted to correct him, but I suspected he was right. "I like helping the patients." Weak.

"You could have interned with Doctor Sanchia." Riley sat next to me.

"I wasn't that nasty. More like grumpy and a little surly."

"Sorry, but no. Nasty is the right word." He held up a hand to stop my protest. "Consider your refusal to take a blood test. She still grieves for her daughter and you could ease her pain."

"What if I'm not Sadie?"

"Then she'll know Karla lied and there's no hope."

"Wait a minute. Karla could be telling the truth and Sadie is living in the lower levels right now."

"Doctor Lamont already tested every girl born close to Sadie's birth week. All fifteen of them. No match. You're the last one."

Oh. "Are you going to counter all my comments?"

"Yes."

"Why? Her betrayal could have sent us all to Chomper, including your father."

"You keep forgetting, she didn't tell Karla *everything*. Her information made it difficult for us, but we won." He ran a hand through his hair, pulling his bangs from his eyes. Riley stared into the past. "Besides, if Karla had offered me the chance to see my mother again, to hug my mother and tell her I love her… I would have been mighty tempted. And you had been ready to exchange your life for Cogon's. Remember? Lamont's actions aren't as despicable when you look at it that way."

I grumbled, but couldn't respond. He had a point.

"Will you at least think about it?"

"I will. Later." I scooted closer to him and he hooked his arm around my shoulder.

"Do you want to stay with us?" Riley asked. "You'll have a shower close by."

I glanced around the storeroom. "Eventually I'll want to, but right now this place is…comforting and familiar. Do you understand?"

He smiled and I realized just how much I missed his smile. This was the first time in weeks that we had complete privacy.

"Yes, I do. And so does Sheepy. He was just reminiscing about those hours we spent in here with you before the rebellion." Riley turned to me. "In fact your uniform is bringing back those memories of the first time I met you." He trailed his fingertips along the slippery material of my arm as he cocked his head, considering. "Something's not quite right."

Reaching around with both hands, he pulled my hair from its braid. His touch sent shivers through me. When he finished, he mussed my hair. "There, that's better. Now you look like the wild scrub that fell into my life."

"Because *you* loosened the vent's screws."

"Best. Decision. Ever." He combed his fingers through my hair and laced them behind my neck, pulling me in for a kiss.

Heat burned inside me as he deepened the kiss. I snaked my arms around his shoulders and pressed against him. The thin material of my uniform chafed and when he tugged at the zipper along the back, I broke our kiss long enough to whisper an encouragement for him to keep pulling. Reclaiming his lips, I worked on unbuttoning his shirt.

He peeled the top of my uniform down, exposing my breasts. One of the benefits of being on the smaller side—no uncomfortable support garment. His surprise at encountering nothing but smooth skin lasted mere microseconds, before his thumbs sent tingling waves through me.

This was farther than we've ever explored before, but I wasn't about to complain. I yanked his shirt off and ran my hands along his muscular arms. He abandoned my lips to nibble on my neck, pushing me back so I reclined on the couch.

"Trella, are you there?" Logan's voice squawked from my earring. I groaned in annoyance and was about to switch it off when Logan said, "Trell, I need you at the Power Plant's control room now." Logan's panic rang loud and clear.

Riley pulled away. Concern creased his forehead.

I fumbled for the transmitter clipped onto my uniform. "What happened?" I asked.

"Sabotage."

4

ALL TINGLY WARMTH FLED MY BODY. "SABOTAGE?" I asked. "I didn't feel—"

"Come to the control room, and I'll explain," Logan said.

"Why can't you tell me now?"

"This frequency isn't secure."

The click from Logan switching off sounded in my ear. I met Riley's resigned gaze. He buttoned his shirt. I pulled up the top of my uniform and zipped it.

"Promise me we'll continue this...conversation later." Riley's mournful tone made me smile.

"That's an easy promise to make."

I glanced at the air vent in the ceiling. Riley's broad shoulders would never fit. Gesturing toward the door, I asked, "Did anyone see you come in here?"

"Nope."

"The corridors should be patrolled by ISF officers."

"They are. I told them I was checking the wiring. As soon as they lost interest in me, I ghosted down our hallway."

"Ghosted? You've been hanging around Logan too much."

"I'd rather be…exploring with you." He ran his hands down my sides and rested them on my hips. "There may be other surprises under your jumpsuit just waiting to be discovered."

I slipped from his grasp and stood. "Key word, waiting."

He groaned. "If Logan's exaggerating, I'll pound him."

Picking up my tool belt, I clipped it into place. "Can you leave here without being seen?"

"Yep."

"Great. I'll meet you in the control room." The ladder I had used before leaned against the far wall. I set it up under the air vent and climbed. Before I pulled myself into the duct, I caught Riley staring at me. "What's wrong?"

"Nothing. Just wondering."

"About what?"

"If you'll keep your promise."

"When have I *ever* broken a promise?"

"What about leaving the Committee?" he asked.

"I didn't promise them anything, just offered to help."

"I didn't mean the Committee members, but the people of Inside. By freeing them from the Travas' control, you promised them a better life."

"First off, the Force of Sheep freed them, not me. And second, they have a better life. No Pop Cops, grueling work schedules and we'll soon have plenty of room. How could you possibly see that as breaking a promise?"

"There wouldn't have been a rebellion or the Force of Sheep without you. You started everything and you need to finish it."

Words jammed in my throat. How could he think I didn't finish it? I shook my head. "We can argue about this later. Logan's waiting for us." Before he could reply, I slid into the air duct, heading toward the control room.

Riley's voice followed me, echoing through the metal shaft. "Logan called *you*, Trell, not *me* about the sabotage. Think about that."

As I traveled in the duct, I dismissed his comment. It was a matter of semantics, nothing more.

I arrived at the control room and took a few seconds to see who worked below. Logan sat in front of a computer, frowning at the monitor. Riley hadn't arrived. No one else was in sight.

The noise from opening the air vent should have alerted Logan to my presence, but the poor guy jumped a meter when I landed behind him.

"Would you stop doing that?" he asked. "You're going to give me a heart attack."

"You knew I was coming." I studied him. He still had bags under his eyes, but he no longer looked as if a hundred-week-old could knock him over.

Logan flinched when the door opened, but relaxed when he spotted Riley. Something had him rattled.

"Time to explain," I said.

He typed on the keyboard for a minute. The screen changed to tables and charts that meant nothing to me.

"The explosion in the power plant was caused by sabotage," Logan said.

"That's—"

He cut me off. "It's the only explanation. My first clue was the location of the blast. Damage to the plant itself was minimal, but it hit the Transmission in the perfect spot."

"The Transmission?" Riley asked.

Logan glanced at me. "Didn't you tell him?"

"You made me promise not to." I shot Riley a look. "And I *keep* my promises."

"Oh. Well you could have told him," Logan said.

"Then next time you swear me to secrecy, you need to include that exception." I quickly explained the Transmission to Riley. "Did you fix it yet?" I asked Logan.

"No."

"What about being on a collision course?" Riley asked.

"We should have plenty of time to avoid it. As I was saying, the Transmission's controls were damaged, but not the equipment. Repairs should be easy if we knew how the controls worked."

"I could look at it for you," Riley offered.

"It couldn't hurt," Logan said.

"How do busted controls lead you to sabotage?" I asked.

"Second clue is this." He pointed at the screen.

Riley bent closer, but I wasn't going to try and decipher it. "And?"

"Operating data for the plant right before the explosion," Riley said.

"And?"

"All the machinery was operating within normal parameters," Logan said. "There is nothing here to warn of an impending explosion. No spike in power, no jammed valves, no fire or anything unusual."

"But the computer might not have registered it in time. Did you examine the plant?"

"Of course. Went over it with a couple of the supervisors. They're equally puzzled about the cause."

"But that isn't enough to suggest sabotage," Riley said.

Logan uncovered a glass container. "Final clue. At the explosion site, I found an oily residue coating the walls, and pieces of a timer and switch. And before you try to explain them, I tested the residue and it's a flammable substance not found anywhere in the power plant. It's used in the recycling kilns on level one."

Riley picked up one of the twisted hunks of metal from the container. As he examined it, a shocked horror filled his eyes. "This could detonate a bomb."

A bomb. Spoken aloud, the words slammed into me. Someone had set off a bomb, killing people on purpose, risking all our lives—thousands of people. I let the stunned outrage roll through me. It took me a few minutes to pull my emotions together and think.

"Who did this? Why?" I asked.

"Who would have to be someone who knew about the Transmission, and had enough knowledge to make and place the bomb so it didn't blow a hole to Outside," Logan said. "As for why, I can only guess. Since the Transmission was the target, either someone doesn't want us traveling through Outer Space or someone wants to get our attention."

"Do you think they will make demands or threaten to damage another system if we don't comply?"

"I've no idea, Trell. This is all new territory for me."

"If they plan to make demands, it should be sooner rather than later," Riley said. "Actually, if they do contact Logan or the Committee, we might be able to find out who they are."

"Have you informed the Committee?" I asked Logan.

"No."

"Why not?" I demanded.

"I just connected the clues. And this information needs to be handled with care. Knowing we're dealing with a saboteur gives us an advantage. If nothing is said, maybe the person will relax and give himself away."

"And if word gets out, there could be panic," Riley added.

"This is too big. The Committee needs to know."

"Nineteen people can't keep a secret. It's statistically impossible," Logan said.

"What if the saboteur makes a demand?" I asked.

"The Committee will know then, won't they?"

I huffed in frustration. "You need to tell someone," I said.

"I did."

"Besides us."

"I think that's unwise."

"Do you have any suspects?" Riley asked.

"Don't encourage him," I said.

"He's right and you know it."

"I can pull together a list of all those who know about the Transmission for you and Trella," Logan said.

"Us?"

He ignored me. "Anne-Jade is still trying to find out which Travas worked on the Transmission equipment. Once we have those names, I'll add them to the list. It's doubtful the Travas pulled it off, but one of them could have given the information to someone who isn't under constant surveillance."

"I can talk to the maintenance scrubs, see if they know more than they're letting on," Riley offered.

"Are you going to tell Anne-Jade?" I asked.

"Of course. She can be trusted."

Still not convinced we were doing the right thing, I knew when I was outnumbered. "We're going to need Jacy's help. He has kept his network of contacts."

"Is he trustworthy?" Riley asked. "He's on the Committee."

Remembering how he had bartered and traded for services and favors, I said, "I'll talk to him."

From the air shaft, I searched for Jacy among the Committee members' offices in Sector H3. Each of the nineteen had been given a small space and computer to use when they weren't sitting in meetings. Using the ducts had been a cowardly act on my part. I didn't want to encounter any of the other members. I didn't want to be questioned about why I left or guilted into returning.

Jacy's office was empty. I debated waiting or leaving a note. Neither appealed to me, so I found a vent in the main corridor between Sectors and dropped down. He could be in the upper's dining room next door in Quad G3, but my skin-tight jumpsuit would draw everyone's attention. Since I needed regular clothes anyway, I headed down to the laundry in Sector B1 via the stairs in Quad I.

When I reached level one, I almost tripped. Huge mounds of glass, metal and clothing filled most of the floor space. The recycling plant in Quad I1 remelted glass and metal and turned clothing back into thread. Usually a busy place with scrubs sorting and carting items to the kiln or the furnace or to Chomper, only a few people worked among the piles.

I put my moccasins on, but was still careful to avoid the sharper objects as I skirted the heaps. The recycling scrubs were required to wear thick boots for a good reason.

After the mess in the recycling plant, the condition of the laundry room failed to surprise me. Bins overflowing with soiled garments and uniforms had been lined up. The line snaked around the room. Rows of washers and dryers stood silent and unused. The bins for clean clothes were empty. One person loaded a washer. Another folded clothes. A few picked through the dirty bins, searching for sizes. Otherwise the place was empty.

I crossed to the lady shoving sheets into a washer. She wore the drab green jumper that the scrubs wore when off-duty.

"Where's everyone?" I asked. By necessity, the laundry had the most workers in the lower levels.

She shrugged. "Not here. If you want clean clothes, you have to do them yourself."

"How long has it been like this?" I asked.

"Where've you been?" The woman paused to look at me for the first time. "In the upper levels, I'd bet." She swept her hand out. "The laundry scrubs stayed for a few weeks, but none of the uppers came down to help them. Eventually they stopped. They're not washing the uppers' clothes. We're all supposed to be equal, but as far as the scrubs are concerned nothing's changed."

I bit back my reply about the lack of Pop Cops patrolling the hallways and kill-zapping dissenters or about not having to report to the hundred hour assemblies. Instead I said, "You have to be patient. It's going to take some time to get everyone organized. And we outnumber the uppers ten to one."

"So? Can't a few come down and help? How hard can it be?"

Opening my mouth to respond, I closed it. She had a point. But it wasn't like the uppers sat around doing nothing. Yet another problem for the Committee to address.

The woman waited for my reply.

"The Committee—"

"Has caused more problems than they solved. This is a big ship, right?"

Confused by the change in topic, I said, "Sort of, but—"

"We had a captain, right?"

"Captain James Trava. But he was relieved of duty. All the Trava officers were." We also had an admiral and a fleet admiral. Although I didn't know why since one ship didn't equal a fleet.

"So? Appoint another."

I smiled. "Just like that?"

"Why not? Can't be any harder than taking the Travas out, right? Unless you're afraid?"

My humor died. "I'm not afraid of anyone."

"I don't doubt that, young lady, but I wasn't talking about a person."

"Then what—"

She poked a finger at a bin half hidden behind the washers. "You'll find clean clothes in there. They're too small for most of the scrubs." Scooping up an armful of clothes, she added them to the washer. Conversation over.

I sorted through the uniforms and jumpers. Finding a few shirts and a pair of pants the kitchen scrubs wore, I tucked them under my arm. The nearest washroom was in Sector E1, which also housed the barracks, along with Sectors D1 and F1. Bluelights lit the rows and rows of bunk beds stacked three high.

Unlike the laundry and recycling areas, many scrubs lounged in the barracks. Some gathered in groups, others slept despite the noise and a few played cards. The place was packed and the stench of them nearly knocked me over. I hurried to change my clothes in the washroom, but as I dashed through the barracks on my way out, I spotted a number of ISF officers patrolling the barracks.

I felt as if I had just slammed into a wall. Why were they here? The scrubs didn't like their presence either. They threw snide and nasty comments at them, mocking and taunting them. Horrible. I wondered if Anne-Jade knew what was going on down here. Or was she like me, avoiding the lower levels? I hadn't been on levels one or two in weeks and I didn't have a good reason either.

Sick to my stomach, I paused in the corridor and breathed in the clean air until my heart slowed to normal. Going with a hunch, I braced for another assault on my senses as I entered the barracks in Sector D1. Jacy used to hold court in a corner.

Not as bad as E1, there were less people and ISF officers. Also the general mood seemed stable and not as tense.

Sure enough, Jacy and a few of his followers huddled together. When I approached they broke apart.

"Hello Trella," Jacy said, but his tone was far from welcoming. "What's the emergency?"

"There isn't one. Why would you think that?"

"You're here with the scrubs so it must be something big."

I ignored his snide comment. "Did you mention what's going on down here to the Committee?"

"And just what is going on?" He acted innocent.

"The piles in recycling and the dirty laundry. How no one is doing their jobs."

"Of course."

"And?"

"And nothing. It's not a high priority. The Committee thinks once the extra levels are completed and the scrubs get more space, everyone will be *happy* to return to work." His sarcastic tone implied otherwise.

"Is it the same for all the systems?"

"Except for maintenance and security, they're busy and productive. Why? Do you care now?"

I laced my hands together to keep from punching Jacy. "Okay, tell me. What should I be doing?"

He jerked as if I surprised him. "Truthfully?"

"Always."

"Disband the Committee. Appoint a few people to be in charge."

I laughed. "Is that it? And here I was ready for something that would be hard to do."

"You asked." He kept his expression neutral.

"I don't have the power to appoint people. I'm just a—"

"A scrub?"

"No. A citizen of Inside. I've done my part. It's time for other people to step in and set up a better system. I wouldn't know the first thing about running a society."

"Uh-huh." Jacy leaned against a bunk. "And you're here because…"

"I need to talk to you."

"So talk."

I glanced around. There were too many people nearby who seemed interested in our conversation. "Some place private."

He frowned with annoyance then snapped his fingers at his men. They cleared a wider space around us. Impressive.

"Better?"

"Yes." But I hesitated. His hostility worried me. Plus he acted like he had before the rebellion—as if we were enemies. Yet he had been a key member, rising to the occasion and being invaluable. I suppressed my doubts and asked him if he knew or heard of an expert in explosions.

He whistled. "You think someone damaged the power plant on purpose?"

Trust Jacy to put the pieces together so quickly. "Let's just say I'd like another opinion."

"Uh-huh. And what if this *expert* is the one you're searching for?"

"There is always that possibility."

He tapped his fingers on the bunk's metal support beam as he considered my request. "I do know one scrub that would be regarded as an expert, but you need to do something for me in return."

No surprise. "And that would be..."

"Remember those microphones you planted for me in air duct seventy-two?"

"Yes."

"I need you to plant more in another air duct."

"Why?" I asked. "The Pop Cops are gone and you should know everything that's being decided from the Committee meetings."

"Let's just say I like another opinion. Deal?"

"Yes, I'll plant the mics for you." But I didn't say *where* I would.

"Good. I'll get them to you soon."

"And that expert?"

Jacy grinned. "His name is Bubba Boom and he works for maintenance."

"You got to be kidding me."

"Nope. He probably had a real name when he was born, but his care mates gave him that nickname at a young age. Bubba Boom can set fire to anything, and he loved setting off little explosions. Drove his Care Mother crazy, burning up various things in the care facility. He was the youngest scrub to be a member of the fire response team since he's equally adept at extinguishing fires."

He sounded familiar. "Is he the guy who rigged that container of casserole to explode?"

"Yep. He had to help the kitchen scrubs clean green goo from the walls and ceiling for a week."

I remembered hearing about his pranks. My care mates used to delight in telling the stories, but I had never learned his name. By the time I graduated from the care facility, he had stopped his mischief. "Did working for the fire response team settle him down?"

"Nope. The Pop Cops took care of that."

Understandable. Vinco could convert anyone after a couple sessions with his knife.

Hank worked on repairs to the pipes below the blasted section of the power plant between levels three and four. He shouted orders and the others rushed to follow them. A few faces weren't familiar and I hoped that meant more of the lower level citizens had volunteered. My optimistic assumptions burst when I spotted a number of armed ISF officers nearby.

Anne-Jade didn't waste time. She had mentioned using Travas for the repairs a mere twelve hours ago and here they were.

When Hank took a break, I asked him about Bubba Boom.

He chuckled. "I haven't heard that name in a long time. We just call him Bubba and he's up on level four welding the ruptured water tank."

I thanked him and headed for the water storage tanks located in Sector B4. When I entered, the humid air reminded me of hydroponics except there was nothing living growing here—only rust. The spilled water had been cleaned, but not before some of it had dripped down to the infirmary.

The crackle and hiss of a torch sounded in the corner closest to the explosion. Sparks flew, pointing out Bubba even though he wore a metal shield over his face. He worked on a long crack along the seam of the metal tank. Wearing gray maintenance coveralls streaked with dirt and peppered with holes, his large frame reminded me of Cog.

Looking at the damage to the tanks, I wondered how Cogon would have reacted to the explosion. He would've been angry and upset and I would have had to force him to take breaks. He'd have every single person of Inside helping until the damage was repaired, and they would have been happy to do it for him.

Not for the first time, nor for the last, I thought it should have been me, not him that floated away into Outer Space.

I waited until Bubba finished before I cleared my throat, letting him know I was there. He pulled off the shield, revealing messy light brown hair that seemed to stand on end. Sweat trailed down the sides of his face and freckles sprinkled his cheeks and nose. Close to my age, I figured he couldn't be more than a hundred weeks older than me.

"Need something?" Bubba Boom asked.

Going with the second opinion ruse, I asked him if he had a chance to see the point of the blast.

The edges of his mouth dipped as a guarded expression covered his face. "Everyone in maintenance has looked at it. I wondered when one of you would start asking about it."

"One of us?"

"Committee upper."

"I'm not..." Correcting him would be a waste of time. Since Lamont had changed my eye color back to its original blue, I had difficulties convincing people I had been raised in the lower levels like them. "Are all your colleagues wondering or just you?"

Again he masked his emotions. "Just me."

"And you didn't say anything to Hank?"

"No."

I waited.

Wiping the sweat off his chin with his shoulder, he jabbed the torch in my direction. "I knew this would happen if I said anything."

Just in case he decided to attack me with his torch's white-hot flame, I planned which tool I would grab from my belt. Hopefully, my outward calm remained. "This?"

"Stop with the dumb act. You figured out a bomb set off the explosion, you talked to Jacy, and now I'm your primary suspect."

Guess I needed to work on my investigative skills. Even though I wasn't an expert in reading people, I noted the edge in his voice when he said Jacy's name. "You would have looked less guilty if you reported your concerns to Hank."

He shrugged, but there was nothing casual in the movement. "Force of habit. I've learned to keep a low profile." Bubba Boom absently rubbed his hand along the bottom of his rib cage.

"If you didn't build that bomb, who did?"

I surprised a laugh from him. "I don't know. And if I did, I wouldn't tell you."

"Why not? You like welding up ruptured tanks? Sanding out rust spots and re-painting the walls? What if he sets off another one? What if someone you care for dies in the next blast? What if he blows a hole to Outside and—"

"Impossible."

"Which one?"

"Damaging one of the Walls. We measured them, they're two meters thick."

"How?"

"Cogon's Gateway. That inner room between the doors is as wide as a Wall."

Interesting and good to know. "My other points are still valid. There might be another explosion."

"And I still wouldn't squeal on a fellow scrub."

"You do know the Pop Cops are no longer in charge, right?" I didn't wait for his answer. "The worst thing we'd do is incarcerate the saboteur. He wouldn't be fed to Chomper. And he wouldn't be tortured into submission either."

A stubborn tightness hardened his gaze.

I couldn't say when I decided he wasn't guilty; it was an internal instinct. "You think I'm an upper."

A slight confused nod.

"My clothes and eye color gave me away."

"Yes."

"Do you think being called an upper is better or worse than my old nickname of Queen of the Pipes?" I asked him.

He stared at me.

"I like Queen of the Pipes better. It doesn't have any prejudices or wrong assumptions associated with it. And the best thing, the Pop Cops didn't give me that name. I earned it. Just like these..." I pulled up the bottom of my shirt, and showed Bubba Boom the line of round scars that followed the edge of my ribcage where Commander Vinco had gouged out my skin. "And if I knew the bastard who was blowing holes in *our* home, he wouldn't need to worry about Chomper. Oh no. He'd need the ISF to protect him from *me*."

Bubba Boom's Adam's apple bobbed as he swallowed. "Or she would need protection. Even the Queen of the Pipes can make wrong assumptions."

I smiled. "Never said I was perfect. And I'm not going to accuse an innocent."

He held up a hand to stop me. "I didn't get a chance to fully examine the blast site. Did you find any shrapnel that looked like it didn't match any of the surrounding equipment?"

"Shrapnel as in pieces of the bomb?"

"Exactly."

"Yes."

He set his torch and mask down. "Okay, I'll look at the site first, and then I'll need to see what you found."

I followed him to the blast location. He squinted at the damage, ran his fingers along the scorched marks, sniffed the wreckage, and sorted through the rubble. Filling his pockets with odd bits of metal and wires, he straightened and asked to see what we had collected.

The control room was empty when Bubba Boom and I entered. I showed him the pieces Logan found. He set everything out on a table, including the fragments he had gathered. Arranging and turning the bits, he scrutinized each one.

Logan arrived, but I hushed his questions. He stood next to me as we waited for Bubba to finish.

"This doesn't look familiar," Bubba said. He held the biggest chunk up to the light.

"Not one of yours?" Logan asked. His tone was almost nasty—very unusual for him.

"I stopped building these. You know that better than anyone," Bubba said.

These two had a history. Wonderful.

"The Pop Cops aren't around. You could have returned to your old ways."

Bubba Boom huffed in exasperation. "You're still mad at me? I never told the Pop Cops about you and your sister. *That* was more important than the fact I stopped helping you design your little gadgets."

"Those gadgets—"

"Logan, that's enough," I said. "He agreed to assist us with finding the bomber."

Giving me an odd look, Logan said, "How did you find out about him?"

"Jacy."

Logan and Bubba exchanged a glance.

"What?" I demanded.

"A distraction?" Logan asked him.

"Could be."

Fear sizzled up my spine. "Another bomb?"

"No," Logan said. "More like keeping you busy and away from the real culprit."

"Why would Jacy do that?" I asked.

"Don't know," Logan said. "He's hard to read."

"Anything that doesn't have numbers scrolling across it is hard for you to read," I teased.

"Real funny. At least I didn't fall for Jacy's disinformation."

"Not quite," Bubba Boom said.

"What does that mean?" I asked.

"Just because I stopped playing with fire, doesn't mean I ignore what's going on around me." He held up a twisted piece of metal. "I recognize this."

5

"DO TELL," LOGAN SAID.

I swatted Logan on the arm. "Cut it out." He acted like a two-hundred-week-old, and I wondered if he had looked up to Bubba Boom only to be disappointed when the man caved in to the Pop Cops.

"There's a couple of scrubs," Bubba said. "I wouldn't call them Tech Nos as their devices are rudimentary, but they've gotten together and built a few incendiary apparatuses."

"Could they be responsible for the damage in the power plant?" I asked.

"Possible. One of them works in the wastewater treatment plant, the other in hydroponics. As far as I know they've only set off a couple stink bombs. One time they cleared everyone out of Sector E2 due to the stench." He smiled at the memory. "They also helped keep the Pop Cops occupied while you were busy rebelling."

Which meant Jacy knew about them. "What are their names?"

Bubba Boom squinted at the warped metal in his hands. He turned it over and over. "What if they're innocent?"

"Then we keep searching. We're not like the Pop Cops," I said.

"Really? Then why are there ISF goons patrolling the barracks all the time?" he asked.

"Because of the fights," Anne-Jade said from the doorway. "They're not working so they're bored. Nine times out of ten boredom leads to trouble. We did our share of proving that theory didn't we, Bubba?"

A wide grin spread on his face, matching Anne-Jade's. "We sure did," he said.

Logan's displeasure deepened. "As much as I'm not enjoying this little reunion, we need the names of the two stink bombers."

Bubba Boom met Anne-Jade's gaze. "Promise me you won't do anything rash? That you will be one hundred percent sure they're guilty before you arrest them?"

"When have I ever done anything rash?" Anne-Jade asked.

He gestured to me. "When you risked *everything* helping her."

"That wasn't rash," she corrected. "Risky, dangerous and suicidal, but not rash. We studied the situation carefully before offering our assistance." She winked at me. "Stubborn scrub almost turned us down, but it worked in our favor."

Bubba Boom tapped the metal piece against his leg as he considered. "All right. Kadar works in waste management, and Ivie is one of the gardeners in hydroponics."

"Thanks," I said. "Can you keep our...suspicions quiet for now? I don't want people to panic."

"Sure." He hesitated and glanced at Anne-Jade before leaving the control room.

"He's full of sheep's manure," Logan said. "A woman

named Ivie who just happens to work in hydroponics. Come on, how dumb does he think we are?"

"At least he didn't say Crapdar," I said.

Logan laughed. "Close enough."

Anne-Jade frowned. "I think he's telling the truth."

"You would," he said.

"What's that suppose to mean?"

Before they could launch into an argument, I asked Logan, "Can you look up those names in the population records, see if they do exist?"

"I don't have the time, but you can do it. It's easy," he said.

I tried to object, but Anne-Jade said, "I need you first."

Her tone didn't give me a warm feeling. "For what?"

"None of the Travas will tell *me* who worked on the Transmission."

Cold fingers gripped my stomach as I braced for the rest of her news.

"However, ex-Lieutenant Commander Karla Trava is willing to cooperate. But she'll only negotiate with you."

"Do I want to know why?"

"I think it's obvious," Anne-Jade said. When I failed to respond, she added, "Gloating over our problems for one, and just being difficult because she can. Plus she sees you as her ultimate enemy. If it wasn't for you, she would still be in command of the Pop Cops."

"Does she know I don't have the authority to grant anything she asks for? That I would need the Committee's approval?"

"Yes. And that may be part of the gloating."

"Wonderful," I grumbled. "Do I have to talk to her in the brig?"

"No. We'll bring her to my office and secure her, then give you two privacy."

This kept getting better and better. "When?"

"Now."

The thought of negotiating with Karla Trava sapped my energy. I rubbed my hand over my eyes.

Logan said, "Trella, each second we stand here brings us closer to a collision. We need to fix the Transmission."

"All right." Let the fun begin.

Anne-Jade had commandeered half of Karla's office in Quad A4, including her large desk and multiple computers. The other side held two smaller worktables for her lieutenants. The room remained almost the same from when Karla occupied it. Weapons and handcuffs hung from the side wall, Remote Access Temperature Sensitive Scanners (RATSS) lined a shelf and a bench with chains and cuffs bisected the area.

The couch had been removed and a variety of high-tech devices filled the long table. Anne-Jade's little receivers and microphones made the Pop Cop's communicators look clunky and old.

While Anne-Jade and her lieutenants fetched Karla, I paced the room. I automatically noted all the points of escape— two air vents in the ceiling and four heating vents near the floor.

When the door banged open, I steeled myself for the encounter. Sitting on the edge of a hard metal chair, I fidgeted with the buttons on my shirt. Wedged between the two ISF officers, Karla's smirk didn't waver as they cuffed her to the bench. She had twisted her long blond hair up into a knot on the top of her head. Her gaze swept my face and clothes, sparking amusement in her violet-colored eyes.

Now that I knew the doctors could change a person's eye color, I wondered if Lamont had tampered with hers.

"We'll be right outside." Anne-Jade handed me a stunner. "Just yell if you need us."

The door shut with a metallic clang that vibrated in my heart, matching my rapid pulse.

Karla laughed. "Still afraid of me?"

"Don't flatter yourself. It's disgust and not fear on my face. You reek of the brig."

"And you should know, having spent many hours there."

"Yes, I spent about thirty hours in your custody before I escaped. You're up to...what? Fourteen hundred at least and counting. Big difference."

Her humor faded. "We underestimated you. Something that won't happen again. But who could blame us? Look at you. Leader of a rebellion and you're still a scrawny little scrub."

"What did you expect?"

"Better clothes." It was my turn to laugh, but it died when she said, "And more power. You risked your life for them, yet you have to beg for the Committee's permission to do anything."

"Unlike you, I'm quite content with my role as support personnel. I never desired power, just freedom," I said.

"Uh-huh. And do you have your freedom?"

"Of course."

She opened her mouth, but I cut in and said, "Let's skip the small talk crap. We need the names of those who know how to repair the Transmission. What do you want in exchange?"

A sly half-smile teased the corners of her mouth as she leaned back, crossing her legs. "We never had that type of trouble when we were in charge. I think some of the scrubs miss us. And when you combine unhappy scrubs and bored prisoners, you can get an explosive reaction."

I studied her. Was she guessing about the sabotage? And was her comment a hint of more problems to come? Either way, a quick negotiation didn't seem likely.

"Should we recycle all the Travas to avoid any more trouble?" I asked.

She shrugged. "You obviously need a few of us to help with unexpected repairs, but this indecisiveness over what to do with us will only cause more problems. Which I'm more than happy to sit back and watch."

Anne-Jade had been right about her desire to gloat. "Thanks for the tip," I said. "But I'm here to get names and not a lecture."

Annoyance flashed in her eyes before she returned to acting casual. "Fine. In exchange for fixing the Transmission, we want the people in the brig to be released to our quarters, and we desire trials to determine degree of guilt in your warped little minds. There is no reason the entire Trava family should be confined."

I hated to admit this, but she had a point about the Trava family. However, releasing the upper officers from the brig would be a mistake.

Karla waved her hand as best she could while cuffed to the bench. "Run along to the Committee now and deliver my request like a good little scrub."

I couldn't suppress my grin as I toggled on my button microphone. Repeating her demands to the Committee, I waited as they discussed them. She rested her hands in her lap in an attempt to disguise the fury pulsing through her body, but her rigid posture betrayed her. I slid back in my chair, relaxing.

As expected the Committee was willing to review each

family member's actions prior to the rebellion to determine degree of guilt for each, but they refused to move the brig prisoners. I relayed this to Karla.

"Next?"

She scowled and my heart stuttered for a few beats—an automatic response.

"My terms are not negotiable," she said.

My temper flared. This had been a waste of time. "Then we're done." I stood to leave.

"You *have* to fix the Transmission." Karla's voice held a bit of panic. "The survival of our world depends on it."

I pressed a finger to my ear as if listening to a message. "The Committee is willing to include those in the brig in the review process."

"No. We want out of the brig."

Keeping my hand near my ear, I cocked my head and furrowed my brow. "Okay, then you'll be taken out of the brig and sent to Chomper."

Shock bleached her face. "That's not what I meant. What about the repairs?"

It was hard not to snigger over her reaction. "I'm sure once the others see how we cleaned out the brig, they'll be more cooperative."

Her hard stare burned like acid on my skin, but I kept my face neutral.

"You're lying," she said.

"Doesn't matter if you believe me or not." I strode toward the door.

"Wait," she said.

I paused but didn't turn around.

"I'll tell you the names if you do a review for all the Travas, including those in the brig."

Glancing over my shoulder, I said, "All right."

I rummaged for a wipe board and marker and returned to Karla. "Don't lie," I said. "If the names are wrong, you'll be the first to be sent to Chomper. I'll do the honors myself."

Karla rattled off three and I wrote them down. I didn't recognize any of them, but I hadn't been expecting to. Without saying goodbye, I left the office. Anne-Jade waited in the hallway.

"Well?" she asked.

I handed her the board.

She whistled. "Last I heard, the Committee was waiting for a counter-offer. What happened?"

"She pissed me off."

Feeling rather satisfied over my meeting with Karla, I changed into my climbing clothes and returned to the Expanse. I found the mark I had left on my last trip. The safety equipment hung nearby, so I strapped it on and made another attempt to reach the ceiling.

The new route looked promising and, after finding plenty of handholds, I climbed higher than ever before. I rested at twenty-three meters above level ten. Craning my head back, I shone my light up into the blackness. Still no ceiling. Logan had found a few diagrams in the computer system, and from them he estimated Inside's height to be about seventy-five meters, which would put it about two meters above my head. Either the computer or Logan had been wrong.

I yanked on the safety line and guessed I had another couple meters before I was literally at the end of my rope.

When I felt strong enough, I continued and discovered why meter seventy-five was mentioned in the computer. A bottom rung of a ladder started at that point. I grabbed the wide cold bar, hoping the rung would hold my weight. The smooth and rounded shape fit nicely in my hands. And my light illuminated the ladder which continued up with more rungs disappearing into the darkness.

I climbed on the ladder another meter, confirming the metal hadn't rusted or deteriorated with time. Squinting, I shone my light higher, but the ceiling still remained out of sight. However, I thought I spotted a dim gleam of a reflection. Wishful thinking or my imagination, it didn't matter. It was enough to justify my decision to unhook my harness from the safety line.

Despite the cold, sweat soaked the fabric of my uniform. I rubbed my moist palm on my arm before grasping the next rung. Continuing up the ladder with slow and careful movements, I tested each before allowing it to bear my weight. In the silence of the Expanse, my breath sounded loud and mechanical. My heart thudded with urgency as it reminded me of the danger. One slip, and…I wouldn't think about it.

Instead, I focused on keeping a tight grip and my balance on the rungs. Concentrating so hard on my hands and feet, I bumped my head on the ceiling. I clung to the ladder in surprise, and when my muscles stopped trembling, I scanned the flat expanse of metal over my head. Finally!

I checked the altimeter. Inside was eighty meters high, which meant we could build six more levels for a total of sixteen. Wow. That was mind-numbing. I hoped our systems could service all those levels. And what about keeping them clean and in good condition? And when did I turn into such a worrier?

Eventually, someone would need to explore the entire ceiling. Logan had read about another Outer Space Gateway in the computer files. By the way he described the file system, it had sounded as jumbled as the infirmary's supplies after the explosion. Between the Travas' attempts to erase files and the sheer amount of information, Logan had said—with his usual glee over a technical challenge—that it was an utter mess.

With one last look upwards, I steeled myself for the descent and stopped. Moving the beam of light slowly, I searched for the almost invisible indentation I thought I spotted from the corner of my eye. I swept the beam back and forth over a square meter-sized section. When I was just about to give up, the light skipped over a line.

I found a near-invisible hatch! Pleased over my discovery, it took me a few seconds to understand the full ramifications of my find. Above each of the four levels we have been living in, was a near-invisible hatch to the Gap between levels. This meter and a half space housed pipes and wires and room for someone like me to move between levels without being seen.

I had thought I reached the ceiling. But the presence of a near-invisible hatch meant there was *something* on the other side.

6

***SOMETHING ON THE OTHER SIDE.* I REPEATED IT IN MY** mind in order for the logical side of my brain to catch up. No black rubber ringed the hatch, which meant it wasn't a Gateway to Outer Space. There could be another Expanse and room for additional levels. I laughed, but it sounded strained and metallic as it echoed. I had thought sixteen levels incomprehensible.

Only one way to know for sure, I hooked my legs through the rungs on the ladder to anchor my body. Stretching my hands up, I felt for the release.

The pop-click reverberated through the bones in my arms. I pushed the hatch. The metal groaned and creaked, setting my teeth on edge. A dusty stale smell drifted down.

When the opening was big enough for me to fit through, I shined my light inside. The ladder continued another meter before stopping. Odd shapes decorated the wall. Taking a risk, I climbed into the space. The floor seemed solid so I stepped down, but still held on to the ladder just in case.

The good news—the floor didn't disintegrate under me.

The bad—a strange tingle zipped through my foot and daylights turned on.

Blinded by the bright white light, I squeezed my eyes shut. Even through my eyelids, the harsh brilliance stabbed like a horrible migraine.

It felt like hours before my vision adjusted.

When I could finally see, I saw a giant monster.

I screamed and hopped onto the ladder before logic took control. The huge thing was a thing, not a living breathing creature. It didn't move. No sounds emanated. No lights shone from it. It appeared to be made of an odd black metal without rivets.

Unable to stifle my curiosity, I stepped closer. About nine meters tall and a hundred meters wide, it was too long for me to guess with any accuracy. A colossal sheep without a neck had been my initial impression. Or a long sock filled with round balls. Or glass balls all stuck together in a rectangular shape.

Either way, the whole oddity rested on eight thick metal legs with massive wheels. The head—for lack of a better word—had two large glass panes for its eyes, which reflected the daylights set into the ceiling. If the roof above this strange level was indeed the ceiling for Inside. At this point, I wouldn't be surprised to find yet another level and perhaps a whole other society living above us.

I ringed the structure and spotted its tiny twin right next to it. Not as scary as its super-sized brother, the smaller… what to call it? A lamb? A bubble thing? It appeared to be a conveyance of some type.

Once the shock of my discovery wore off, I realized that the room I stood in was indeed a room. Inside was approximately two thousand meters wide, by two thousand meters long. This area was a fraction of that size. In fact, my body's internal sense of measurement suspected the room's dimensions equaled one Sector or Quadrant—six hundred and sixty-six point seven square meters. One ninth of a level. Or to convert it into Inside's designation system so it matched the levels below, this area would be Quad G17.

Which meant, there was potentially four Sectors and three more Quadrants in this level. Did that mean eight more bubble monsters? I shuddered, sending a horde of goose bumps across my skin. Feeling as if I would float away, I leaned against the bumpy wall.

Remembering the patterns and symbols covering its surface, I straightened to examine them. The pictures and diagrams made as much sense to me as one of Logan's computer screens.

I walked along the walls, seeking a doorway. The strange markings continued, filling every centimeter without a break on three of the four walls. In the middle of the north wall, which would be shared with Sector D17, was a Gateway outlined in the familiar black rubber seal. But this one extended almost to the ceiling and was at least two hundred meters wide. Big enough to fit the bubble monster. In the northwest corner, sheets of the black metal had been stacked. I touched the smooth surface. It felt like glass, but seemed too thick. Prying the first sheet up, I expected it to be heavy. But it peeled away with a staticky-crackly sound. It weighed nothing compared to metal or glass. And the edges drooped like cloth, but not cloth. It reminded me of a slice of Outer Space—black, cold and weightless.

The floating dizziness returned full force. I dropped the sheet, and sat on the floor, holding my head in my hands. Discovering the Expanse paled in comparison to this find.

And then a thought stopped my heart. Should I tell the Committee? The rapid pace of changes in our society has

been overwhelming to the majority of the people. Some
even had trouble accepting the Expanse and new levels. And
what about the saboteur or saboteurs? If they were upset over
the fact we traveled through Outer Space to an unknown
destination, what would they do when faced with this new
discovery?

Perhaps we needed to deal with our current problems
before I added more to the mix. I returned to the ladder
and climbed down below the floor, replacing and resealing
the near-invisible hatch. I wondered about the daylights and
hoped they would turn off.

I had no memory of the rest of my descent other than
the tricky maneuver of reattaching my harness to the safety
line.

By the time I returned to the storeroom, it was hour thirty.
Only two hours had passed since I had left Karla and gone
exploring. It seemed as if weeks had come and gone.

I perched on the edge of the couch's cushion and tried
to decide between showering and sleeping. But each time I
forced my thoughts to the matter at hand, the image of the
Bubble Monster reclaimed all of my attention.

When Riley arrived an hour later, I hadn't moved. He sat
next to me and I collapsed against him. Should I tell him?

He wrapped his arm around my shoulders, supporting me.
"You look like you had a close encounter with Chomper.
What happened?" he asked.

I opened my mouth, but the words jammed in my throat.

"Logan told me you talked to Karla Trava. If she upset you,
I'll…"

Wrenching my thoughts away from my discovery, I focused
on Riley, looking up at him. A hard stubbornness radiated
from his blue eyes and the muscles in his neck strained.

"You'll what?" I asked.

"I'll put her in the same cell with Vinco and smuggle a knife to him."

"Although she tried, she failed to unnerve me. But it's so sweet of you." I tapped my chest. "Nothing says you care for me better than offering to torture my enemies."

He grinned. "No sense doing things halfhearted. And to think, some girls have to endure listening to poetry."

"Poor things." I tsked, but couldn't stop a smile.

Riley stroked my cheek with his fingers. "That's better. Now you have some color in your face. Did something go wrong with searching for the bomber?"

Glad to have a topic I could handle, I said, "No. Jacy sent me to a guy named Bubba Boom." I held up a hand to stop his snort of disbelief. "Just wait, the story gets better." Telling him about the stink bombers, I filled him in on what I had learned.

He fiddled with a piece of ripped fabric on the couch's arm. "Not much to go on. You can use the computer in my rooms to research the names Bubba Boom gave you. Logan assigned you a ten-degree security clearance so you can access the entire network."

"Why would he do that? I barely know how to use the computer."

"You're kidding, right?" Riley stared at me as if I had told him Sheepy could talk.

I ignored his question. "Your computer is fine. I also need a shower. Is your dad working? I don't want to bother him."

This time Riley gave me a slow conspiratorial leer. "What a coincidence. I need a shower as well. Good thing my father's busy for the next couple of hours and you have a promise to keep."

★ ★ ★

Taking different routes to Riley's rooms in Sector E4, I figured my path through the air ducts would be quicker than his through the corridors. But when I reached the vent for suite number three-six-nine-five, he waited below, standing on the table.

I opened the cover and dangled my legs. Riley caught me around my waist and I slid down him the rest of the way. He didn't let go when my feet touched the table. Dipping his head closer to mine, he kissed me for a long time.

When he tugged at my uniform, I pulled away. Breathless for a moment, I sucked in a few deep breaths.

"Are you sure your father won't be back soon?" I asked.

He answered with the metallic trill of my zipper unzipping. Cool air caressed my sweaty back. A nervous shiver raced over my skin. His lips found mine and his hands stroked my exposed back. Heat from his touch burned all the doubts away.

When he began to pull the fabric of my jumpsuit down, he paused. "Shower?"

A big step, but my heart beat its approval. And the desire to see him naked and soapy overrode all logic. I imagined cold reason melting and steaming away in a puffy cloud.

We left a trail of clothes to the washroom. Warm water, the scent of soap and slippery skin made for an exhilarating combination. I worried about the ugly scars crisscrossing my torso, arms and legs, but no hint of disgust or pity darkened his expression.

He wiped the water from my eyes. "You're beautiful. I—"

I covered his mouth with mine, afraid to hear him utter words I couldn't repeat back to him. Grabbing the soap, I worked it into a frothy lather. I explored the hard ridges of his stomach, the smooth lines of his back and his nice grab-able butt as we kissed under the spray of hot water.

His hands were equally busy and quite distracting. And when his lips moved to my neck, I lost all track of time and location. However, Riley kept an eye on the clock in the washroom, and he stopped way too soon with a sigh.

"Dad's due in a few minutes. Although..." He trailed a finger along my ribs. "He wouldn't just barge in here. He'd think I was alone in the shower so we could continue."

"And what happens when we both come out?"

"He would grin like an idiot, beaming with happiness."

I pushed Riley's hand away before it could move any lower. "No. I'm not ready for your father to get any ideas."

"Too late. He's been full of ideas ever since I started talking about an intern named Ella." Riley pulled me close. "The rebellion distracted him, but he's back to being way too nosy about our relationship."

"He needs one of his own."

Riley dropped his arms and turned off the water. "It would be nice, but he says my mother was the only one for him, and he hasn't met anyone who drove him as crazy as she did." He grabbed a couple of towels and handed one to me.

"Drove him crazy in a good way or bad?" I dried my body and wrapped the towel around my torso.

He paused as if struck by an amazing notion. "He always said both good and bad, but I never really understood how it was possible..." He met my gaze. "Until now."

I looked away and rummaged for a comb. My question had almost been in jest, and I didn't want to start a serious discussion. The knots in my hair resisted the comb's efforts, but I managed to smooth them out. I braided my hair without drying it. A certain amount of patience was required to dry it first. Patience I didn't have. Never did.

Glancing at Riley, I watched him run his fingers through his wet mop before he dressed. I never cared about my appearance prior to meeting Riley, and he'd seen me at my worst. So why would I waste precious time to fuss over my hair? I studied my reflection in the washroom's mirror. A stranger stared back. Even after fourteen weeks, my blue-colored eyes still seemed like they belonged in another face. The blue had been my original color; otherwise, the reversal drops wouldn't have worked.

According to Domotor and a few others, I had my father's eyes. They also claimed my father was Nolan Garrard Unlike Lamont's name, his didn't make me cringe. In fact, I would be proud to be his daughter. Even though the Force of Ten's attempt to change our world failed, his final defiance by saving those ten files had been vital. Without them, we wouldn't have found Gateway. And their existence impressed Logan—hard to do when it came to technology.

Perhaps settling the matter of my birth parents wouldn't be so bad. So what if Lamont's my mother? It's not like I'd be forced to live with her or to forgive her. Nothing would change.

I hurried to dress before Riley's dad returned. Riley already sat at the computer in the living area. The apartment had one bedroom, a washroom, a small space for the computer, a table and couch. Posh accommodations from a scrub's point of view, but still not the huge suite of rooms I had imagined when the Pop Cops kept us from going above level two.

Riley typed for a few minutes before relinquishing the chair. "I logged you on. You'll need to pull up the population records to search for those names."

Reluctance kept me from claiming the seat. "Can't you look them up for me?"

"Sit." He pointed. "You need to learn how to access the computer files."

Not happy, I plopped in front of the screen. He leaned over me as he explained how to navigate the network. I might look like Nolan Garrard, but I didn't have his knack with computers.

After more than a few frustrating minutes, Riley almost growled at me. "Think of the network as a map of Inside and the files are stored in different Sectors and Quadrants. In order to find the right file, you need to know the location."

"But what if it isn't there? Logan said—"

"That the files had been jumbled, but I'm used to them that way. If I can't find what I'm looking for, I request a search."

"From who?"

"The computer."

"Oh. Like from the Controllers in the network?"

"No. Yes."

I turned my head to see him. He squinted at the screen as if in pain.

"Which one is it?"

Riley ran a hand over his face. "We learned that the Controllers are really just an operating system. It connects all the information in the network, lets you know if you can do something or not. It protects certain areas. And it will search for files and tell you where they are." He swept his arm out. "Everything in Inside is all connected to the network. Technically, I could run all the systems from one computer."

This fact seemed to impress him, but, considering the recent sabotage, it scared me. "What happens if the network breaks down?"

"It can't."

"Why not?"

"There are backup systems and everything has been saved in protected files."

"But what if they're compromised as well?"

He dismissed my concerns. "Won't happen. And you're trying to distract me so I don't teach you how to navigate through the network."

"I'm not. I'm just worried another bomb might blow apart the network."

"Don't worry, there are many safeguards in place. Unless you want me to have Logan explain—"

"No! I trust you."

He clutched his hands to his chest. "She… Gasp… Trusts me! Call for medical aid stat!"

I swung at him, but he grabbed my wrist and pulled me to my feet.

Snaking his arms around my waist, he said, "We need to celebrate this momentous occasion."

"What are we celebrating?" Jacob Ashon, Riley's father, asked from the doorway.

I pushed Riley away to greet his father. But the damage had been done. He grinned at us like an idiot. Joy beamed from his brown eyes as his gaze went from Riley's wet hair to mine. I suppressed a groan.

"We're celebrating Trella learning the computer system," Riley said.

The wattage from his grin dulled a few kilos. His slightly disappointed expression reminded me of Riley. He had his father's solid build, sense of humor and mannerisms, but, according to Jacob, Riley's black hair, blue eyes and stubbornness had been inherited from his mother, Ramla Ashon.

She had been another casualty of the failed Force of Ten rebellion along with Nolan Garrard, Blas Sanchia and Shawn Lamont. Four brave souls who would be honored with a plaque or memorial along with Cogon once our world settled back into… What? Not like we would return to life before. I guessed just when our society settled into a new routine.

"Oh," Jacob said then recovered his brightness. "Don't teach her too much. She tends to leave a wake of trouble behind her, and I don't want to spend hours trying to decipher the carnage."

"Not funny," I said, plopping back down in the chair. The diagram of file names on the screen hadn't gotten any more understandable with Riley's explanation.

Riley attempted another round of frustrating instruction before giving in and swapping places with me. I paid attention for a few minutes, but soon lost interest. As he worked, I studied Jacob. He straightened the mess of wires and gadgets Riley had strewn about the room, collecting them into a neat pile.

Jacob had been thrilled to be reunited with Blake, Riley's younger brother. Having to send a child to live in the lower levels must be difficult especially since Jacob reveled in the whole family experience. I wondered if Blake's decision to return to living in the barracks upset him. If I did test my blood to determine if Nolan and Lamont were my parents, I knew Jacob would be happy. Despite Lamont's first betrayal costing him his wife, and the second one almost killing his son, he stayed friends with her. Crazy.

"…paying attention, Trella?" Riley asked.

"Uh…"

"You're impossible. Here's the file you need." He stood. "*You* can search through it."

Back in front of the computer, I scanned the directory of names with birth weeks, barrack locations and other stats listed next to them. The file contained all the lower level scrubs. All eighteen thousand and change. Ugh.

As I scrolled down the page, Riley asked his father why he was late.

"I visited your brother," Jacob said. "The Committee heard rumors of the kitchen workers threatening to cook only enough food for themselves. I thought I'd check into it and see if I can resolve the issue."

I tuned out their conversation, glad I no longer had to deal with the Committee's problems. Concentrating on the list, I thought there must be a reason why the names had been put in this particular order. It wasn't alphabetical, by barrack location, birth week, by Care Mother or by care unit. At the end of the stats for each were the same letters: AS.

When my name jumped out, I stopped. Did AS mean air scrub? I didn't recognize the other names with AS, but I hadn't learned the names of my fellow workers either. After I scrolled a few more pages the AS turned into a CS and I found my Care Mother's name in that section.

The list had been organized by work area and they had been alphabetized. I quickly bypassed the other workers until I reached the hydroponics scrubs. Sure enough, Ivie was listed. After I wrote down her stats on a wipe board, I found Kadar and copied his as well.

They had been care mates. No surprise. They were also a few centiweeks older than me, putting them closer to Cog's age. And they slept in Sector D1, Jacy's barrack. I tapped the marker against my teeth. This information didn't mean anything other than they existed. Bubba Boom could have picked their names at random.

To really find out what's going on, someone would need to follow those two around. I couldn't do it as I was too recognizable with my blue eyes and small stature. The best way would be to recruit someone not in Jacy's network and who I could trust.

"Trella?" Riley interrupted my train of thought. "Did you hear what's going on in the lower level kitchen?"

I turned. "A little. I found those names, and I think we—"

"There might be a food strike. Don't you care?"

"Of course I do, but your dad and the Committee know about it. They can deal with it. Plus they have Blake to..."

Riley crossed his arms. A danger sign. "To what?"

"To warn them." And he would be perfect to spy on Ivie and Kadar for me. "Does Blake come up here often to visit?"

"Why?" When I hesitated, he said, "I recognize that look. Tell me what you're planning."

By the tension rolling off Riley, I knew to tread carefully. "We need a reliable person to keep an eye on Ivie and Kadar for us. I thought Blake cou—"

"No. You're not putting him in danger."

"It won't be that dangerous."

"What if Ivie and Kadar are the bombers and they notice Blake's interest in them? He could be their next target. Besides, he'll be needed to report to the Committee about the food situation. Trella, you've got to keep in mind the big picture, not just the next thing you want to do."

The big picture. I almost laughed, remembering what I had said to Jacy about being a big picture girl. Drawing in a deep breath, I held it along with a sarcastic reply. My search for the saboteurs was important, but I suspected his ire went deeper than the recent kitchen crisis, and I had no energy to fight with him. The climb to the ceiling of the Expanse had sapped my strength.

Instead, I swiveled back to the computer screen. Not sure how to log out, I picked up the wipe board. Before I could stand, a bright whiteness flashed on the monitor, erasing the list. Then it faded to black. It seemed odd, but when I glanced at Riley, his attention remained on me.

I stood and waved the wipe board. "I'll find someone else to help me with my problem." Hurrying toward the door, I had almost reached the handle when he called my name.

"Who are you going to recruit?" he asked.

"I'm sure Anne-Jade knows a trustworthy person. I'll see you later." I slipped out of the room before he could say anything else.

When the door clicked shut, I leaned against the hallway's wall and considered my next move. No one was in sight. The corridors in the upper living sectors never had much traffic and they tended to be a bit of a maze. I was already on level four and Anne-Jade should be working in her office in Quad A4. Pushing off the wall, I headed to the right and froze.

Gray smoke rolled along the thin carpet. I recovered from my shock and ran, following the clouds. They thickened and blackened as I drew closer to the air plant in Quad I4. Halfway there, the shrill fire alarm sounded, assaulting my ears. Soon shouts and shrieks joined in the cacophony.

The smoke blocked my vision as it stung my eyes. I dropped to the floor and crawled to the entrance of the plant. The heat reached me first. Then I gawked at the fire. Erupting from the units that housed the air filters, flames licked at the ceiling. Water rained down from the sprinkler system, the streams hissed and steamed on the hot metal, but nothing sprayed from the nozzles directly over the air filters.

A few workers ran past me, emptying the room. About to do the same, I spotted a figure sprawled on the floor near the control panel. His legs draped over pieces of a broken chair. It looked as if he had fallen backwards. Dead?

I strained to hear any sounds that meant the fire response team had arrived, but the roar of the blaze dominated. Then he rolled to his side and I saw his face.

Logan.

7

WHAT THE HELL WAS LOGAN DOING IN THE AIR PLANT?
His shoulders shook as he coughed and I realized the flames
burned closer to him. It didn't matter why. All that mattered
was saving him.

I ripped two strips of fabric from the hem of my shirt. Lying
on the floor, I pulled myself toward him as if I squirmed
through a tight air shaft. When I encountered the warm
puddles of water from the sprinklers, I rolled, soaking my
clothes and dipping the strips in them. I tied one around my
nose and mouth.

Logan's lips moved, but I couldn't hear what he shouted.
Blisters peppered his face. He squeezed his eyes closed as
another coughing fit racked his body.

Sliding as fast as possible on my belly, I finally reached
Logan. He jerked in surprise when I touched him. At this
distance, the heat from the fire was almost intolerable and
breathing was all but impossible.

"It's Trella," I yelled in his ear. "Can you walk?"

He clutched my arm. "Yes, but I can't see!"

"Here." I wrapped the other strip around his face to filter

the smoke. "Stay low and keep—" Hot air choked me. Thick black smoke engulfed us and stung my eyes. A brief thought that perhaps I should have waited for the fire response team flashed. But the air cleared for a nanosecond and I tugged Logan toward the entrance.

We crawled, rolled and stumbled. The heat intensified, evaporating the water from the sprinklers before it reached the floor. The hot metal seared our skin. Halfway there, Logan collapsed and I yanked him another meter before I joined him.

Air refused to fill my lungs and my throat burned. Blackness danced in my vision, swirling with white sparks. It reminded me of the brief glimpse I had of Outer Space before Cogon floated away. Except then it had been ice cold and this time it was my turn to drift off.

A blast of water hit me, rousing me and rolling me over. Strong arms peeled me from the floor, carried me. Voices yelled and admonished, but I had no breath to respond. Tucked against my rescuer's chest, I stared as the walls of Inside streaked by.

Then the familiar curtains of the infirmary surrounded me. I was laid on a bed as a mask covered my nose and mouth, forcing cool air down my lungs. I sucked it in despite the sharp pain in my throat. My skin felt like the flames still licked at it. The small prick in my arm a mere nuisance in comparison to the rest of my body.

Only when the dizziness started did I realize what the prick meant. Too late to resist, I let my world spin out of control. It wasn't a new feeling. Not at all.

At least when I woke, the pain was gone. But the mask remained—a good thing since my lungs strained to breathe.

My arms and legs had been wrapped in bandages. Soft white gloves covered my hands. Faces came and went as I drifted in and out of consciousness. I recognized Lamont's frown, Riley's worry and Bubba Boom's scowl. I understood the words *painkillers, idiot, brain damage, reckless* and *growing skin grafts*. But I didn't see the one face I worried about or hear the one voice I wanted to hear or heck, I'd even settle for someone mentioning his name. Logan.

Without him, Inside would be lost. Besides the high-ranking Travas, he alone knew how to run this ship. The Captain in all but name. I suspected he had been the primary target of the fire for just that reason. I tried to yank the mask off to ask, but Lamont slapped my hand and threatened to inject me with a sedative if I touched it again.

Hours or weeks later—hard to tell—I woke into the quiet stillness of bluelights. They shone through the fabric of the privacy curtains. I no longer felt as if a person made of solid metal sat on my chest so I removed the mask, but kept it close just in case.

Sheepy was tucked in next to me. Smiling, I moved him so he wouldn't fall on the floor as I struggled to sit up. The effort winded me. I sucked a few deep breaths from the mask. Moving with care so I wouldn't make a sound, I slipped through the overlap in the fabric. I paused to let my eyes adjust and my legs solidify under me. The clock read hour ninety-two, which would mean I had been out of it for sixty hours. Losing hunks of time just had to stop, I felt as if I spent more time in the infirmary than anywhere else.

A robe hung over a nearby chair as if someone suspected I'd be creeping out of bed—Riley probably. Wrapping it around my shoulders, I scanned the other beds. A couple of patients slept in the next two, but the third had also been isolated from the room by the curtains. Logan's, I hoped.

I shuffled-stepped—all I could manage with my bandage-wrapped legs and tight skin—over to the hidden patient. Ducking under the curtain, I almost fainted with relief. Logan slept in the bed. Or at least I think he was sleeping. Bandages covered his eyes and a mask rested over his nose and mouth.

He tugged it away from his face. "Who's there?"

"Trella," I whispered.

Logan reached with his free hand and I took it in mine. He also wore the special white gloves. "Thanks," he said.

I shrugged, but realized he couldn't see the motion. "I just got you closer to the door. Someone else did the true life saving." And I would need to find out his name. "Besides, you'd have done the same for me."

"Probably." His smile didn't last long.

"What's the damage?"

"Ten air...filter bays. The computer—"

"I meant you."

"Oh. Burns over fifty percent—" he puffed "—of my body." He pressed the mask to his face and inhaled deeply for a few minutes. "Lost my vision...but it might be...temporary."

Horror swept over me and I squeezed his hand. "Might? That's vague."

"Doctor Lamont...will know better...in time."

"How much time?"

He shook his head. "Don't know."

I waited as he drank in more of the oxygen-rich air flowing from the mask. "I have a million questions, but I'll ask you them later. Just answer this one. Do you think the fire was an act of sabotage or an attack aimed at you?"

"Both."

The news inflamed the burns on my skin, sending a hot surge of fear. "Why aren't you surrounded by guards?"

"He's protected," Anne-Jade said. She poked her head in between the curtain's overlap.

I jumped. "How long have you been listening?"

"I've been here the whole time."

"Why didn't you say something sooner?"

She smiled. "I didn't want to interrupt."

"Yeah right. You were hoping to overhear something juicy."

Parting the fabric, she stood next to her brother's bed. Anne-Jade glanced at him and then me. "And just how much juice do you think I could get from a couple of overcooked mutton chops like yourselves?"

Logan's laughter turned into a coughing fit.

"Okay. Point taken. Who else knows about the attack?"

"The Committee has been informed of both sabotages and the attempt on Logan's life."

She gripped the rail on Logan's bed as if a great weight rested on her shoulders. All humor fled her eyes and I realized she teetered on the edge of exhaustion.

Even though I was reluctant to ask, and I could probably guess the answer, I had to hear it from her. "And the Committee's response?"

"Lockdown and search of all levels."

Now I had to grab the rail or risk falling to the floor. We had come full circle. Instead of Pop Cops policing the lower levels, we now had ISF officers. They would confine everyone to their barracks until they could do a thorough search for evidence. At least, they included the upper levels.

Anne-Jade said, "Do you have any better ideas? We can't let them keep blowing and burning up vital life systems. We also brought Ivie and Kadar in for questioning."

"How did—"

"We found your wipe board in the hallway outside the

air plant. I remembered the names from our discussion with Bubba Boom."

"But you don't have any proof they're involved. Just his suspicions."

"Doesn't matter. There could be another explosion or attempt to get to Logan or you."

"Me? Why would they—"

"To prevent you from discovering any more surprises. They're still reeling from the fact we're in a big ship and we have all this extra room to spread out."

Good thing I'd kept the bubble monster to myself.

Anne-Jade then asked me how I had gotten to the air plant so fast. "Did someone ask you to meet there?"

"No." I explained about leaving Riley's, but omitted the fact I had been going to find her. Any chance to discover what Ivie and Kadar had been up to had been ruined. And if they had been working with anyone, it would be impossible to find out now.

"A lucky coincidence," Anne-Jade said. She smoothed Logan's hair. "By the time the fire response team arrived they could only go a few meters into the plant. If you hadn't dragged Logan closer…"

"Who pulled us out?"

"Bubba Boom carried you and Hank from maintenance grabbed Logan."

"How's the plant?"

"Bad. Smoke spread throughout Inside and made a bunch of people sick. Half the air filters are burnt to a crisp. The air workers are rigging up a temporary cleaning system, but it won't last long. When you're feeling better, they're going to need you to help install filters in the air ducts. It's another temporary measure."

Logan lifted his mask again. "Plant fire also…a distraction."

"And a lure to get you in harm's way," Anne-Jade said.

"No. A distraction from…computer."

Dread twisted and I wished I had stayed in my bed. "What's wrong with the computer?"

"Compromised."

My chest felt as if my body had gotten stuck in a tight pipe. "How bad?"

"Don't know…I need to…see."

I considered. Besides the burning from the smoke, my vision hadn't been affected by the heat. "Logan, was there an explosion in the air plant before the fire?"

"No. Light exploded from—" Another coughing fit seized him. "From…the computer monitor. It burned…my eyes."

Anne-Jade and I shared a horrified look.

"Who could…?" I couldn't even say the words.

"I could," Logan said.

"Who else?" his sister demanded.

"A few…of the Travas. Maybe Riley." He drew on the mask for a few breaths. "Domotor. Trella's father."

"Nolan's been fertilizer for over fifteen centiweeks," I said, dismissing him.

"According to…Karla Trava." He shrugged. "She didn't recycle you—"

"We don't know that for sure." I squelched any and all hope. It was ludicrous. "Besides, he would have revealed himself after the rebellion."

Another shrug. I mulled over his list. Not Riley and I doubted Domotor, so that left the Travas. "Are there any working computers in Sector D4?"

Anne-Jade scowled at me. "Do you think I'm an idiot?"

"We disabled them," Logan said.

"Could they have hooked them back up?" And before Anne-Jade could snap at me, I added, "They don't have anything else to do. And you and Logan made a number of amazing devices just from recycled parts so it's a valid question."

She scratched her arm absently. "I guess it's possible. I'll have a team go in and check." Huffing in annoyance, she slid her hand under her sleeve and rubbed harder.

Logan reached out blindly and touched her arm. "Stop it. Doctor Lamont said...to leave it...alone or it'll get infected."

"But it itches," she said between gritted teeth.

"What happened?" I asked her.

She pushed up her sleeve, revealing white bandages like the ones on Logan and my arms. "I donated skin so the Doctor could grow my brother a new coat."

Logan smiled. "I'm covered with girl germs...don't tell Riley."

"Maybe you'll be smarter now," she quipped. "I'd like to think you will appreciate having a sister more, but I doubt it."

I remembered he had said he had been burned on over fifty percent of his body. "He needed skin grafts from you to live. Didn't he?"

"Yes. I matched his skin type, which doesn't always happen with siblings."

Glancing at my own bandaged arms, I wondered how badly I had been burned. I met Anne-Jade's steady gaze.

"You weren't as bad as Logan, but you needed skin grafts to survive as well," she said.

She shifted her stance as if challenging me to ask her who donated skin cells for me; either that or she prepared for a fight. I didn't have the energy to deal with either so I said goodbye and shuffled back to my bed.

The effort to visit Logan had exhausted me. Grateful for the flow of clean air, I inhaled large lung-filling breaths from my mask. Funny how I had taken something as vital as breathing for granted—not paying it one bit of attention until it had become a problem.

The next time I woke, the daylights brightened the infirmary and half of my curtain had been pushed back. Lamont rolled a small table toward me. Stocked with clean bandages, salve, a bowl of water and a sponge, I grimaced in anticipation. She planned to change my dressing and clean the burns.

Hour two glowed on the clock. Another ten hours lost to injury. Another week gone. We were now on week 147,022.

Lamont tried a smile, but thought better of it. She kept her tone and mannerisms all business. Doctor to patient. "How are you feeling?"

"Like I've been stuffed into an oven and twice baked."

Amusement flashed on her face. She tucked a long strand of her hair that had escaped her braid behind her ear. Wearing her light green shirt and pants, she looked ready for surgery. "You know I need to—"

"Just get it over with…please."

With deft fingers, she peeled the bandages from my left arm, starting at the wrist. "You might not want to see your skin. It's not fully healed yet and will look like…"

I waited.

"Raw meat. But it will return to normal healthy skin. I even removed the scars on your arms and legs from… before."

"You can do that?"

"It's considered cosmetic surgery. I normally wouldn't do

it for arms or legs. Faces, yes. But since you needed so much skin already…"

"Oh. Thanks."

Without the dressing the air stung my skin. I braced for the touch of water and it didn't disappoint, feeling like liquid fire as it ran down my arm. I hissed in pain.

"Do you want a pain pill?" she asked.

"No…thank you. They make me sleepy and I've slept enough." Why was I being so polite? *Because this woman saved your life.*

I kept that thought in mind as she changed all the bandages. My extremities fared the worst. When she finished my bedding and gown were soaked, and so were her sleeves. She pushed them up to help me switch to a clean bed and I froze.

White bandages peeked out from under the wet fabric on both of her arms. I stared at them, knowing what they meant, but not wanting to really believe it. Finally, I pulled my gaze away and met hers.

"You were going to die," she said. "We needed to find you a match."

8

"AND YOU MATCHED MY SKIN TYPE?" I ASKED.

Struggling to keep her professional demeanor, Lamont nodded. Impressive considering I stood less than a meter from her. The fact we matched meant I was her daughter. The daughter she had thought had been fed to Chomper over fifteen hundred weeks ago. Alive and…not quite well, but living and breathing.

How would I feel if Cogon returned from Outer Space and he hated me for leaving him out there? Thrilled and awful at the same time.

But I couldn't get the image of her standing with Karla Trava in the main Control Room out of my mind. She had searched all the faces in the room and didn't recognize me. Shouldn't a mother recognize her own daughter no matter how old she was? Plus the fact that she had been there with Karla in the first place, cooperating with her, endangering thousands of people for her own selfish desire.

However, if I was being fair, I endangered everyone with our rebellion. Was I being selfish as well?

Too confused to say anything but thanks for the skin cells,

I collapsed on the clean bed and closed my eyes. Too much of a coward to meet her gaze.

Riley visited me around hour ten. He smiled and sat on the edge of the bed. "How are you doing?"

"Great. I'm ready to go. Do you think your dad would mind if I sleep on your couch?"

"Nice try. But you're not leaving here until Doctor Lamont gives you permission." He took my hand gently in his. "Did you even stop and think about the danger to yourself before you rushed in to save Logan?"

"No time. I hope you didn't come here to lecture me."

"Actually, I came to see how Sheepy is doing. He doesn't like sleeping in strange places." Riley picked up the stuffed sheep and smoothed his gray fuzzy hair made from real sheep's wool. The little toy had been sharing my pillow.

At my age—1535 weeks or 17.5 years in the old time—it seemed silly to lavish so much affection on a toy. But with a limited amount of playthings available while growing up in the care facility with nine others, and the all-work-and-no-free-time structure of my upbringing, Sheepy filled a void.

"Sheepy's been keeping me company," I said. "Thanks."

"He does have an ulterior motive," he said with a sly smile.

"And that would be?"

"Spying on you. Making sure you're listening to the Doctor's orders and not... What's that?" Riley put Sheepy up to his ear as if listening to the toy. "Not staying in bed? Bothering Logan?" He tsked.

"Anne-Jade really needs to learn the difference between her job and basic friendship." I grumped. "I don't suppose she has any suspects for the attack on her brother?"

"She's questioning the two stink bombers, but that's all she has right now." He fiddled with his shirt. "Inside has been locked down. It's worse than when the Pop Cops had been in charge."

An outrage on her behalf surged through me. I struggled into a sitting position. "She's dealing with a very different type of rebel than the Pop Cops ever did. We didn't blow anything up, or kill any innocents or set fires. The only people to get hurt were our own and a few Pop Cops."

He refused to meet my gaze. "There has to be a better way."

"I'm sure she's open to ideas. Have you talked to her?"

"I would if I had one. I'm more of a support person." He finally looked me in the eye. "You're the one who has the knack for coming up with new ideas."

I flopped back. Not *this* again. Time to change the subject. "What have you been doing since the fire?"

Pressing his lips together, he swallowed his obvious ire over my dodge. "Once I knew you and Logan would live, I've been checking the computer network. Logan said it had been compromised, but I've yet to find evidence."

"Did Anne-Jade search the Travas' rooms?"

"Yep. None of the computers they found were connected to the network."

Interesting word choice. I asked, "Do you suspect they have a hidden connection?"

"It's possible, but not probable. I think we have another person or persons with Logan's ability to ghost through the network. He or she would be all but impossible to catch."

This conversation felt familiar, and I wondered if eighteen weeks ago, Karla Trava had a similar discussion with her lieutenants. The arrival of Lamont to check my vitals was a welcome distraction. Although she declared they were all strong, she remained vague about when I'd be able to leave the infirmary.

When she went to check on Logan, Riley raised his eyebrows. "You were...civil to her." He sounded surprised.

"With my tendency to end up as her patient, there's no sense being nasty. Besides, everyone else seems to think she's okay."

"Oh no. I'm not going to believe you'd be influenced by others. That's not the Trella I know. Are you sure it isn't because she saved your life?"

I shrugged. "Well...it helps."

"Uh-huh. And how about the confirmation that she's your mother? Did that help?"

"Not at all."

"Whew! I was beginning to worry the fire had burned more than your skin," he teased.

Glad to see Riley smile, I relaxed. Too often lately, our conversations had transformed into...not fights, but arguments. Right before the fire, he had accused me of not caring about Inside, and I had... A memory pulled on the edges of my thoughts.

"The scrub file," I said.

"What?"

"White light flashed on the screen probably the same time Logan was attacked. Then it erased the list."

He leaned forward. "Are you sure?"

"You might be able to find evidence of tampering in that file if it is still there. Or perhaps where those files are stored."

"It's a starting point." Energized, he kissed me on the forehead, tucked Sheepy next to me and left the infirmary.

Happy to contribute to his search, I squirmed into a comfortable position. But it didn't take long for me to miss him and wish for something to distract me from the sting of my injuries. Perhaps I should ask for a painkiller.

I scanned the infirmary for Lamont and spotted Jacy. None of his goons accompanied him. Guess he felt safe visiting a half burnt scrub. That or he didn't want to make an impression on the two ISF officers stationed next to the door. Now why did I automatically think scrub? Whenever I saw him, he always reminded me of the time before the rebellion. Even though he helped, I always wondered why. Jacy's life had been better than most under the Pop Cop's control.

He swiped his bangs from his eyes and sat in the chair next to my bed. "You look terrible," he said.

"Gee, that really cheered me up. Thanks for visiting."

He flashed a grin. "You do know the Committee is unhappy with you. Don't you?"

"I figured they weren't keen about us keeping our suspicions to ourselves."

"Keen is such a…mild word."

"Jacy, if you keep trying to scare me, I'm going to have Lamont toss you out of here."

Not bothered by my threat, he shifted into a more comfortable position. "Just trying to warn you."

"How about you tell me who's been endangering our world instead?"

He tapped his fingers on his leg. "Wish I could."

"You're lying. You know—"

"Nothing." The word tore from his mouth as if it hurt him to speak it. "I *used* to have eyes and ears in every Sector and Quadrant. But my sources turned blind and deaf after I joined the Committee. I have a few loyal supporters, but not enough to discover who set off that bomb in the power plant."

I studied his expression. He seemed truly disgruntled, but

it could be an act. "If you didn't know, why did you tell me Bubba Boom's name then?"

"You asked for an expert. You didn't ask for a suspect."

True.

Jacy pulled a small bag from his pocket and tossed it on my stomach. I couldn't open it with the gloves on. When Lamont had changed them earlier, my palms were still raw.

"Your part of our bargain," he said, pitching his voice lower. "I need you to plant them in air duct seventy-two, ninety-five and eighty-one."

His list of ducts targeted all the critical areas of Inside—the main Control Room, Anne-Jade's office, the brig and the Sector full of Travas. I hefted the bag, calculating how many microphones might be inside.

"That's three different shafts. You only gave me one name," I said.

"I told you I don't—"

"I don't need names. How about locations?"

"Locations of what?"

"If you could have eyes and ears in the lower levels again, where would you want them?"

His expression smoothed as he caught on. "Sector F1, waste handling and maintenance."

I waved the bag of mics. "Why not ask me to install these there?"

"Because the scrubs didn't know about the Transmission, and they don't necessarily know Logan's the brains of our operation, so I think they're just following orders. Besides, I have a limited number of mics."

"Well, it may be a week or more before I can install these," I said. "It depends on Lamont and how much help the air plant workers need."

"Let me know when they're in place." He stood, but

paused. "I also suspect the explosion in the power plant and the fire in the air plant were done by two separate groups."

Double the trouble. Wonderful. "Why?"

He spread his hands out. "A gut feeling. Before the rebellion, I've dealt with many scrubs that broke the laws, and they get comfortable with one method or one type of defiance and rarely move beyond that. A bomb and a fire are two different methods."

"But the results were the same."

He studied me a moment. "No they weren't. Think about it."

Jacy had given me plenty of information to mull over. The explosion had targeted the Transmission, which only a limited number of people knew about. It affected our travel through Outer Space and killed many. To me, the sabotage screamed a message that someone wasn't happy about our situation and wanted to be noticed. I wondered why they hadn't made any demands yet, or announced the reason they damaged our world. Perhaps the Travas engineered the explosion and didn't want the Committee to know they still had connections with...who? Uppers or scrubs? It didn't matter.

The fire had targeted Logan. Most Insiders knew he was a member of the Force of Sheep, but only a few were aware of his brilliance with the computer network. No one was killed, and I wondered about the timing of the fire. The attack on him felt more intelligent and part of a greater plan. Unfortunately, I couldn't fathom why anyone besides the Travas would desire the problems that would be caused by Logan's inability to access the network.

Even though I failed to solve anything, I understood the logic behind Jacy's two-group theory. I played with the cloth bag of microphones, turning it over and over, and listened to them clink together. Jacy had been quick to mention those three areas when I had asked him where he'd like eyes and ears. Two of them made sense. Scrubs filled Sector F1, and the waste handling workers had the worst jobs. They would desire change. But maintenance didn't fit with the others.

Why not? Jacy had mentioned maintenance before. I searched my memory and remembered his comment about how maintenance and security were the only systems working. Busy and productive had been his words. Which was opposite to the two things that led to trouble—bored and destructive.

I changed tactics. Chasing the reason those two systems kept working despite all the chaos, I found the answer. Anne-Jade and Hank. They led their people, and they weren't on the Committee but reported to them. And then I considered "their people." A mix of uppers and lowers. Riley and a bunch of his cousins helped Hank all the time. Anne-Jade had recruited from both as well.

What did all this mean? Perhaps one of the uppers working in maintenance wished to cause trouble. And one of Jacy's ducts crossed over Anne-Jade's office. He could suspect the uppers working in those two areas—that would be one group. The waste handling scrubs and those living in Sector F1 could be the other.

But which one was which?

My restless agitation inflamed all my burns. Before I helped myself to a pain pill, I visited Logan again. He no longer needed a mask—a good sign. I said his name in a soft voice in case he slept.

"Done with all your visitors?" he asked.

"I only had two."

"Two more than me," he grumped.

"You had lots of visitors, but they were all quiet."

"Oh real funny. Tease the blind man." But a grin tugged at the corners of his mouth.

"Any better?"

"I've gone from seeing nothing but white to seeing large black spots on white. Doctor Lamont's pleased voice indicated this is a step in the right direction."

"Good. At least your hearing has improved. Did you hear what my visitors said?"

"Most of it. Except for Jacy's last bit. What jingled and what does he want you to do?"

I told him.

He whistled. "Cheeky of him. He'd be privy to more than he should. Are you going to plant them?"

"I promised to in exchange for information, but didn't agree to where I put them. It just doesn't feel right. We shouldn't have to spy on our own people."

"True, but I think bugging the Trava apartments and brig is a good idea," he said. "Before you plant them, ask Riley to get the frequencies from them. We might as well listen in, too."

"Should we tell Anne-Jade?"

"Not yet."

"Is that wise?"

"Probably not, but I'll blame the pain medicine and say it clouded my thoughts if she finds out."

"Good luck with that, I've seen her mad and it's not fun." Her new profession suited her. As soon as she had donned that stolen Pop Cop uniform, she'd fit right in. Then I remembered. "Logan, do you have any mics not being used?"

This time his smile broadened. "I have a few stashed in my room. Take what you need."

The itch drove me insane. Every centimeter of my arms and legs felt as if tiny invisible bugs crawled over my skin.

Lamont claimed it was part of healing. If given the choice, I preferred the pain.

Riley visited, but he seemed distracted and never stayed long. I endured another fifty hours as a patient. Finally Lamont released me at hour sixty-two with so many instructions on how to care for my newly healed skin, I almost jumped back into bed. Almost.

"Are you staying with Riley?" Lamont asked as she packed a few meds and a salve into a bag for me.

"No." I carefully pulled on the shirt and pants she had brought me. The curtains had been closed; otherwise I would have flashed the ISF officers. Logan's vision had improved, but he still had another week in here at least.

"The barracks?" Surprise laced her voice.

"Don't worry about it."

She stopped and pierced me with her doctor stare. "You need to sleep in a clean environment for another week. No pipes or air shafts or—"

"I know."

Lamont touched my arm. No longer in doctor mode, she said, "Stay in my extra room. No strings attached."

"What if you find an intern?"

"At this point, it's highly unlikely, but if I do, then we'll wheel an extra bed into the sitting room. Once we move to the medical center on one of the new levels, we'll have plenty of space."

I considered. "Does no strings mean if I have a gaping wound, you won't try to stitch it up for me?"

"No. I'm still your doctor. It means I won't try to…mother you."

"Okay, I'll stay."

She nodded as if I just agreed to take my pills on time and pushed the curtains back.

"Doctor?"

Lamont tightened her grip on the fabric and wouldn't meet my gaze. "Yes?"

"Thanks."

I contacted Riley through my microphone. His terse reply indicated he was in the middle of something and would catch up with me later. Heading up to the main Control Room in Quad G4, I planned to fetch those mics from Logan's room.

The double metal doors failed to hiss open when I approached. Odd. A mechanical voice asked for identification. I said my name and they parted just wide enough for a large ISF officer to poke his head out.

"What do you need?" he asked.

"For you to get out of my way," I said.

He didn't move. "Only authorized personnel are allowed in unless you have a reason for being here. I'm sure *you* understand the need to protect the critical equipment and personnel inside the Control Room."

Was that a slam? In an icy voice, I asked, "And *you're* the protection?"

"Yes. No one gets by me."

"Uh-huh. Tell Takia I'm here."

"She's at a Committee meeting."

Figures. "Fine. I'll come back."

As the door clanged shut, fury simmered in my blood. I understood the need for security, but to prevent *me* from entering was borderline paranoid. No, not borderline, but outright paranoid. I was the last person the Committee had to worry about.

Or was I? I alone knew about level seventeen, and there weren't many places I couldn't get to. Actually there was no place I couldn't get to. Scanning the hallway as I walked away from the Control Room, I found a perfect heating vent. And the beauty of the heating system was the vents were all close to the floor—easy to access.

I had left my tool belt in our storeroom so long ago it felt like a centiweek instead of a week and a half. In a pinch, the thin flat disks of Jacy's microphones worked as well. Most of the vents popped on and off, but the ones on the fourth level had screws as well. I wiggled into the shaft and pulled the vent back in place.

Warm air flowed around me as I swam toward the control room—pulling with my arms and pushing with my feet. It was harder to do with regular clothes and a pocket full of mics. Plus my skin burned with the added friction.

The familiar smell and hum reminded me of when I had slept in the heating ducts. Combine that with muscles that had been doing nothing but lie in a bed for the last hundred and thirty hours, and the trip turned into an endurance test.

Finally, I reached the control room. Through the slats of the vents, I saw legs of seated workers and rows of computers. Bypassing them, I found Logan's rooms. In no time, I popped open the vent and tumbled into his small living area. The Captain had occupied this space when he was on duty but not needed. I imagined problems had been few and far between until Domotor recruited me.

Glad to have room to stretch, I glanced around. No surprise the place was a mess of computer parts, wires and gadgets. It took me longer than I hoped to find his stash of mics. Pocketing them so I was balanced, I debated about returning through the heating system. The bigger air ducts would be easier to navigate, but I would have to climb to the ceiling.

My newly healed skin hadn't liked my recent activities and I doubted I had the strength to scale the wall.

Instead, I walked from Logan's rooms and through the control center. Most of the workers just nodded a greeting unperturbed. A few seemed surprised. The oversized ISF officer's glare could have burned a hole in sheet metal. But he didn't try to stop me.

I waved to him as the doors opened for me to leave. "Guess I should change my name to No One, since *no one* gets by you." It was not a mature thing to do, but I never claimed to be an adult. And I never could resist a challenge.

Tracking down Riley proved to be a challenge as well. I found him at his old work station, banging on the keyboard in irritation. He monitored electrical usage and since the power plant produced all the electricity in Inside, his station was located in the office next to the plant's control room.

"Not now, Trella. I'm—"

"Busy. I know. I'm starting to understand how you felt when I attended back-to-back Committee meetings."

My comment earned me a glance and a brief smile.

"This is critical. The computer…" He slammed a fist on the keys. "Damn it. There goes another one."

"Has the network been compromised?" I peered over his shoulder.

"Sort of. Files are just disappearing as if they never existed."

"Is that possible? I thought—"

"Lousy son of a Trava!"

White light filled the monitor. Without thought, I covered Riley's eyes with my hands and dipped my head, blocking mine with my upper arm.

After a few seconds, Riley pulled my hands down. "It's okay. I think." A strange hitch cracked his voice.

I peeked. White still dominated the screen, but big black letters shone from the center. Squinting at them, I read: *All access denied by order of the Controllers.*

9

I BLINKED A FEW TIMES, BUT THE WORDS REMAINED ON
the screen. *All access denied by the Controllers.* "Please tell me it's
a joke," I said to Riley. "Or Logan's idea of a sick prank."

"Wish I could. But this is the third system that has disappeared."

A dizzy weakness swept over me. "Critical systems?"

"Not yet."

"Yet?"

"I can't stop it. Takia and a few others tried as well."

"Does the Committee know?"

"Yep. They've been getting kicked out, too. Mostly infor-
mational systems and not mechanical or life systems."

Good thing. "Can Logan bypass the Controllers?"

"I would think so. Why else would they have targeted
him?" Riley swiveled around to face me. "We need to find
who has hacked into the network."

"How?"

"I don't know. I need to talk to Logan and maybe Anne-
Jade. She might have a few ideas." He rested his elbows on his

legs and put his forehead into his hands. "It wasn't supposed to be like this."

"What?"

"We reclaimed our freedom and we have all this room to spread out and grow. Yet some group is hijacking the network and blowing holes in our world. Why? Why are they destroying when they could be building levels and using their computer knowledge to help Logan?"

I knelt down, pulled his arms away and met his gaze. "Because of fear. Fear of the unknown. Fear of change. Fear of the Committee's decisions."

"Fear can be a big motivator." Riley tucked a loose strand of my hair behind my ear. "Did you think our new life would be like this when we were fighting the Pop Cops?"

"No. I thought we'd be lying on that big green carpet under that huge blue ceiling in Outside relaxing."

He laughed, but sobered. "We won't ever see the real Outside. We have to make the most of what we have Inside. We can't let fear ruin it."

"You've convinced me. Now you only need to convert nineteen thousand others," I joked.

But he wasn't amused. "No, Trella. You're not convinced. If you were, we wouldn't have half these problems."

An icy chill zipped through me. "So I'm to blame for half of these new problems?" I kept my voice even despite my desire to scream at him.

"No." He slid off the chair and knelt in front of me so we were eye to eye. "I didn't mean it that way. It's just you gave up too soon."

"Gave up what?"

"Power. You handed it over to the Committee without thinking about how the Insiders would react."

"The Committee members are Insiders. And they have more experience."

"This is all new to *everyone*."

I balled my hands into fists, tapping them against my thighs. "Yes, but they're older and more knowledgeable. All I know is the internal structure of Inside. Good for moving around unseen and planting mics, but little else." My knuckles knocked against my pants' pockets. The discs inside jingled.

"Planting mics for whom?" Riley asked in concern.

Glad for the change of topic, I told him about Jacy's request. I pulled a handful from my pocket. "Can you get the frequencies from them? Logan wants us to listen in too."

"Where are you sticking them?"

I listed the areas Jacy requested. "But I'm not bugging the Control Room or Anne-Jade's office. And I have extras to plant for us."

Riley sat back on his heels as if bracing for bad news. "Why?"

Explaining Jacy's theory of two groups, I speculated that one of the groups had to be connected to the Travas. "The Pop Cops had moles in the lower levels, spying on the scrubs. They could still be loyal. Perhaps by listening in, we can discover who sabotaged the power plant."

He considered. "I doubt the network hackers worked in the lower levels. With the degree of complexity it needed, I believe there could only be a few suspects with that ability. And the people I'm thinking of are all uppers."

His obvious sincerity didn't stop my instant ire over his statement. "Logan broke into the network and reached the highest levels without a port. He's not an upper so why are you assuming only they could sabotage the files?"

"That's a valid point. Why are you getting so defensive?"

"I'm..." I had been about to protest, but realized I had overreacted. "It was an automatic gut reaction. The Pop Cops had brainwashed us to believe the uppers were superior in every way."

"You know that's not true."

"Knowing and believing are sometimes hard to combine."

While Riley discussed the network problems with Logan in the infirmary, I showered then slept. When I woke, Riley had left a wipe board listing the frequencies of all the mics next to Sheepy.

I reported to the air plant at hour seventy to assist with the clean up and repairs. No surprise to see Hank there, barking orders and organizing workers. Pleased to see so many helpers, I waited until he finished instructing a team before claiming his attention.

"You're in high demand," I said to him with a smile. "Do you even have time to sleep?"

"Sleep? What's that? A new type of casserole?"

I would have laughed, but the craters under his eyes proved he and sleep were strangers.

"You have a big crew now. Can't you take some time off?" I asked.

My comment had the opposite effect. Hank's mood soured. "Yeah, lots of scrubs being forced to help."

"What do you mean?"

Hank shook his head in a slow way as if he couldn't believe I had to ask. "Where have you been, Trella?"

"In the infirmary, growing new skin."

"Oh. Sorry. I forgot." He ran a calloused hand over the

stubble on his face. Dirt and ash stained his coveralls. "The Committee and ISF have commandeered hydroponics and the kitchen. If the scrubs want to eat, they have to work two hours for each meal."

I noted Hank's use of the word commandeered. Even though the Committee was desperate for aid, they had mishandled the situation. In theory Hank should be on their side. He bore all the stress of having to make repairs with a limited crew. They should have asked him how to recruit workers.

"Any work or just repair work?"

"Any. Laundry, recycling, kitchen duty, waste handling… All the jobs that need to be done. Repair work actually counts double—one hour for one meal—because of the critical time-sensitive nature of them."

"Did they set the same requirements for the uppers?"

"What do you think?"

Damn. "But to be fair, the uppers are still doing their jobs. It's just—"

"None of the scrubs has a clue what their jobs are. I know, and the scrubs on the Committee understand, but the rest of them believe all the uppers do is sit in front of a monitor and type every so often. No one is taking the time to explain it to the scrubs." He swept a hand out, indicating the flurry of activity around the air filter bays. "At least there has been one positive thing to all this. I've a few uppers who don't mind getting their hands dirty and they're putting in long hours right beside the scrubs."

The situation felt sickly familiar. "Who's keeping track of a person's hours?"

"The ISF or as we'd like to call them, the Mop Cops."

"Do I want to know what that means?"

"Things are a mess right now, and they're trying to mop it all under the bed and pretend it's not there."

Hank had a point, but I didn't believe the Committee and Anne-Jade had been blind to the mess, just overwhelmed.

I asked for my assignment and Hank sent me to the foreman. He eyed my skin-tight climbing suit and tool belt, handed me a stack of air filters, and listed the air ducts to install them in.

Glad to be productive, I set the filters inside the shafts. The magnets along their edges made the installation easy. The best part, I could plant the mics as I worked. The worst, my new skin protested the activity. And my muscles hadn't returned to full strength. I lasted four hours, which equaled two meals. I found the ISF officer and made sure to report my time.

Over the next twenty-five hours, I installed filters and mics in four-hour shifts. During the last four hours of the week, I planted one of Logan's mics near the air vent above Sector D1 where Jacy tended to hold meetings with his people. An unhappy murmur drifted through the shaft over the barracks.

I slid east over the bunk beds in the barracks in Sectors D and E. With the buzz of voices below, I doubted anyone even heard me. As I crossed into Sector F1, snatches of loud conversation reached me.

"...did you see the piles of laundry?"

"...the air still smells bad. It makes me nauseous."

"...idiots...we need a better Committee."

"...I saw Meline and Bo behind the dryers. They're finally together."

"...still haven't seen Kadar. I bet they tortured him and fed him to Chomper."

"...uppers have it sweet. We outnumber them...can bribe a few Mop Cops, get weapons..."

I froze, then backed up to the last vent, listening to the man.

"...I heard that Tech No is out of the picture and the computers are going crazy. Perfect time to attack. We'll force the uppers to be scrubs and live in their posh apartments. Then feed the Committee to Chomper."

The man's voice grew louder and I strained to see who spoke.

"What about that little scrub who started this whole mess?" a woman asked.

"I heard the Committee's upset with her. Maybe we could..." He lowered his voice.

I pressed my ear to the vent as he mentioned something about recruiting. My tool belt clanged on the metal, but I doubted it was loud enough to be heard amid the general noises below.

Without warning the cover popped free. In the seconds that followed, I caught a brief glimpse of a man then hands grabbed my shoulders and yanked. I fell onto the top bunk a meter below.

It was a soft landing, and I rolled over to my back. The man who had pulled me from the air shaft straddled my hips. He seized my wrists, pinning them to the mattress with his weight. I struggled to no avail—he outweighed me by forty kilograms. Finally, I stopped, but my heart kept up its fast tempo.

"Hello little bug," he said. His smile seemed more amused than sinister. "Do you know spying on others isn't playing nice?"

"Get off me."

"Not until you explain what you were doing up there."

"I was installing air filters so we can all breathe clean air. Let me go."

His round face was close to mine. He had light brown eyes with tiny flecks of yellow, a mustache, and short brown hair. Another man's head and shoulders appeared beside the bunk. He gripped the safety rail, probably standing on the bed below us. "Hey, Sloan, Wera said you wanted—" The scrub noticed me.

"Help me," I said.

"Uh...what's going on?" His voice almost squeaked.

"I caught me a blue-eyed bug," Sloan said. "She *claims* she was installing air filters and is even wearing an air scrub uniform. Can you check the duct for me?"

"Uh...sure." He climbed up to the vent and poked his head in. "It's too dark to see."

I huffed in frustration. "There's a flashlight in my tool belt."

Sloan shifted back so his friend could reach it. Now his weight rested on my upper thighs and wrists.

"There's a filter...don't know if it's new or not." His voice echoed slightly.

"What color is it?" I asked.

"White."

I met Sloan's gaze. "It's new, otherwise it'd be gray."

"Then why did you stop over my vent when I started talking about bribing the Mop Cops?"

"I had to fix my tool belt, it slipped. You heard it bang."

He studied me and I kept my innocent expression.

"Hey! Look what I found." The friend held the microphone I had planted above the vent. Damn! I had hoped he wouldn't look directly up. He rolled it around his palm. "I think it's a mic."

"Care to change your story?" Sloan asked.

"I didn't plant that. Someone else must have."

But Sloan didn't believe me and recognition flashed in his

eyes. "You're *that* scrub. And as I recall, your little group of uppers used those mics to listen to the Pop Cops."

"So? It's probably left over from before. Let me go or I'll scream for help."

"Go ahead and yell, no one in here will care. Cain, check her belt for more of those devices."

A cold and clammy fear spread through my muscles as Cain fumbled through my tools. He found the bag with the remaining few mics.

Sloan's grip tightened as anger shone on his face. "Traitor." He let go of my left wrist and slapped me across the cheek.

Pain exploded as my head whipped to the side. Tears welled. Sloan shifted off my legs. And before I could react, he shoved me with his feet. I slammed into the rail opposite Cain. With another push from him, I went up and over, falling off the bunk.

The landing knocked the breath from me. I curled into a ball and gasped for air. My shoulder hurt. Sloan's loud voice carried over the general din, informing everyone in the barracks about me.

No time to recover. Legs surrounded me on both sides and I suffered two hard kicks to my back. When one clipped my head, I feared for my life. I rolled under the bunk. Too narrow to provide any protection, I kept rolling, hoping to outdistance the scrubs chasing me. Bunk, walkway, bunk, walkway, bunk, walkway.

Yells followed me. The floor vibrated with the rush of so many feet. As I drew closer to my goal—the far east wall, I noticed a line of scrubs waiting along that last walkway. Damn. I couldn't stop and I couldn't change my trajectory. Or could I?

Taking the biggest risk of my life, I paused under a bunk. The scrubs chasing me climbed over and through the bunk

without checking underneath. I knew there would be strag-
glers, but I couldn't wait too long. Changing direction, I rolled
the opposite way toward the west wall. Yells erupted.

But after I reached an empty walkway, I jumped to my feet
and ran toward the south wall. It didn't take long for them to
catch on, but I had a bit of a head start. I poured every bit of
energy into my short legs. Feet pounded behind me. I yanked
a screwdriver from my belt.

No heating vent was in sight so when I reached the wall,
I dove under a bunk and rolled again until I found one. I
popped the cover off and scrambled inside. A hand grabbed
my ankle, tugging me back. I stabbed the screwdriver into
the hand. It released me as its owner swore loudly.

The heating vent would not provide a safe haven yet. I slid,
squirmed, pushed and pulled. Voices shouted and echoed.
Once I felt certain I'd escaped, I stopped. I had reached the
connector shaft that led into waste handling in Sector H1.

Sweat-drenched and huffing for breath, I lay there. As my
heart slowed and my muscles quit trembling, my other injuries demanded attention. My shoulder, wrists and hip ached.
Sharp pain stabbed my back anytime I breathed in too deep.
Overall I felt like I'd been shoved through a pipe too small
for me. However, every stab of pain reminded me of my luck
in getting out of there alive.

I didn't blame Sloan and the others for being angry. But
I wondered if he had said those things about attacking the
Committee because he heard me in the duct or if he had
meant them. If I hadn't gotten away, would they have killed
me? I rubbed my cheek. It still burned from the slap. Sloan
had called me a traitor and by the fury in his gaze, I guessed
that yes, they would have easily vented their anger on me.

Eventually, I continued into waste handling and exited
the shaft at the first opening. I had no energy left to travel

through the ducts. Leaning on the wall, I scanned the plant
for scrubs from Sector F1. No one appeared to be searching for
me. The regular plant workers milled about the equipment.

Emek spotted me, smiled and approached. "Haven't seen
you down here in a long time. Did you come to check up on
me?"

"Yes. I'm making sure you're fully recovered from the
surgery."

He inspected my appearance. "How nice." Yet his tone
implied he didn't believe me. "Rough trip?"

"Yep. Installing air filters is hard work, I better get back."
I pushed off, but just then Rat raced into the plant like
he'd been chased by an angry mob. Or it just could be my
imagination.

"Emek! The scrubs in…" Rat slid to a halt when he spotted me talking to Emek. Two bright red splotches stained his
cheeks and his short brown hair stuck up as if he had ran his
fingers through it.

"Don't keep us in suspense," Emek said.

"The scrubs in Sector F1 are rioting. They're fighting
with the ISF officers, claiming the Mop Cops are spying on
them."

Emek pierced me with his scowl. "Did you know about
this?"

I suddenly wished to hide under the covers of my bed.
"The riot? No."

Rat's gaze jumped from Emek to me and back. "I heard
Trella's name."

Emek groaned. "Do the ISF officers need help?"

"Yes."

"Go get the rest of the crew, Rat. They're cleaning out
the secondary sludge tanks." He hooked a thumb, pointing
toward another room. Rat dashed off.

"Do you need an escort back to level three?" he asked.

"No thanks. I'm fine."

He raised one eyebrow. "Are you sure? You look—"

"I'm sure."

Rat returned with a dozen people on his heels. They sprinted out the door. Emek's gaze followed them.

"Go help the ISF officers," I said.

"No one's in the plant right now so you can use the small washroom in my office before you go."

"Thanks." I shooed him away.

Tucked into the northeast corner of the plant, Emek's neat office seemed very organized. When I considered the raw sewage that flowed into the plant, it made sense for him to have his own washroom. It always amazed me how the machinery and bacteria transformed crap into fertilizer and cleaned our water. Plus the process produced a special gas that was pumped into the power plant to be used as fuel.

I glanced at my reflection in the mirror. Dirt smudged my face. Clumps of dust clung to my hair. My bottom lip was swollen and bloody. And a bright red handprint covered my left cheek. I cleaned up as best as I could, braiding my hair. In my haste to escape I hadn't noticed how dirty the barrack's floors were.

Dirt and rust harmed our world. They weren't as bad as sabotage, but they could do plenty of damage.

I left Emek's office. The hum and whoosh of the machinery sounded louder without the workers. I debated between the risk of walking the hallways or the effort needed to climb into the air shaft. Scanning the ceiling for an accessible vent, I spotted one over the digester, which had a ladder up its side. Perfect.

Halfway up the ladder a clang sliced through the mechanical drone. I hoped it meant the riot had been quelled. Leaning to the side, I peered around the digester. One man, wearing an off–duty green jumper crouched next to the gas collector. No one else had returned.

I waited a few seconds to see if the others would arrive. The man kept glancing over his shoulder. Then he pushed something under the collector, straightened and hurried off.

Odd. Did he come back from the riot just to fix the machine? About to shrug it off, I paused, remembering all of Emek's men wore dark blue coveralls.

Sliding down the ladder, I rushed over to where the man had been. Nothing looked out of the ordinary, but I wouldn't know. I unhooked my tool belt before wiggling under the collector. Yet another unique view of my world. At least the space was cleaner than under the barracks. The irony wasn't lost on me.

I peered up. Hoses, wires, pipes and a strange device wedged between the pipes. The device had a short fat pipe about twenty centimeters in diameter and sealed on both ends. On top of the pipe were two glass containers of liquid. Between the containers was a metal box with a digital display. Each time the four numbers flashed they were one less.

Understanding hit me as hard as Sloan. I'd found a bomb.

10

I GAPED AT THE BOMB'S DISPLAY, WATCHING THE
countdown with a numb horror. Three thousand and fifteen, three thousand and fourteen… When it reached three
thousand, I did the math and fumbled for my microphone,
switched it on and turned it to Riley's frequency.

"Riley, find Bubba Boom and bring him to the waste
handling plant now. There's a bomb that's going to explode
in forty-nine minutes!"

Staring at the bomb, I debated. Should I move it? Where?
Every place in Inside had critical equipment. And people.

I slid out from under the collector. The adjoining Quads
should be evacuated as well as the infirmary and care facility
filled with children directly above the plant. I checked the
clock. Five minutes past hour ninety-nine. The bomb was
set to detonate at the very beginning of week 147,023.

There was enough time to evacuate, but I couldn't leave.
What if Bubba Boom arrived while I was gone? Instead, I
paced and worried and second-guessed myself, sending out a
call to Riley every ten lengths.

When Emek and his crew arrived, I rushed over. Not

caring that they seemed upset to see me. My words tumbled out in a flood as I explained about the bomb. Emek quickly grasped the situation and he organized three teams to evacuate the Quads and Sector H2. Since the explosion would be so close to flammable gases, Emek told them to go to Sector E1 and H3 if they had time. Rat volunteered to find Bubba Boom in case Riley slept through my calls. He still hadn't answered any of them.

I showed Emek the bomb. He barely fit under the collector. Another worry flared in my chest. Would Bubba Boom fit?

"Should we move it?" I asked.

"No."

"How much time left?"

"About thirty-five minutes." He pulled himself out and stood. "I wonder why the bomber left it with so much time. Could this be a distraction?"

"I hope not. Perhaps he wanted enough time to be far away. He did wait until everyone left the plant and probably figured no one would find it. Plus he didn't know I was here since I came through the heating ducts."

"After causing problems in Sector F1." Emek crossed his arms, clearly unhappy.

"If I hadn't been here, we wouldn't know about the bomb." I snapped at him.

"True. Although you being here to witness it seems too coincidental."

"But who would know I'd be here? I didn't know I'd be here. I was supposed to be in the air ducts, installing filters."

"Perhaps someone saw you come in and he placed it here at this time to throw suspicion on you."

"Why would I plant a bomb and then tell everyone about it? That makes no sense," I said, outraged by his suggestion.

"So starting a riot made sense?" Emek asked, but his stern expression had softened.

"Nothing has made any sense since the first explosion!" I paced again. "Where are Bubba Boom and Riley?"

"If Bubba Boom was in Sector F1, then we'll have to find someone else who's an expert with explosives."

"Why?"

"The ISF had to gas the entire Sector, putting everyone to sleep. They're looking for you so you can identify the trouble makers before they wake."

Lovely. I'd go from traitor to snitch. Getting blown to bits didn't seem so bad.

When Bubba Boom finally arrived with both Riley and Rat right behind him, the tight band around my chest eased a bit. Emek showed Bubba Boom where the bomb had been planted.

"Why didn't you respond?" I asked Riley.

"I did." He touched my earlobe. "Your receiver is gone." Blood dotted his fingertips.

"Oh." I must have lost it in Sector F1.

Then Riley cupped my chin and turned my head. "Who slapped you?" Anger flared. "I'll kill him."

"Don't worry, I'll take care of him."

"What happened?"

"She started the riot in Sector F1," Emek said.

I shot Emek a sour look as Riley rounded on me, demanding an explanation.

"We have more pressing problems," I said, gesturing to Bubba Boom as he knelt next to the collector. "A bomb. Remember? I'll tell you later."

Since Bubba Boom was too large to fit underneath, he used a mirror to read the display. The counter read nine hundred seconds, which meant we had fifteen minutes.

Riley insisted everyone else leave, including me.

"I need Trella to stay," Bubba Boom said. "She's the only one who fits underneath."

Riley closed his eyes for a moment. "Fine, then I'm staying too." He shooed Emek and Rat out the door.

As Bubba Boom inspected the bomb with his mirror, I pulled Riley aside and whispered, "There's no reason for you to stay."

"You've been trying to get yourself killed since Cog's death. At least this time I won't have to wait for news or wonder if you'll survive your injuries. If this thing blows, we'll both go."

"I'm not trying to kill—"

"I think I know how to disarm it," Bubba Boom said.

"Think or know?" Riley asked.

"It's a basic mixing design. The glass containers are filled with two stable chemicals. When the counter reaches zero, it removes the barrier between the liquids. They'll pour into the bigger pipe and mix together, creating a highly explosive combination. The counter will then create a spark and good-bye half of waste handling." Bubba Boom met my gaze. "As long as the bomber didn't get cute with the wiring, it should be easy to disarm." He handed me a pair of wire cutters.

Once again, I wriggled underneath the collector. Ten minutes left. My guts twisted and knotted with each second that disappeared.

"Pull the counter gently away from the pipes to expose the wires behind it," Bubba Boom instructed.

My hands shook, but I eased the box out from where it was nestled between the glass containers. I moved the mirror so he could see.

"Interesting."

"Good or bad?" Riley asked. I recognized the tight tension in his voice.

Bubba Boom ignored him. "Trella, I need to see where the second wire on the left ends."

All the wires were covered in black. I pointed to my guess. "This one?"

"No. One over. That's it," he said when I touched the next wire.

Running a finger along it, I followed it until the end and repositioned the mirror. I rubbed my sweaty palms on my uniform.

"Well?" Riley asked.

"I'm thinking."

"Eight minutes left," I said.

"Not helping. Riley, I need a wipe board to draw out the circuit."

"Emek's office," I called, remembering the neat stack of them on the corner of his desk.

The desire to scream at him to hurry lodged in my throat. His pounding feet faded then returned. Through the gap in the machinery, I watched Bubba Boom draw on the board. Riley peered over his shoulder. Dark gray sweat stains covered his gray shirt and strands of damp hair clung to the side of his face.

Bubba Boom instructed me to move the mirror a few more times. He discussed the circuits with Riley as they figured out how to cut off power. I clamped both hands over my lips to keep quiet. The need to urge them to move faster filled my mouth and pushed against my teeth.

Finally Bubba Boom told me to cut the wire I had traced for him. I placed the wire in the cutters and drew in a deep breath.

"Stop!" Riley yelled. He argued with Bubba Boom. "Trell,

you need to cut that wire and the one on the other end at the exact same time," he said.

I found the other wire. "This one?"

"Yes," Riley said.

"No," Bubba Boom said. "He's wrong. Cut only the wire I told you."

"No, don't. I'm right, Trell. He's going to get us all killed."

My fingers refused to work. Who to trust? Bubba Boom, the explosives expert or Riley, the electrical expert. Less than two minutes left. I listened to Bubba Boom and cut his wire.

The numbers stopped counting down, but they flashed red. The box started to beep.

"Break the glass on one of the containers," Bubba Boom yelled. The beeping increased its pace. "Now!"

"Avert your face," Riley shouted.

I rested the wire cutters on the glass with the clear liquid. Turning to the left, I covered my face with my arm and then struck the container as hard as I could. The glass shattered. Shards rained as the chemical splashed on my chest and stomach.

Yanking me out by my ankles, Riley picked me up, threw me over his shoulder and ran toward the shower in Emek's washroom. Shoved under the cold spray, I caught on and helped Riley tear off my chemical-soaked uniform. He ripped his shirt off and we scrubbed our skin, removing the last traces of the acidic substance before it could burn holes into our bodies.

I shivered and hugged my chest. "I've been wanting to take another shower with you," I said. "This wasn't quite how I imagined it."

His lips quirked into a brief smile, but it didn't reach his eyes. And it disappeared just as quick. Turning his back on me, he grabbed a couple of towels, handing me one without looking at me.

I dried off, then wrapped the towel around my body. Riley's shirt lay in a heap on the shower's floor tangled with my ruined uniform. They needed to be disposed of properly so I stuffed them into a hazardous waste bag.

"Trella, I...can't do this anymore," Riley said.

Cold dread stabbed me. "Do what?"

"Me and you...us." He gestured between us with both his hands.

Shivers raced across my skin as I realized Riley wasn't just angry at me for trusting Bubba Boom over him. This ran deeper.

"Trella, you have no qualms risking your life for Inside, sweeping in to save people, yet you don't want to stick around and deal with the cleanup. You'd rather let others come in and decide how to organize our world. It's frustrating and terrifying for me. I keep hoping the Queen of the Pipes will return and put a stop to all the Committee's nonsense. Only you can help them focus on the real issues." Riley dropped his hands. "Plus you don't need me. You've been pushing me away since we won control of Inside. Since you accepted my pendant."

"That's not true," I said.

"Really? How about when you discovered the fire in the air plant? I was right around the corner. You could have easily turned on your mic and called me to help, but you didn't."

"There wasn't any time," I tried, but knew by his cold expression he thought it was a lame excuse. "I called you when I found the bomb."

"You ordered me to fetch Bubba Boom. If he had his own receiver, I doubt you would have bothered and we would be having this conversation in the infirmary while you once again grow new skin. Every time I try to get close to you, Trella, you turn to someone else. You only need me to clean up after you. You don't trust me. I'm sorry, but I can no longer be with you. It's too…painful to watch you self destruct."

Did he believe I cut the wrong wire on purpose? Shocked over his announcement, I couldn't form a coherent response.

Riley left Emek's office and the waste handling plant, ignoring Bubba Boom and Emek who waited for us.

Before they could question me about Riley or before I could fall apart, I asked, "What about the bomb?"

"Crisis averted." With a chagrined expression, Bubba Boom said, "Riley was right. Both wires should have been cut."

"I got that," I said, letting sarcasm edge my tone. "Do you know who built it? Who planted it?"

"I don't recognize it. I'll take it apart and see if I can learn anything."

"Did you get a good look at the man?" Emek asked me.

"Just his back and the side of his face. Short brown hair. No facial hair. Average build. Between 1800 and 2200 weeks old."

"That's a big help." Emek's turn to be sarcastic.

I bit back a nasty reply. "Now what?"

"The Committee's looking for you. And Anne-Jade wants to talk to you," Emek said. "I'm surprised she isn't here now."

The thought of being questioned by Anne-Jade and the Committee made diffusing a bomb seem like a pleasant task. Then I remembered the ISF wanted me to finger Sloan and his friends, which I was loath to do. Add that to Riley leaving me and all I craved was to curl up in a little ball in the quiet solitude of an air duct.

★ ★ ★

Rat fetched a set of clothes for me from the laundry. He had grabbed the green shirt and pants that the infirmary workers wore. I dressed in Emek's office. Anne-Jade's voice pierced my haze of exhaustion. She waited for me beyond the door.

Glad I had taken my tool belt with me, I strapped it on, placed Emek's chair on his desk and climbed into the air shaft. Once again I was avoiding confrontation. I didn't go far. Dropping down into the middle of the recycling plant, I scattered a group of workers. I apologized and headed straight for the stairs. Others had also clumped together and from the bits of alarmed conversation I caught, they discussed the evacuation and bomb.

News of the attempted bombing could either work in our favor or ignite panic. If everyone kept an eye out for unusual activity and strange devices, it might stop the bomber from trying again, which would be good. Panic would bring nothing but trouble and more destruction.

I reached the infirmary without encountering any ISF officers. Unfortunately Lamont took one look at my face and accosted me.

"Trella, what happened?"

"It'd be easier to tell you what didn't happen," I said.

She swept my hair from my face and, for a second, I wanted to press her hand against my cheek. "I need to put a suture in your earlobe." Inspecting my face, she frowned. "Who hit you?"

"Did you hear about the riot?"

"Of course. I needed to be ready in case there were injuries. Were you caught in the riot?" She tried to keep her tone professional, but alarmed concern dominated.

"Sort of. I…uh…started the riot."

Lamont paused. "You're serious."

"Yep."

"Do you want to talk about it?"

"No."

"All right. Come back to the exam room and I'll fix your ear."

As I followed her, I passed Logan's empty bed. "Where's Logan?"

She waited until I sat on the examining table before saying, "He's in protective custody."

"Arrested? The riot was *my* fault. Not his."

Her eyebrows rose, but she smoothed them. "He's not in the brig. With all the troubles, Anne-Jade felt he'd be better protected in a more secured location."

Lamont filled a needle and approached. I flinched away instinctively.

She stopped. "It's lidocaine. If you'd rather not—"

"Go ahead. Numb my earlobe please. I've had enough pain."

"Little pinch and I'm done."

Compared to the slap, falling to the floor, being doused with an acidic chemical and Riley breaking up with me, the pinch barely registered.

As she prepped the sutures, I tried to focus on something besides myself. "What about Logan's vision? Isn't he under your care?"

"I can't do anything more for him. It's just a matter of time."

"Will he regain his sight?"

"His progress is promising, but I can't guarantee it."

"Do you know where he is?"

"No." Lamont looped two stitches to close the tear in my lobe.

By this time, I could have fallen asleep on the exam table.

Lamont trailed behind me as I headed toward my room. I stopped at the threshold. She hovered, rubbing her hands together. I had spent enough time with her to recognize her anxiety.

"No mothering. Remember?"

Although she didn't look happy about it, she nodded.

"I just need to sleep for about a hundred hours. If anyone comes looking for me, can you tell them I'm not here?" I asked.

"Even Riley?"

My hands shook. Doubtful he would be looking for me. "Yes."

"Okay, I'll keep everyone out."

"Thanks." I collapsed onto the bed, crawling under the covers and muffling my sobs. Eventually, I would seek out Anne-Jade and tell her everything about the riot.

Too bad she found me first.

Startled from a deep sleep, I stared at Anne-Jade through puffy eyes. Confusion clouded my mind and her words failed to make sense. I rubbed my face in an effort to focus. My cheek throbbed.

"...hear me?" she asked. Grabbing my arm, she yanked me from the bed. "Do you even know how much trouble you're in?"

I swayed on my feet, but straightened real quick when I spotted her two lieutenants standing behind her. "I—"

"No excuses, Trella. I have orders from the Committee to arrest you."

Wide awake now, I said, "But—"

"You had your chance to explain down in waste handling, but you chose to run away."

"I—"

"Running is an act of a guilty person. I had no choice. Yuri, secure her." Anne-Jade stepped back to let Yuri closer.

With nowhere to go, I could only appreciate the speed in which Yuri slapped a handcuff onto my left wrist, spun me around and snapped the other cuff onto my right. With my arms pinned behind my back, my sore shoulder ached.

"Anne-Jade, the cuffs aren't necessary," I said.

"I disagree. Let's go."

She gripped my arm, propelling me forward as if I would resist. With a lieutenant in front of us and one following, they marched me from my room. Lamont hovered in the sitting area. Hour three shone on the clock.

"You could have at least waited to call Anne-Jade until I got more sleep," I grumped at Lamont.

"Give us some credit, Trell," Anne-Jade said. "No one called us. You weren't that hard to find."

True. If I had known she'd arrest me, I'd have slept in the ducts. She'd been to our storeroom and the small control room where we had hidden Domotor. That was back when I could trust her. I needed to find a new hiding place. The image of the bubble monster sitting on top of the Expanse filled my mind. No one would find me there.

Our little parade entered the lift and went up to level four. When the door swished open, a horrible possibility struck me. I resisted Anne-Jade's pull.

"What?" she asked.

"You're not taking me to the brig, are you?" I couldn't keep the panic from my voice. The thought of being there with Karla and Vinco, even in separate cells, caused me to sweat.

"It's up to you. The Committee has a number of questions for you. If you refuse to cooperate, they'll send you to the brig to think over your decision."

We bypassed Anne-Jade's office and walked down the main corridor to Quad G4. Inside didn't seem so big until I was handcuffed and stared at by every single person we passed in that hallway. The time it took us to reach the conference room off the main Control Room felt like hours.

My relief to be out of the public's eye disappeared in a heartbeat when I faced the nineteen Committee members. They sat around the long oval conference table. Domotor's wheelchair faced the front of the curved end. Scanning the faces, I did a quick calculation. Five members gave me encouraging nods, twelve people wore a variety of unhappy expressions from pissed off to mildly annoyed, one wouldn't meet my gaze—Riley's father—and one kept his face blank—Jacy.

Anne-Jade pushed me into the empty chair at the end opposite Domotor. I perched on the edge since my hands were still cuffed. She stood behind me as if I might try to escape or harm someone. I would have laughed, but I couldn't miss the heavy tension that filled the room. The lines of strain, dark circles and signs of fatigue were the common denominator from all eighteen members. Jacy wasn't giving anything away, and that scared me more than anything else.

Domotor took the lead. It was a good sign as he had been one of the encouraging nodders. The mics sat on top of the bag on the table. Computers were another new feature on the table. Each member had a small monitor in front of them.

Domotor started asking me questions about the riot.

I was honest to a point. Admitting I planted the mics, I got a little creative with why. "I hoped to overhear the saboteurs." Which was the truth.

"Why didn't you and Logan tell us about them?" Domotor asked.

I noted the lack of Anne-Jade's and Riley's names. They were both aware of the sabotage and failed to inform the

Committee. Funny, I had been the one to argue to tell the Committee. "The evidence was circumstantial. We didn't want to accuse anyone without proof." Also true.

"Where did you plant these mics?" he asked.

"The air shafts about Sectors E1 and F1." I pointed my chin at the mics. "I planned to do more, but was…interrupted."

"She means caught," Anne-Jade said. "The scrubs in Sector F1 heard her in the air shaft."

"I haven't climbed through the ducts in weeks. I'm a little rusty," I said in my defense.

A few Committee members smiled at my play on words. I wouldn't go as far to say I was winning them over, but it was better than nothing.

Anne-Jade wanted to know who pulled me from the air shaft and incited the riot.

"I started the riot. It all happened so fast, I didn't get a good look at him." Just because I protected the bastard who slapped me, didn't mean I would forget him. Oh no. I owed him a visit. I just didn't need the scrubs to think I was an informer as well as a traitor.

The questions then turned to the bomb in waste handling. Those I answered with complete honesty. Jacy relaxed back in his chair. His gaze contemplative. Probably wondering why I hadn't told them about his request to plant his mics over sensitive areas. Right now they assumed Logan provided the mics. I'd like to say I had a grand scheme in mind, but at this point, I operated on pure instinct.

When all the questions had been answered, Anne-Jade escorted me out to the main Control Room so the Committee could discuss…I wasn't exactly sure what.

We waited near the door. "Thanks for not mentioning me," she said in a quiet voice. "I owe you one."

"Great. Take off these damn cuffs," I said.

"Not until the Committee gives me permission. Sorry."

I stared at her. "Come on, it's me. You *can't* be happy with how they're running our world."

"Do you really think I like being called the Mop Cops?" She balled her hands into fists. "I worked so hard to *not* be the Pop Cops and look what happened. Bombs, computer failure and someone tries to kill my brother. It's a mess and I wouldn't even know how to fix it at this point." Anne-Jade punched the wall. The Control Room workers glanced at us as the loud bang vibrated. "It's our fault, you know." She rubbed her knuckles absently. "The Force of Sheep gave them the power. It seemed like a good idea at the time."

It did. I mulled over what had happened. Why did the Committee fail? Then I remembered where they sat at the conference table. All the uppers sat along the left side, then Domotor, Jacy and the rest of the scrubs on the right side. Jacy had known the problem all along and so did I, but I'd hoped it would work itself out. That the uppers and scrubs would play nice together and forget all the Pop Cop propaganda.

But they remained divided. And all the current problems just drove them further apart, which didn't make sense. With saboteurs threatening all our lives, we should be banding together, not sitting on opposite sides.

"Trell, you have that look. What are you planning?"

"Maybe we should take the power back and start again," I said, thinking a new smaller Committee could have people like Hank who viewed our world as a whole and not two groups.

"Too late."

"Why?"

"Because someone else beat you to it."

11

"ARE YOU SAYING THE COMMITTEE NO LONGER HAS the power to make decisions?" I asked Anne-Jade.

"Yep. They're just following orders. And so am I." A look of self-disgust creased her face.

Even though I feared the answer, I asked, "Who is issuing these orders?"

"The Controllers. They have hijacked the computer network, shutting down access to all but a few people. If the Committee doesn't do as they say, they'll erase the programs for running vital systems."

"But that would hurt them as well."

"They're in the network, Trell. They don't need air or water. Just electricity."

"Anne-Jade, you know better. Logan said they were an operating system. Nothing more."

"Well, Logan is blind and the Committee has him locked away somewhere. So as far as I'm concerned, I obey their orders." She rubbed her face.

A sudden surge of outrage consumed me. "I can find Logan for you."

"Not from the brig."

Surprised, I gaped at her. "I answered all their questions."

"And the Controllers will tell them what to do with you."

"I haven't been involved with the Committee in weeks. Why would the Controllers consider me a threat?"

"You planted those mics. You helped diffuse a bomb. Those aren't the actions of someone who is uninvolved. And the last thing they want is for *you* to be involved."

My head spun with all the information from Anne-Jade. It seemed like an elaborate joke and I expected Anne-Jade to laugh at me for falling for it. But her shoulders dropped and worry filled her eyes.

"Don't let the Committee know I told you all this," she said.

"I won't."

We were summoned back into the conference room. I noticed the vampire box on the table right away.

I endured a lecture about planting the mics on my own and how I should have come to the Committee right away. No surprise.

"Since you no longer wished to be a consultant to the Committee," Domotor said, "we insist on your cooperation to stay out of our affairs, and to keep out of the air shafts, the Gap and the Expanse. Failure to comply will result in your incarceration in the brig."

Big surprise. How did they plan to enforce... The vampire box. A cold wave of dread swelled in my chest as I remembered those tracers Anne-Jade had invented. She must have told the Committee about them.

Domotor met my gaze. His gray eyes held an impotent

anger. "You're also confined to level three and are hereby designated as Doctor Lamont's intern."

Another shock. While I enjoyed helping patients, being forced to was another matter.

"Do you agree to all these conditions?" Domotor asked.

"What happens if I say no?"

"The brig."

I thought so. No choice. I agreed.

Anne-Jade removed the handcuffs and shoved my right arm into the vampire box. The pricks in my forearm just below my wrist stung more than usual. I wiped the blood on my shirt.

"A tracer has been implanted into your arm," Domotor said. "If you stray from level three for any reason, we will be informed. Should you be tempted to remove the tracer, we will also be alerted. The device monitors temperature."

Damn. He had read my mind. With access to the medical supplies, removing the device would have been easy. However, body temperature was approximately thirty-seven degrees centigrade while Inside's ambient temperature was kept at twenty-two degrees centigrade.

The meeting ended and the Committee members either milled about or filed out. Returning to my seat, I had to wait for Anne-Jade to escort me to level three. She discussed the lockdown with Takia. No one spoke to me. Jacy remained in his seat, studying me. I ignored him. Let him wonder.

After most of the others had left, Jacob Ashon approached me. By the uncomfortable stiff-armed way he stood, combined with his queasy expression, I knew this wouldn't be pleasant.

"Trella, I…uh. I'm sorry things didn't work out with Riley." He cleared his throat, then his words rushed out. "It's best if you make a clean break and forget about him."

True. And that's when the full realization of no longer being with Riley stabbed me deep into my heart. Unable to utter a sound, I reached behind my neck and unfastened the clasp. Hooking it back together, I handed the pendant to Jacob.

"I didn't mean…you don't need…"

"Give it to him…please."

Jacob's fingers closed around it. The edges of my vision blurred as black and white spots danced in front of my eyes. I closed them and inhaled deep, calming breaths, concentrating on that simple act only.

When I opened my eyes, Jacob was gone along with Jacy. Anne-Jade tapped my shoulder, gesturing me to follow her. I did.

The trip back to the infirmary occurred without incident. Lamont spotted me, but she continued to wrap bandages around a patient's hand.

"Do you want to inform the Doctor about your assignment or should I?" Anne-Jade asked.

"Feel free." I kept walking.

"Where are you going?"

Annoyance spiked. "To my room. Do I need to file a request with the Committee first?"

"In triplicate."

I turned and made a rude gesture. She laughed. I couldn't help but grin. It lasted a microsecond. All memory of it was erased when I entered my room.

Sheepy was gone.

Sitting on the edge of my bed, I stared at the cuts from the vampire box. I ran my finger along the skin, but couldn't feel the tracer buried inside. If I hadn't been there, I would never have believed if someone told me that helping diffuse a bomb would send Riley and Sheepy away.

I lay in bed, curled under the sheet. Action was required. Plans needed to be made. A tracer to trick. I couldn't let the Controllers or the Committee ruin what I had worked so hard for. What Cogon had died for. I hadn't wanted the responsibility. No. If I was being honest, I had been...or rather was still terrified of the responsibility. And despite what Anne-Jade had said, it wasn't too late.

But for now, I needed to grieve for the loss of the world I had imagined with the Committee in charge. For the loss of Riley. And Sheepy.

Lamont woke me. "An ISF officer is here to check on you."

"Why?" I blinked. Her presence had triggered the daylights.

"You haven't moved in eighteen hours."

An impressive amount of sulking time.

Standing behind Lamont, an ISF officer nodded to me. "Just making sure you're okay," he said.

"Yeah right. You're more worried I've found a way to fool the tracer," I said.

He dropped the pretense. "AJ warned us not to underestimate you."

"AJ?"

"Anne-Jade."

"Cute. Yet you still waited eighteen hours."

"The Doctor's word was sufficient until she also became alarmed as well."

"Guess I was tired." I stretched my stiff muscles—the downside of being inactive for so long. However, my shoulder no longer ached, the swelling in my cheek had gone down and scabs covered the two cuts—the upside.

"You should shower and eat. When you're done, I need

help with a couple patients," Lamont said. She shooed the ISF officer out as she left.

Ah, the glamorous life of an intern. I pushed the covers back and padded through the sitting area to the kitchen. Rebel that I was, I ate first then showered. Sad and pathetic.

The water cleared my mind. I considered how to bypass the tracer as I helped Lamont with routine tasks. Rolling clean bandages, I figured I needed to find a way to keep it at a constant thirty-seven degrees and to move it around, but only on level three.

Inserting it into another person would work. The next time Lamont has surgery, I could slip it in. Except as soon as the patient left this level, the ISF would pounce on the poor unsuspecting person. Avoiding the brig was imperative.

I could use the newborn warmer, parking it in my room when I wanted to explore. But if it didn't eventually move, the ISF would be suspicious. Absently, I reached to play with my pendant only to encounter smooth skin. The jolt of pain reminded me of when Vinco's knife had found a sensitive spot.

I wrenched my thoughts back to my current problem. The warmer could work if I moved it around the infirmary, wheeled it to the cafeteria and other areas on level three. Searching the patient area, exam room and surgery, I couldn't find it.

"Looking for something?" Lamont asked when I exited the surgery.

"The newborn warmer."

She gave me a rueful smile. "Confiscated by the ISF."

Damn. "What if we need it?"

"They'll bring it back only when I have a newborn. We do have a few pregnant patients, but they're not due for weeks."

So much for that idea. Again I grabbed for the pendant without thinking.

Lamont noticed the gesture. "Did you lose your necklace in the riot?"

"No. I lost it diffusing the bomb."

"Bomb?" Her voice squeaked. "The one found in the waste handling plant? You were there? But I thought the riot..."

"I had a busy week."

She stared at me for a few seconds. "I can only imagine." She gestured to my neck. "Is Riley upset that you lost it? Is that why he hasn't come around?"

Normally, I would have snapped at her, telling her to mind her own business. But I couldn't produce the energy. Instead I had a moment of weakness and told her about the choice I had made when disarming the bomb.

She drummed her fingers on the exam table. "I think I would have done the same thing. This Bubba Boom is an expert in explosives after all."

"Yeah, but it was a wiring problem. That's Riley's area of expertise." I rubbed the spot where the tracer had been inserted. "Riley thinks I have a death wish. He may be right." I stared at the floor. "Ever since Cogon floated away...I keep thinking it should have been me. He wouldn't have been afraid to guide us through all these changes. He would have united the uppers and lowers by now. Sabotage and riots would never have happened if Cog was here."

"And what would killing yourself accomplish?" Lamont asked. When I didn't answer, she continued. "It won't bring him back. Cogon is gone. And from a purely medical point of view, you don't have a death wish. If you did, you wouldn't have fought for every single breath in those first critical hours after the fire. Your skin wouldn't have healed as fast as it did."

Even though I hated to admit it, she had a point. And damn it. I felt a little better. Looking up, I was going to thank her, but she had her doctor's purse on her lips as if reviewing a diagnosis in her mind.

"Who also has Cogon's way with people?" she asked.

"Hank from maintenance. Emek's people love him. And Riley. He's been able to work with both uppers and scrubs."

"Then you need—"

I waved my arm. "I can't do anything. Remember? I'm stuck here."

"Let's pretend you don't have the tracer. What would you do first?"

"I'd find Logan, rescue him and set him up at a computer terminal to bypass the Controllers."

"What if he can't see?"

"Then I'd find someone who knows enough about computers to sit next to him and be his eyes."

"Riley?"

"No. He's good, but not Logan good." I considered.

"Your father was Logan good." Pride filled her voice.

I waited for the pain and anger to flair inside me, but only sadness touched. However, his name reminded me of another. "Domotor would be perfect."

"Would he agree to help?"

I remembered his anger. He couldn't be content taking orders from the Controllers. "Yes."

"Then it's an excellent plan. Let's get started." Lamont headed for the surgery, pushing through the double doors.

Curious, I followed her. "But—"

She handed me two syringes. "I think a local anesthetic should be enough. Grab the lidocaine and alcohol wipes."

Then she collected a few other supplies—sutures, scalpel and long curved tweezers.

Understanding hit me hard; I grabbed the operating table to steady myself. "You realize the risk you're taking?"

"There's no risk to me. You're the one who will be in danger of being thrown into the brig. And you'll still need to work here so you're visible to others. Otherwise, they'll get suspicious."

"You'll have to stay on level three."

She shrugged it off. "I'm always here anyway."

The final concern was mine alone. Could I trust her? No. But she offered the only possible solution. If I wanted to make Cogon…and Riley proud of me, I couldn't give up.

With the two of us working together, it didn't take long to remove the tracer from my arm and implant it in Lamont's. The device had only been exposed to the ambient air for a second.

Just to be sure, I stayed and worked in the infirmary for the next six hours. Then we went to the cafeteria in Quad G3 with the intent to eat and then stock up on food for our kitchen.

Riley's brother Blake worked behind the counter, serving soup. His resemblance to Riley sent a flash of pain across my heart.

I wondered what he was doing up here. "New job?" I asked him, trying to sound casual.

"Same job, new location." He shrugged then tilted his head to the people sitting at the tables. "Change of scenery. Change is good. Right?"

"Uh…yeah." I wondered what he was implying. Was he glad Riley and I were no longer together? Hard to tell. I didn't know Blake that well.

After our excursion to the cafeteria I took a brief nap, then changed into my skin-tight uniform. As long as Lamont stayed in our suite or in the infirmary the ISF shouldn't suspect anything.

I climbed into the air duct, grinning.

The Queen of the Pipes has returned.

There weren't many hiding places in Inside. I doubted the Committee knew the locations, but I didn't want to leave anything to chance so I ruled them out right away. They had probably taken him to an empty apartment. Since I had been confined to level three, I suspected he would be on level four. The Travas filled Sector D4, so that meant I had to search Sectors E4 and F4. Doable in the time I had.

I tried not to think about apartment number three-six-nine-five in Sector E4 as I carefully traveled through the air shafts and peered into rooms. At least there weren't any air filters to bypass.

After the rebellion we discovered that scrubbing air shafts and water pipes had been one of the jobs created purely for busy work. With a simple programming adjustment, the trolls cleaned the shafts and pipes without a scrub minder. Which worked well for me now.

When I reached Riley's apartment, I paused for only a moment. The empty living area and bedroom matched the hollow feeling in my heart. I didn't see Sheepy and wondered where he was. Moving on, I finished searching Sector E4 and crossed into F4.

I found Logan in a small room in the far northeast corner of Sector F. Sprawled on the couch, his arm covered his eyes. His space also had a bed, refrigerator and a tiny washroom. The computer station had a screen, but no keyboard or box.

No guards, but I checked the hallway to make sure. A complex series of locks had been installed on his door. And when

I returned to the air vent, I noticed the thick bolts securing it. What I worried most about were microphones and other sensors.

The air shaft was free of any sensors, and knowing Logan, any sensors within his reach would be dismantled by now.

So taking a chance, I said his name.

He sat up and squinted. "Trella?"

"Up here," I said.

He jumped to his feet and whooped. "I knew you'd find me!" No microphones then. "Come down! It's safe."

"I can't." I explained about the bolts. "Next time I'll bring my diamond wire."

"Oh." He dropped back onto the couch. "I can't escape anyway."

"Did they inject you with a tracer?"

"Yep. Nothing like having your own technology bite you in the ass. If you see Anne-Jade can you punch her in the face for me?"

"She didn't lock you in there." I explained about the Controllers.

"The Travas have a link into the network," he said right away.

"That's what I thought. How's your eyesight?"

"Better, I can see about a meter so I can read the monitor if I had a working computer."

"Could you fix the damage to the network?"

"Of course. First thing I did when we gained control of the computer systems was to secure backup in case something like this happened."

I considered his problem. "You can't leave, but I can bring you what you need. Will you be able to hide it when your keepers come to check on you?"

"I should with proper warning." He surged to his feet,

excited. "I have a sweet little sensor you can install in the ceiling of the hallway, and I'll need—"

"Slow down, Logan. Remember it's me. Start with the most important and we'll work from there."

He listed several items and I determined how many trips I would need.

"Zippy can pull the skid I rigged," Logan said in excitement. "Then you can bring more."

"Where's Zippy?" I hadn't seen the little cleaning troll since the rebellion.

"Under the bed in my room."

Ugh. Too close to the Committee for my comfort, but almost all the gadgets he needed could be found there, including the computer.

"Okay, Logan. I'll be back with your supplies, but it may be a while." I used more time to locate Logan than planned so I hurried back through the shafts as fast as I could without making noise, which wasn't very fast at all.

At least I arrived in my room without encountering trouble. It was hour thirty-five. I changed my clothes and joined Lamont in the exam room. She helped an elderly man down from the table.

"I'm not sure when your ears will stop ringing, Ben," she said. "You were close to the blast and are lucky you didn't lose your hearing." Lamont handed him a bottle of small white pills. "Try these, one pill every ten hours. They might help."

He thanked her and shuffled through the patient room.

She watched him go then said, "When we move to a bigger place, I'd like a separate waiting room for walk-ins."

"You should be the one to design it," I said. "Do you know how to use the blueprint program?"

"No."

"Here, I'll show you." I went into her office and sat at the computer. The blueprint program was the only one I used. After the rebellion, Hank had me draw out the layout of the Gap between levels.

"You might have trouble," she said. "Something's wrong with the network. I can't access patient records right now."

I wondered why the Controllers would block them. No idea, but the program I sought popped up without hesitation, and I demonstrated to Lamont how easy it was to draw lines and type in labels.

I surrendered the chair to her. She caught on pretty quick. "This is fun."

Her comment reminded me of my trip through the shafts. I asked her if she had any problems while I was gone.

"Not really," she said.

"That's not an answer."

"One man stopped by to talk to you, but I said you were asleep and he said he'd come back later."

"ISF?"

"No. Big guy with freckles. Kind of cute."

Bubba Boom. I wondered why he came by.

"No trouble from him," she said. "But what if the ISF comes by and you're not here?"

That could be a problem.

"I need a way to contact you," Lamont said.

I touched my earlobe, but remembered I'd lost my receiver in the riot, and the microphone on my uniform had been thrown into a hazardous waste bag. "I'll see what I can find."

"Did you locate Logan?"

"Not yet." I lied, but thought the less she knew the better.

★ ★ ★

I spent the rest of week 147,023 fetching supplies for Logan. Sneaking into his room next to the main Control Room caused my pulse to race. And even though I had been here two times before, I still sweated.

This last trip was for me. I had planted all those mics and they remained in position. Why not listen in? Logan had a device I could use. I also picked up a set of communication buttons and receivers for me and Lamont. Logan would program them so no one could overhear our conversations.

Back in the duct, I used Zippy to haul the supplies. Round with cleaning brushes and a vacuum, he rolled along, pulling the skid. The noise hadn't bothered anyone so far. I'd encountered a few other cleaning trolls in the air ducts.

I reached Logan's without incident and opened the vent. The diamond wire had sawed through the bolts and we had rigged them to appear as if they still secured the vent. I dropped the supplies I brought to him, then swung down. He had managed to disguise most of his new toys. I hoped his keepers wouldn't check under his bed or under the couch.

"Who brings your food? ISF?" I asked him.

"No. The same two guys. Uppers, but not part of the ISF and I would know. Anne-Jade had me check into the background for all her officers to make sure they were trustworthy." He chuckled. "They're armed with stunners, but they have no idea their weapons won't work in here."

"Any luck?" I pointed to his computer. It looked the same, but according to Logan, he had installed all the important components behind the screen and the keyboard could be hidden before all the locks on the door were opened.

"No. They have built a wall around the important systems. I'm trying to find a way to slip inside without anyone noticing, but it's been difficult." He rummaged in the cushions of the couch, pulling out a long glass tube. It resembled a light bulb. He handed it to me. "A Trava computer in Sector D4 has to be connected to the network. Use that to find which one."

"How?"

"Get as close as possible and if the tube glows green, you've found it. Then…" He knelt next to his bed and reached under the mattress. Logan tossed me a small box. "Insert that into Zippy's undercarriage and he should be able to knock out that computer."

"Like when I used him to disable all the weapons in the Control Room?"

"Yep." He straightened and wiped the dust from his pants.

"Why not use a stronger pulse and hit all the computers in Sector D4 at once?"

"It's too risky over a large area."

"But after the computer's zapped, you'll be able to take back control?"

"Don't see why not."

Between sleeping, working for Lamont and searching Sector D4, I didn't have much time for listening to the mics or for implementing the other part of my plan—talking to Hank and Emek. I tried to think of a better way to organize my time.

Logan picked up the button mic I had brought and fiddled with it. He snapped it onto my uniform. "All you have to do is turn it once to the right and it'll go to this receiver only." Dropping a small earring into my palm, he grabbed the other mic, adjusted it and gave it to me. I placed the set into my tool belt.

When he handed me the other receiver, I went into the washroom. The cut on my earlobe had healed, but a tiny hole remained. It wasn't big enough, but it was better than nothing. I pushed the receiver through my earlobe in one quick motion. It stung and I guess I could have waited until I returned to the infirmary and used lidocaine. Oh well. Waiting had never been one of my best traits. And looking at my reflection in the mirror, keeping my hair neat seemed to be another impossible task.

I contemplated cutting my hair as I untangled my messy braid. The knots in my hair resisted my fingers and I couldn't find a comb. When I peeked out to ask Logan, he sat cross-legged in the middle of the room with one of his gadgets nestled in his lap. I noticed how he squinted and brought objects up close to his eyes.

The computer beeped. He hopped up and sprinted to the monitor. "Someone's coming," he said.

My cue to leave. "See you later." I crossed the room and climbed up the wall to the open shaft.

"Trella, wait."

"Why?"

"It's not my keepers. Look."

I glanced over and almost lost my grip. On the screen was a moving picture of Anne-Jade and Riley walking down the hallway. They kept peering back over their shoulders as if worried someone followed them.

"Wow, Logan, that's amazing! How did—"

"They're here to rescue me," Logan said. He grinned, but an instant later alarm replaced his excitement. "If they mess with the locks, we're done. They're wired to set off an alarm if not opened in the proper order. You have to stop them!"

12

"WHAT'S THE PROPER ORDER?" I ASKED.

"No time and it doesn't matter." He waved his arm.

The tracer. How could I forget?

"Hurry," he said.

I pulled myself into the air shaft and crawled the short distance to the hallway in front of Logan's locked door. Anne-Jade's hushed voice drifted up. Without hesitation, I popped the vent open and dropped down almost on top of them.

They both jumped back in surprise. Anne-Jade pulled her stunner. I braced for the sizzle slap of the weapon, but she lowered it.

"Trella?" Her shocked expression didn't last long. "What are you doing here?" she demanded. "How—"

I held up a hand. "If you try to open Logan's door, you'll set off an alarm."

"How—"

"He can't be rescued anyway. He has a tracer."

"Really?" Anne-Jade didn't sound convinced. "Yet you managed to circumvent the tracer in your arm."

I noticed she didn't put her weapon away. Although I felt

Riley's gaze burning on my skin, I resisted glancing at him. "What I did won't work for him."

"I already anticipated the tracer. We're planning to cut it out," she said.

"And alert the Controllers?"

"We have a safe place to hide him," Riley said.

Now I met his gaze. Even though my insides twisted—I missed him more than I realized—I kept my voice even. "You'll still alert the Controllers, who will be on guard. Right now they think Logan isn't a threat."

"Think?" Anne-Jade asked.

"He's been busy."

"I'm assuming so have you," she said.

"I'm not at liberty to say."

"Why not?"

I glanced at her weapon. "You still haven't put that stunner away. And I don't know if you're going to arrest me or not."

The tension in the hallway pressed against my skin.

"They've been using Logan to force my cooperation," she said. "If I had him somewhere safe—"

Logan's door swung open. He poked his head out. "Get in here before someone sees you."

We hurried inside and he closed the door. Wires hung down from below the knob. Anne-Jade rushed to her brother, wrapping him in a hug. Not wanting to intrude on the siblings, I inspected the wiring by the door.

"Interested in electrical circuits now?" Riley asked. The tone in his voice bordered on sarcasm, but could be teasing.

Looking at him was too painful so I traced the loops of wires instead. "Yes. I thought I'd try electrocution next. Since a bomb, a fire, Vinco's knife and a brief encounter with Outer Space didn't kill me."

"There's not enough juice in those. You'll just get a nasty shock. The best place to get electrocuted would be in the power plant."

"Thanks for the tip."

He huffed. "Trella, what are you doing here?"

"Visiting Logan."

Riley stepped in front of me. "You know that's not what I meant. Why are you helping him? You didn't care what the Committee was doing before. Why now?"

I stared at his chest. "I always cared."

"You didn't act like you did. You let—"

"Everyone down. I know. It's because I cared too much."

"That doesn't make sense."

Now I met his gaze. "I didn't want to screw it up. It was terrifying to have the entire population of Inside counting on *me* to make our world a perfect place. It was too much responsibility. Too much to expect me to suddenly know exactly how to combine a society that has been divided and brainwashed for so long."

"What changed?" He whispered the question.

"They *ordered* me to stay away."

He laughed.

I punched him in the stomach. "I'm serious."

"I know, but you have to admit, it's funny."

"What's funny?" Logan asked.

Riley gestured to him and Anne-Jade. "This. Us. Trying to find a way to bypass the Controllers... Again."

"That's easy," Logan said. "Trella's gonna find the active computer in the Trava Sector and disable it."

Unease rolled through me as I remembered when Anne-Jade had commented that the Pop Cops' downfall had been due to overconfidence. Lamont had said the same thing about my father. His confidence had made him cocky and sloppy, leading the Pop Cops right to him.

"And then what?" Anne-Jade asked.

"We regain control of the network and start over with a new Committee," Logan said.

"What about the saboteurs?" I asked.

"We're close to finding them, and there haven't been any more attempts," Anne-Jade said.

"Was it the stink bombers? Ivie and Kadar?" I asked.

"No. They taught a bunch of maintenance scrubs how to build bombs. The suspects sleep in Sector F1. I just need to narrow it down." She peered at me as if I were one of the bombers.

Logan shooed us out so he could repair the locks before his keepers came to check on him. "They usually come every twenty hours, and the new week starts in thirty minutes."

Anne-Jade and Riley headed back through the corridors, while I climbed into the air shafts.

Before Riley left, he shot me a significant look. I mulled over what he tried to communicate to me as I crawled through the ducts. Did he want to talk about us? Or just about the situation? At least he knew I had realized my fears and acknowledged my mistakes.

I returned to the infirmary to make an appearance. My mind remained on the task of finding the live computer in the Trava Sector while I disinfected the examination table.

"...see you. Trella, are you listening?" Lamont asked from the doorway.

"Sorry. What did you say?"

"That Bubba Boom is here. He's waiting out in the patient area."

I peeked past Lamont. No missing the big uncomfortable

man who tried to stay out of everyone's way, but ended up in the wrong place each time.

Curious, I joined him. "You wanted to talk to me?"

Relief flooded his features and he smiled. His pleasure at seeing me was a nice change of pace. Plus he reminded me of Cogon.

"Is there somewhere private we can go?" he asked.

"Sure. Come on back." I led him through the exam room and to our sitting area.

He settled on the couch and I perched on the edge of the chair.

"What's going on?" I asked.

"I examined that bomb." Bubba Boom shifted with unease, focusing on his hands in his lap. "I think I know who built it."

"Why aren't you telling Anne-Jade?"

"It's complicated." He laced and unlaced his fingers together.

"One of your colleagues?" I guessed.

He glanced up. "Yeah. And…it's hard. He works with me sometimes. But…I don't want him to damage any more systems."

I waited, letting him work through the logic.

Taking a deep breath, he said, "It's Sloan. He's getting everyone in Sector F1 riled up and has been talking about forming a resistance and storming the upper levels."

I'd never forget that name, but it seemed a little too convenient. "Sector F1 was rioting at the time."

"Exactly. They planned it as a distraction."

Which made sense, yet they didn't know I would be in the ducts. "But I started the riot."

"Yes, but how did Sloan know you were there?" he asked.

"He heard me in the shaft."

"You? The Queen of the Pipes?"

"My tool belt banged the metal. I'm out of practice."

Bubba Boom shook his head. His shaggy hair puffed out with the motion. It reminded me of when Cog had decided to grow his hair as long as mine—what a mess.

"If you had spent any time in the barracks, you would know it's too noisy in there to hear anything, let alone a bump in the air duct. Sloan knew you were coming."

"How?" I still wasn't convinced.

"Jacy rigged the bag of mics he gave you with a little sensor, tipping Sloan off."

The bag I no longer had. "Why would Jacy set me up? I was supposed to be helping him."

He leaned forward. "Supposed to be? There you go. Jacy doesn't take kindly to people who lie to him or double-cross him. He makes the Pop Cops seem nice."

I scoffed. "You're exaggerating. Jacy helped with the rebellion."

"Of course. All so he can get more power." His cheeks flushed, causing his freckles to almost disappear.

"No. He doesn't even have enough people to maintain his information network."

"Because they're all afraid." He sagged back against the cushions. "Why would I lie? I'm gonna tell all this to Anne-Jade."

"Good." Confusion tugged. I thought I could trust Jacy.

"You need to know Jacy isn't your friend. He hoped the angry mob in Sector F1 would send you to Chomper."

An icy finger of fear touched the back of my neck. I rubbed my cheek, remembering the fury in Sloan's gaze.

Bubba Boom scooted closer to me. "Be very careful." He rested his warm hand on my knee. "I know you're confined to level three, but you shouldn't stray from the infirmary. When I save someone's life, I expect them to stay safe."

"Which time? Helping to diffuse the bomb or rescuing me from the fire?"

He laughed. "Maybe I'm expecting too much from you."

I swatted him on the arm. "Well, thanks for both."

"Anytime. In fact, I think I should visit more often just in case you need saving again." His hand inched up my thigh.

Oh no. Just when I thought I might have found a friend who wasn't incarcerated or the head of ISF, I thought wrong. And I really didn't need another person keeping track of me. I moved my leg away. "Don't worry. As you said, if I stay close to the infirmary I should be fine."

His good humor died. "I thought you and Riley…"

News traveled fast. "We did, but I'm not ready to get involved in another…friendship. Besides, with all the troubles and sabotages, it's best if I just concentrate on helping Doctor Lamont for now."

He studied me as if I was a complicated explosive device, seeking weaknesses. I resisted the urge to squirm. Instead, I stood and said, "Make sure you tell Anne-Jade about Sloan and Jacy." I held my breath. Would he take the hint?

Bubba Boom ambled to his feet and grinned. "Okay. I'm willing to wait until everything is mended. I'm sure all these troubles will soon settle down." He gave me a mock salute and left.

I collapsed back into my chair. My mind swirled. Between his accusations about Jacy and advances, I had no idea what to think. The thought of being close to another man… No. I couldn't even contemplate it without my skin crawling.

Why could I run into a burning room, climb up sheer walls, diffuse a bomb and defy the Committee without hesitation, yet be terrified to admit my feelings for Riley? My own fear had really screwed up not only my life, but Inside's potential for peace and harmony. I hoped it wasn't too late for all of us.

The glass tube didn't glow during my first sweep through the Trava Sector. I had covered about half of the Sector before I needed to return to the infirmary for my shift. Lamont had created a schedule in keeping with the intern ruse. It worked, except I spent my free time crawling through air and heating vents searching for an active computer.

And as the hours passed, I felt more pressure to accomplish something. Anything besides how to determine if a wound was infected or not. Halfway through week 147,024, I completed the fourth and final sweep through the Trava Sector. Still no results. However, by spending so much time in the ducts above the Travas, I learned a few things.

One—they were dangerously bored. Two men had pulled apart a heap of computers to build a couple of hand-held devices. They could be weapons or a way to communicate, I had no idea. But my glass tube didn't glow so it wasn't a link to the Controllers.

Two—they planned to escape and release their comrades in the brig.

Three—they wanted to regain control of Inside and protect something or somebody. Which didn't make sense to me. They already had control. So why didn't the so-called Controllers tell the Committee to release all of the Travas?

My agitation grew and the tension in Inside filled every space. Fights broke out and a number of riots erupted. Anne-Jade's ISF officers were swamped and many were injured.

When she stopped by the infirmary to check on Yuri, I pulled her aside and informed her about the Travas' plans.

"They can have it," she snapped. "Nothing is getting done besides the repairs to the air plant, and everyone has reverted to acting like the Pop Cops are back. They're keeping to themselves and not helping despite the food rationing."

"And the Committee—"

"Does nothing! They're too afraid. I wish the Controllers would just lay it on the line and tell us what they want."

Interesting strategy. "Is the Transmission working?" I asked.

"No. The three Travas who Karla named had no clue how to work it."

"If the Transmission isn't fixed, eventually it won't matter who has control."

"You don't need to tell me, but the Controllers don't seem worried about that."

Odd. "What about Hank? Can he fix the Transmission?"

"He's busy with the air plant repairs. And trying to help us find the saboteurs."

"Did Bubba Boom tell you who they are?" I asked.

"Yeah. But the five of them disappeared when we tried to arrest them."

They could have been tipped off. "There aren't many places to hide."

"You think? Such stellar intellect, I'm going to promote you to captain."

"No need to be nasty."

Anne-Jade rubbed her eyes. Exhaustion had etched deep lines into her face. "Sorry. I don't have the manpower to search those places. If it wasn't for Hank's offer to keep an eye out, Sloan and his cohorts could be lounging in the dining room without having to worry about the ISF."

"At least with them on the run, there shouldn't be any more attacks."

"One good thing," she said.

"One thing at a time." Which reminded me of my task. "Anne-Jade, I know you're swamped, but can you search the Trava Sector for the active computer? I've done all I can through the shafts and came up with nothing."

"We do regular inspections. Too regular from what you've told me." She sighed. "I think it's time for a surprise visit."

"Take the glass tube with you. It should pick up anything that is hidden." I hurried back to my room and retrieved the detector and Zippy for her.

She raised her right eyebrow. "You keep Zippy in your room?"

"In case I need him. Can you bring him back when you're done?"

Anne-Jade left muttering about smoke damaged wits. I had told her the truth about Zippy, but not the entire reason I kept the little cleaning troll near my bed. He's been with me through some tough times. And he filled the void left by Sheepy.

At hour sixty, Anne-Jade returned with Zippy and the glass detector. Although her surprise inspection had netted her an interesting and scary array of illegal devices, weapons and contraband, she didn't find a computer linked to the network.

Which meant another person or group were the Controllers. Not good. Two hours later, I hurried over to Logan's room.

Faint voices rolled through the shaft as I neared his vent. I slowed, keeping as quiet as possible as I slid the final meter.

Logan's aggravated tone was easy to recognize. The other two sounded calmer and were harder to discern.

"...long are you going to keep me here?" Logan demanded.

"...safe...saboteurs...life," a man's voice said.

"I'll stay in the Control Room. No one can get in there." Logan's anger rang clear.

"...rebellion...easy..."

"That's because we were all helping her. Besides, Trella's not a danger to me, you unrecyclable idiot. She's my friend."

More murmuring and I strained to hear the rest. The voices stopped and the door clicked shut. Metallic snaps and clangs followed before silence filled the room. I waited a few minutes until I was certain Logan's keepers had left, then I dropped down to the floor.

Logan stared at the closed door, hugging his arm to his chest.

"Logan, if you want to leave here, just say the word and I'll find you the perfect hiding place."

He spun around. "No worries, I'm fine. I just have to whine and complain to my captors or else they'll suspect I'm up to something. Did you hear my little tantrum about being bored to death?"

"No."

"Too bad, it was quite the performance." He crossed to his computer and pulled the keyboard out from its hiding place. Tapping a few keys, the screen lit up and displayed the picture of the hallway. The two guards walked down the corridor.

Still impressed by the moving pictures, I asked, "Do I even possess the rudimentary knowledge to understand how you invented a device that sees?"

He puffed up his chest. "No. You need to be a genius like me."

"I'm glad your sense of self worth hasn't changed," I teased.

"If you must know, I found the information and schematics in the computer. It's called a Video Camera."

"I remember them now. They were all over Inside, and a room full of computer screens for watchers to keep an eye on everyone. But I thought they were all destroyed."

"Those were. They were about fifteen centimeters long, by five centimeters wide, by three high. Bigger than mine, easier to spot and to smash."

"You can't blame them. It's creepy having someone spying on you."

"Not that different from the mics we're using."

"I disagree. It's a big difference." I shuddered.

Logan shrugged. "I was hoping to make more of these, but..." He closed his eyes and touched his eyelids with his fingertips, smoothing the skin as if he could wipe the injury away. "There are a few Video Cameras pointed toward Outside. They hadn't been damaged by the riots. I'd show you the pictures, but access to them has been blocked. Too bad, as they're really fascinating."

Another shudder shook my body. "No thanks. I've already seen Outside and I'm not fascinated at all." *Horrified* would be my word of choice. To rid myself of the image, I studied the screen. "The big guy on the left seems familiar," I said. "Too bad I missed their faces."

Logan's fingers danced on the keyboard and the men walked backward, disappeared and appeared again, but this time facing forward. They continued to walk backward for a few steps, then froze.

"How's that? Or do you want them closer?"

"That's good." I leaned forward and peered at the monitor. "The guy on the left reminds me of...someone. I've seen him before, but I can't place him." I hoped his name would eventually click.

In the meantime, I updated Logan on the search for the computer linked to the Controllers'. "Not in the Trava Sector. Where should I look next?"

He drummed his fingers on the edge of the keyboard. "Every Inside computer is suspect now."

"That's..." I couldn't even calculate a number.

"Two thousand, four hundred and nine computers."

My emotions warred between being impressed by Logan's memory and astounded by the sheer number of computers. "I couldn't—"

"Impossible to check them all." His fingers tapped again. "Did you bring the detector with you?"

"No."

"Next time you come, bring it along. I might be able to adjust it to hone in on the Controllers' signal over a wider area." He then added a number of other items he needed me to fetch for him.

Heading back to the infirmary through the air shafts, I concentrated on remembering Logan's list. When Doctor Lamont's voice sounded in my ear, I almost hit my head on the top of the shaft.

"Trella, Bubba Boom is here and he insists I wake you," she said. "What should I do?"

I fumbled for the button mic. "What's so important?"

"He wouldn't say."

Curious. "Tell him you woke me and I'll be out in a couple minutes. I'm almost home."

"Okay." She clicked off.

It wasn't until I had swung down into my room that I realized I had called the infirmary home. I really needed to return our world to a more normal state before I started calling Lamont Mom.

Changing into my green long-sleeved medical uniform, I pulled strands of my hair from my braid to appear sleep tousled. No need to act tired—sleep remained a low priority.

Bubba Boom wasted no time with hellos. He took my hand and pulled me from the infirmary and out into the hallway.

"Let go." I yanked, but he wouldn't release me. "What's going on?"

"I'll tell you in a minute." He kept his quick pace through the corridors.

The few people we passed gave us either curious stares or smirks, or ignored us. Bubba Boom dropped my hand as soon as we reached a quiet corner.

"I know you don't believe me about Jacy." He held a finger up before I could interrupt. "He's in his office and you should see for yourself who he's been…collaborating with."

"Why can't you tell me?"

"Better this way." He pointed to a vent above our heads. "This will take you over the Committee members' offices in Sector H3."

"I'm not supposed to go into the air shafts. The tracer—"

"Isn't that accurate. It'll appear as if you walked through the Sector. You need to hurry before he finishes his meeting."

I glanced up. The vent was in the middle of the ceiling. "I'll need a boost."

He squatted down, holding his hands out. "Stand on my shoulders."

I kicked off my mocs, grabbed his hands for balance, and stepped onto him. He stood with ease and steadied my legs. The vent was within reach and I pushed it open. As I squirmed into the duct, I marveled at Bubba Boom's strength and height. He didn't appear to be that tall, but I doubted even Cog could boost me that high.

"I'll wait here for you," he called.

It took me a few minutes to get my bearings and head in the right direction. Despite Bubba Boom's suggestion to hurry, I slowed as I crossed over the Committee's offices. Bluelights glowed from most of them. No sounds or voices drifted, but that didn't mean no one was below.

The bright square of daylights reflecting off the metal duct marked Jacy's office well before his voice reached me.

"...don't know...she...problem," Jacy said.

Two almost-familiar male voices answered him, and I crept with care for the last two meters. The front half of Jacy's desk and two sets of legs facing it were visible from my vantage point. I strained to match the voices with faces and names.

"All your plans sound feasible, but you need to repair that Transmission before you can do anything else," said an authoritative and scary voice. Why scary? I searched my memories.

"We tried," Jacy said. "Karla sent us a trio of idiots."

"No surprise. She was having fun with that little scrub. *I'll* send you the right people."

I tucked that tidbit away for now.

"How do we get them past Hank?" asked the third man.

My hand flew to my cheek. I couldn't forget that voice. Sloan. Bubba Boom was right. Jacy had set me up!

"He has people in the power plant all the time," Sloan said.

"How long would they need?" Jacy asked.

"A couple hours at most," Authoritative and Scary said.

"We'll stage a distraction. If they wear the maintenance coveralls, they'll blend right in," Jacy said.

While Jacy working with Sloan was a bad thing, fixing the Transmission wasn't. I guessed Jacy had used the sabotage and the attack on Logan as a distraction so he could grab control of the computers and therefore Inside. It would make sense that he'd want to fix the Transmission once he gained power.

"What happens once the Transmission is repaired?" Sloan asked.

"We implement your plan," Authoritative and Scary said.

That comment supported my mutiny theory. Sloan and the other man stood and each shook Jacy's hand over the desk. I willed the unknown man to turn left to leave instead of right so I could see his face.

For once, I had my wish. I caught a glimpse of his beak of a nose and black mustache. His features were familiar. An upper, but not one I've seen more than once or twice.

I chased the logic as I traveled back to where Bubba Boom waited. Scary had been one of my initial reactions, which meant I must associate him with a frightening event. Perhaps he had been a Pop Cop. But from the commanding tone of his voice, he was used to giving orders. Unfortunately, I knew most of the higher ranked Pop Cops. The answer slammed into me.

The other man was Captain James Trava.

13

AS SOON AS I PULLED THE VENT OPEN, BUBBA BOOM appeared below. I hung down. He grabbed me around my waist and lowered me to the floor.

He stared at me a minute before releasing me. "Now do you believe me?"

"Yes. How did you know about the Captain?"

"Hank never trusted Jacy, and one of our guys found a maintenance panel that had been tampered with in Sector D4."

"Maintenance panel?"

"There're these covers on the walls that blend in and are easy to remove in case you need to get to the pipes and wires inside. It's better to pop off a panel than cut a hole in the wall. The Travas have been using the one in Sector D4 to sneak in and out."

"But there are ISF officers all over the place."

"Not up here. Heck, anyone wearing an upper's shirt and pants can stroll around levels three and four without any problems."

Sounded familiar. I had traveled the halls of the upper levels without notice when the Pop Cops had been in charge. Why? Not enough Pop Cops and people who kept to themselves too scared to get involved. Same thing, different names. There had to be a way to break that cycle, to unite us. The answer eluded me.

We headed back to the infirmary. I mulled over the information.

Jacy could no longer be trusted so everything he had told me should be considered a lie. The biggest threat to Jacy and Captain Trava was Logan. Even though it had been for the wrong reason, the Committee had actually done the right thing when they put Logan into protective custody.

As we neared the infirmary, Bubba Boom asked me to accompany him to the dining room. Since we needed to make plans, I agreed. I poked my head into the patient area to inform Lamont. Because of the tracer, she had to tag along, but she claimed it was a good idea.

Bubba Boom had been quick to hide his frown, but she noticed and said, "Don't worry, I won't sit with you two."

No one spoke as we turned south toward Quad G3. My thoughts still sorted through all that I had learned in the last few hours. Lamont filled her tray and joined a group of friends while Bubba Boom and I found an empty table as far away from everyone as possible. My plate contained a greenish-colored casserole, but I had no memory of scooping it.

I watched my mother. She appeared relaxed and when she smiled it changed her whole face, reaching all the way to her eyes. I realized she hadn't been happy in a very long time. Which should seem obvious, but I held no memory of her ever showing any joy or peace even before she betrayed us.

What was different? Her daughter was alive and despite her tendency to downplay the risk, she put herself in considerable danger by carrying the tracer for me. I thought about what I'd done without hesitation for my friends.

I'd been willing to sacrifice myself for Cogon. Would I have done it for some stranger? While I'd like to think I would, if I was truly honest with myself, the answer would be probably not. And why were we strangers at all? We lived in a giant metal cube. Granted, the Pop Cops had separated us, but if we went back far enough, we were all related to one of the original nine families.

A little zip of understanding jolted me. Could the solution to our problems be that simple?

"…look. Should I be worried? Trella?" Bubba Boom waved a hand in front of my face.

"Sorry. I was just…"

"What?"

"Thinking."

"I already figured that out." He tilted his head toward Lamont. "Are your deep thoughts about your birth mother?"

"Yes, but they don't help the situation with Jacy. Do you know what they're planning?"

"No. We've just connected him to Sloan and the Captain recently."

"We?"

"Me, Hank, Phelan, Kren and Ange. The maintenance soups…supervisors."

"Aren't you a little young to be a soup?"

He shrugged. "After the rebellion, not many people were willing to step up and take charge."

Guilty of the same thing, I played with my food. At least I realized my mistake.

"We think Jacy and his cohorts are trying to hack into the

computer network," he said. "It hasn't been working right the past two weeks. And if they gain control…"

"They already have."

Bubba Boom's expression flickered in surprise. "How do you know?"

Time to decide. If I wanted to fix the mess, I needed Bubba Boom and Hank's help. They had already figured out a few things on their own. I explained to him about Jacy's group using the mythical Controllers to give orders to the Committee and Anne-Jade. But for some unknown reason, I didn't tell him about Logan.

"You've been confined to level three. How did you find out about all that?"

An interesting question. He didn't seem too upset about the Controllers, but he did suspect something wasn't right. "I'm allowed visitors."

He studied me a moment. "If they truly have the network, there's nothing we can do."

But Logan could. I hoped. "At least Jacy and the Captain plan to fix the Transmission. That gives us one less problem to worry about."

I surprised him again. "When?" he asked.

"I don't know. But I think you should give them a predictable time when Hank won't be nearby so they don't have to create a distraction. And it will also give you an opportunity to see who else is involved." Spoken like a true Pop Cop. They had enjoyed baiting and trapping as many scrubs as possible in their schemes.

"But without control of the computers, it won't matter if we know who's involved or not," he said.

"We might be able to reclaim the computer systems."

"Might? Do you really think we have a chance?"

"I've done more with less."

He laughed. "So you're asking us to trust you."

"Yep."

"I'll talk to Hank. He's been saying we need to start over so I'm sure he'll agree to give you all the help you'll need."

Logan was thrilled to hear the Transmission might be repaired. He gave me one of his new tiny Video Cameras to plant so he could watch when they started working on the machine. Between my supply runs, he spent his time building gadgets. And I spent my free time with Bubba Boom. Since Hank and his crew had agreed to assist me, Bubba Boom acted as our go-between.

Modifying the glass tube detector, Logan returned it to me. Since I didn't have the time to sweep all the Sectors and Quadrants in Inside to search for the active link to the Controllers, I passed it along to Hank and his crew to check them.

"You want to start doing what?" Lamont asked me.

"Using the vampire boxes," I said again. It was hour fifteen during week 147,025, and the last fifty hours of traveling back and forth to Logan's had been physically draining. I perched on the edge of the examination table while Lamont sorted through her supplies.

"Why?"

"The files with all the blood test data are…unavailable, so I want to do tests on everyone."

Lamont stared at me as if I displayed symptoms of a high fever. "What do you want to test for?"

"Family bloodlines."

"Why?"

"I think it'll help us regain a sense of community. Instead of being the uppers and lowers we can be the Ashons and

Minekos. Then each family can vote for a representative to be in the Committee of nine. But I think we still need a Captain. Someone like Hank."

"Or you," she said.

"I don't have any technical knowledge of the ship."

"You don't need it. You have Logan, who you trust. A Captain can't do everything, that's why she has a support staff of trusted people."

"The people of Inside might not be too happy to see me in that position."

"You have good ideas. When you get us on the right track everyone will be happy."

She had a lot of confidence in me. I waited for the familiar twist of fear in my stomach, but nothing happened. At least the thought of people relying on me didn't scare me anymore. Instead, it gave me a push of motivation. Much better.

"The only problem with using the vampire boxes is we can't put the results in the computer, and we don't have enough wipe boards," I said.

"Then we'll do it the old-fashioned way." Lamont gestured to the white metal walls. "They're just giant wipe boards and we'll have plenty of space."

I laughed.

"Do you want to test everybody? Even those who know their family names already?"

"No. Just test the people in the lower levels. Will the boxes be able to tell which family they belong to from the blood sample?"

"The families have been mixing together for the last 145,027 weeks in the lower levels. It might be hard to find a clear match. We could do hybrid families like the Ashekos?"

"That would give us too many groups. I'd like to keep the

numbers small. If possible, pick the dominate family and tell each person his or her family name."

"And if I can't?"

"Pick a family. Preferably one that is short on members."

Lamont grinned then sobered. "One last problem. I can't leave level three."

"I'll have to send them to you."

"All eighteen thousand? How?"

"I'm not sure. Maybe Bubba Boom or Hank will have a suggestion."

But I didn't have a chance to ask them because soon after I finished my shift for Lamont at hour twenty, a series of loud metallic clangs rolled through Inside. The walls and floor shuddered with each, clearing the shelves and tripping anyone standing, including me. I had been in my room debating between sleeping and visiting Logan.

It wasn't as severe as the Big Shake. More like Little Trembles.

I joined Lamont in the exam room.

"You think it was another bomb?" she asked.

"I hope not, but unless a piece of machinery malfunctioned there aren't many other ways to cause that much movement." And then I remembered Jacy had talked about creating a distraction. Bubba Boom had assured me Hank had changed his schedule and eliminated the need for a distraction. Perhaps Jacy suspected an ambush. Otherwise, it meant Jacy risked all our lives just because he could.

Helping Lamont prep for casualties, I worried about my friends. I would have liked to search for them, but already a few injured people had arrived.

I felt better when it became obvious that most of the injuries were minor. Cuts, bruises, a few broken arms and legs, a couple concussions and a number of sprained ankles and wrists. Nothing like the overwhelming deluge after the Big Shake. And no burns.

Sometime during the next ten hours, Bubba Boom stopped by. He had a small cut on his arm, but wouldn't let me clean and bandage it.

He waved away my efforts. "It's fine."

When I asked about the others, he said, "I haven't heard of any fatalities." He pulled me outside and a few meters away from the infirmary. He lowered his voice. "The Transmission blew again. Jacy's Travas either overloaded it by mistake or incompetence. Or they did it on purpose."

"I heard them say *fix*."

"Maybe that meant *fix* it so it won't run again."

"That bad?"

"It's a mangled mess. We won't know for a week or more."

I wondered if Logan had watched the Travas with his Video Camera. Hank and Bubba Boom still thought he was in protective custody. They hadn't asked how I would bypass Jacy's Controllers, but at least they hunted for the active link.

"Any news about the link?" I asked.

"Nothing. And we'll have to postpone the search until we can figure out what to do about the Transmission."

Just what we needed—more delays. Jacy was bound to clamp down on our freedoms soon and release all the Travas. It still puzzled me why he hadn't by now.

After the last of the injured had been seen and I had slept for over eight hours, I climbed into the ducts and visited Logan.

He pounced on me as soon as I dropped down into his room.

"I've been calling you for hours," he said.

"I turned my receiver off so I could get some sleep. Sorry. Are you hurt?"

"No." He twisted the bottom of his shirt, coiling it tight.

"What's wrong? Did you see what happened—"

"Of course! I saw it all and I've been dying to talk to someone about it." He paced and twisted. "I'm bored."

I glanced at all his half-completed devices. "No. You're lonely. I should stop by more often."

He waved my comment away. "I'm sure you were busy." He sprinted to the computer and tapped a few keys. "Come see what happened before the Video Camera died."

The screen showed the long cylinder and control panel for the Transmission. Bluelights glowed in the empty room. Then the daylights flooded as three men dressed in maintenance coveralls approached the control panel. Logan pressed a key and the men moved super fast as they went back and forth from the panel to the machine.

"They worked on the Transmission for about an hour," Logan said. "Here's where it gets interesting."

Their actions didn't make sense to me, but there was no missing the bright flash just before the panel exploded. The men flew back and the screen turned dark.

"The energy pulse blew the Video Camera." Logan swiveled around to me.

"Did they cause the explosion?"

"No. I studied that whole hour and it appeared to me they were repairing the damage from before."

"What happened then?"

"The panel must have been rigged to blow when they reached a certain point."

"Rigged by who? Did you see anyone else work on the machine?"

"No. The booby trap was in place before you installed the Video Camera."

Booby trapped prior to the explosion? It didn't make any sense. Everyone wanted the Transmission fixed. I pointed at Logan's screen. "That first explosion set off a bunch of others."

"Overkill, for sure. One was enough to obliterate the controls. Can you place another Video Camera in there for me? I'd like to see the extent of the damage."

"A mangled mess, according to Bubba Boom."

Logan sniffed. "I'd still like to see it for myself."

"Okay."

He gave me another Video Camera and a list of supplies. I climbed into the air shafts and crossed to the power plant. The Transmission was located in the southeast corner and the damage to the floor and walls from the first explosion hadn't been repaired yet.

Finding an intact shaft was difficult, but I switched to the heating ducts, and managed to circumvent the open areas. As I drew closer, the sound of an argument reached me. Strained, worried and upset voices shouted at each other. I doubted anyone heard the replies if there were any.

I peeked through the vent. Most of the Committee members gathered around a hole in the middle of a control panel. The metal had been peeled back as if a giant fist had punched through the panel. Black scorch marks streaked along the sides and water dripped from everything. At least the sprinkler system had doused the fire. Unlike the fabric in the air filters, there wasn't much here to burn. It looked bad, but not quite the mangled mess of Bubba Boom's description.

Hank and a few of his crew stood together, enduring the ire of the Committee members. I waited until they left and placed the Video Camera just below the vent.

★ ★ ★

I returned to the infirmary and helped Lamont change bandages and feed patients. The follow-up care wasn't as interesting to me as the initial treatment. Surgery fascinated me, but I'd be happy to let someone else take charge of a patient's recovery. All part of my impatience. Another aspect of my personality that led me into trouble.

A few hours into my shift, Domotor wheeled himself into the infirmary. Three shades past pale, his haggard expression regarded me with desperation. I yelled for Lamont and ran to him, asking him to list his symptoms, checking his pulse.

He gave me a weak smile. "I'm fine."

"Are you sure?"

"Well...I'm physically as fine as possible considering the broken back."

Lamont arrived with her scanner. "What hurts?"

"My ego. Apparently, I don't look well."

She paused. "That's putting it mildly."

"Nothing a good meal and ten hours of sleep won't cure, Kiana," he said.

I winced at the use of her first name. It had been so long since I heard it. To me, that name equaled pain. They pretended not to notice.

"Are you here for a checkup then?" she asked.

"No. I need to talk to Trella. Do you have a few minutes?"

I glanced at Lamont. She nodded and returned to work, giving us some privacy.

"Here?" I asked.

"If you'd be so kind as to wheel me over to the dining room, we can talk there."

Interesting how no one wanted to talk in the infirmary. I wondered if someone had planted a microphone here. Perhaps it was due to the patients. Lying around with nothing to do, they would enjoy eavesdropping on our conversation.

Domotor remained quiet as I pushed him to Quad G3, helped him fill his tray and found an empty table far away from those who eyed us with curiosity. Blake wiped off tables, ignoring us, but I had the strange feeling he'd been keeping track of the people who shared my table. I wondered if Riley had asked his brother to keep an eye on me. I hadn't seen Riley since our conversation in Logan's room.

While I pushed my food around my plate, Domotor attacked his food as if he hadn't eaten in weeks.

"If you need a break from Committee business, I know a little place in Quad C1 where no one would bother you," I said. "You'd probably eat more often, too."

He laughed. "Tempting, except for the black dust and roar of the power plant."

Domotor finished his meal. He wiped his mouth with a napkin, but kept the cloth clutched in his hand. A little color had returned to his face. No spark lit his blue eyes. Even during the worst moments of the rebellion, he'd never looked this bad.

"What's wrong?" I asked.

"Everything. But first tell me how you bypassed the tracer in your arm."

Was he guessing? Or did he know? I kept my expression neutral. "I didn't bypass the tracer." The truth.

"You can tell me. I'm no longer on the Committee."

A sinking feeling of unease stroked my stomach. "Why not?"

"There is no longer a Committee. The Controllers have taken over Inside."

"But the computer—"

"They have the network and all system controls. Except the Transmission's."

"All systems?" Fear swirled and I fought to keep from grabbing the chair's arms in panic.

"Yes. If they decide to cut off our air, we're dead."

"Did they release Karla and Vinco?" Funny how I was more terrified of those two than the threat of suffocation.

"No."

Surprised, I asked, "Why not?"

"The Controllers are *not* the Travas."

"Not all of them," I said. "Jacy's in charge, but he's working with them."

Domotor laughed. "Jacy? Where did you hear that?"

"I have my sources."

"Well your sources are wrong."

"Really? Then who are the Controllers?"

"Outsiders."

14

"OUTSIDERS." I REPEATED THE STRANGE WORD. "YOU think the Controllers are Outsiders? How... Why..." The concept was so outrageous, I couldn't say more.

"Logan isn't the only one who is good with the computer, Trella," Domotor said. "I've been trying to find a way around the Controllers since they showed up. I managed to isolate a small part of the network, and I traced where the link is coming from. It's not from anywhere in Inside."

"Are you sure? Jacy—"

"He could be helping them. It wouldn't surprise me. That boy's an opportunist."

"Do you know what the...Outsiders want?" I asked.

"To come in."

I felt as if I had drifted into Outer Space—unable to breathe as ice stabbed deep into my bones. "Can they?" My voice squeaked.

"Yes, they can and will."

No wonder he looked so haggard. "Maybe it would be a good thing. They could be in trouble or need our help."

"Then why didn't they ask? They infiltrated our network,

they ordered us to lock down our people and they told us they're boarding. Not the actions of a friendly group."

"Can we stop them?" I asked.

"I've been trying, but since this last explosion they've shut down all access. I can't get into my isolated system."

My head spun. "Why are you telling me all this?"

"You need to give this…" He handed me a small round disk. "To Logan." Domotor studied my face. "He needs this disk to get to the isolated system. I know you've been visiting him so don't lie to me and say you can't. This is vital to our world."

"What can Logan do that you can't?"

"Work his magic, get control back and stop the Outsiders from coming in."

"What if he can't?"

"Then we're all at the mercy of the Outsiders."

Logan didn't mince words. "Holy crap, Trella, this is bad." He had inserted Domotor's disk into his computer and had been typing away.

"How bad?"

"We're screwed." He tapped the screen with a fingernail. "No wonder we couldn't locate the link. I never considered an Outside source."

His fingers flew over the keys as he murmured and cursed under his breath.

"But now that you know what's going on, you can stop them. Right?" I prodded.

"No can do."

My knees refused to hold my weight. I sank into a nearby chair.

He pushed back from the computer. "We're blocked out

of everything. Domotor isolated an area, but I would need an untainted computer to access it."

"Untainted?"

"One that hasn't been hooked into the network."

"What about the computers in the Trava Sector?" I asked. "Anne-Jade said they were cut off from the network."

Logan fiddled with the ends of his hair. He hadn't bothered to cut it while in protective custody. "It would depend on when those computers were unhooked. If the Outsiders had already gained access, they won't work."

"How do we get you there without anyone knowing?"

His face lit up. "I rigged a device that feeds off the heat from the lamp. It'll keep the tracer at a constant temperature."

"If we wait until right after your keepers leave, we'll have about twenty hours before the game is up."

I considered the steps needed to get Logan to Sector D4. After I scouted out a computer, he could travel through the air shafts with me. However, what would we do with the Travas in the room?

Time to pay Anne-Jade a visit.

"You want to borrow what?" Anne-Jade sat behind her desk and blinked at me as if she could clear me from her vision.

I had waited until the ISF office emptied of her lieutenants before dropping in on her. Keeping close to the heating vent in case one of the others returned, I repeated my request. "A stun gun, Anne-Jade. Not a kill-zapper. I need it to help Logan." And when she didn't answer, I added, "Trust me."

"Stun guns can kill if set high enough."

"I know." Cogon had killed a Pop Cop by accident because the Pop Cop's gun had been set to maximum. "Can't you lock it at a certain level?"

She crumpled. There was no other way to describe it. One second sitting straight and being stubborn, the next a defeated slouch. "You have the worst timing." Anne-Jade spun her monitor around so I could see it. The white screen had a row of black letters that read, *Collect all the weapons Inside and lock them in the safe, including your own.*

"Is that—"

"Yes. Orders from the Controllers."

"Do you know they're not—"

"Yes. And they know exactly how many weapons we have because our inventory was in the computer."

"But if you're locking them—"

"The floor of the safe has a weight sensor in case anyone decides to try to steal anything."

My mind raced. "Then add in extra weight. You can't lock up all the weapons! That's suicide."

"I don't have much time." She pointed to the bottom of the screen. A small clock counted down. She had less than an hour. "If I don't do as they say, they'll gas Sector D2."

"Sleeping gas?"

"I wish."

I sorted through the potential problems. "If I find you the weight, will you loan me a stun gun?"

"Sure."

Anne-Jade gave me the approximate weight of each weapon. While she called in her officers, I returned to the air shafts.

As I slid through them, memories of other panicked scrambles through the tight shafts replayed in my mind. I had hoped never to be in this situation again. In order to put a positive spin on my rushed descent to level one, I considered this trip practice. If the Outsiders did gain entry into our world, we would have one advantage of being in familiar territory.

The best place to pick up items of various weights was in the recycling plant. I peered through the vents, searching for a pile away from the bustle of activity and near a vent. Part of me was glad to see people working to recycle the large amount of waste that had collected during the last six weeks, but the other half worried one of the workers would recognize me. Too bad I didn't have time to don a pair of the drab gray overalls and boots.

A few people picked through a couple piles as if searching for something so at least in that regard, I wouldn't be calling attention to myself. I spotted a mound of broken glass items. They would be heavy enough to stand in for the weapons.

Easing from the air shaft, I dropped to the floor with a light thump. My heart added its own thumping that I swore the entire recycling plant could hear. A couple people glanced over, but resumed working. Careful of where I stepped, I tried to keep the glass pile between me and the others.

I filled my bag with a hefty amount—enough, I hoped, for three or four weapons. The beauty of taking glass was Anne-Jade could break off pieces if they didn't match the weight. Tying the bag to my belt, I climbed the wall, using the rivets. In the recycling plant, the air vents were at the top of the walls and not in the ceiling.

When I reached the vent, I pulled my body in. Except before I could draw in my legs, a hand clamped around my ankle and yanked.

I used my elbows to stop my fall. With the lower half of my body dangling from the vent, I glanced down. Sloan held my ankle and gave me a smirk. Damn.

"Come on out, little bug," he said. "You aren't supposed to be down in this level. You're a bad little bug that's about to get squashed, and not by Chomper."

The graphic image propelled me into action. I kicked back

with my other foot. My heel connected with his eye. Not hard because of my awkward position, but it doesn't take much force to temporarily damage a person's vision. He yelled and let go of my ankle. I didn't hesitate to haul the rest of my body into the shaft.

His curses followed me, echoing in the thin metal duct. The good news, I escaped. The bad, Jacy would soon know I had bypassed my tracer. Although with the Outsiders poised to enter Inside, I doubted anyone would care about me.

By hour fifty-nine, I returned to Anne-Jade's office. Through the vent, I spotted a wall gaping open. It was the door to the safe. I had never noticed it before, which made sense.

A line of very unhappy ISF officers relinquished their weapons. One of Anne-Jade's lieutenants kept track of the number. I was about to squirm into a comfortable position to wait when I noticed the stun gun. Light from the office illuminated the dial. It had been set to level five intensity— enough force to stun an average-sized man. I tucked it into my belt and left the glass for Anne-Jade.

I needed to swing by the infirmary to gather a few supplies before going back to Logan's. Lamont found me stuffing a syringe, tweezers and sutures into a cloth bag.

"Are you here to help me?" she asked.

"No."

"What's going on, Trella?"

I hesitated.

"I think I've been more than understanding and patient with all your trips these last two weeks, but something zapped the computer and Domotor's face…" She shivered and wrapped her arms around her torso. "I figured you already found Logan. Did he get into the network?"

I considered what to tell her. "Logan's working on it and I'm helping him." I added about the Controllers disbanding the Committee.

A crease of concern lined her forehead as she watched me as I finished packing the bag.

"I can see you're spooked. What else is going on?" she asked.

"I'd rather not say." It was an honest reply.

"You're being smart. I shouldn't have asked and I don't want to know. Because if someone threatens to harm you, I'll do or say anything to protect you. Go on. I'll cover for you."

"Thanks."

"You will warn me if I need to prep for casualties?"

If the Outsiders come in, there could be panic and injuries. "Yes."

"Good. Now shoo."

I arrived at Logan's room a few minutes after his keepers had left. So far, they kept to their twenty-hour schedule, which meant Logan and I had that much time to find him an untainted computer.

Over the next hour, I learned a few things about Logan. He hated needles, he vomited at the sight of his own blood and he acted like a baby when it came to pain. Removing the tracer turned into an unexpected ordeal. I wished for Lamont's cool confidence that surfaced whenever she dealt with a difficult patient.

Finally, Logan and I crept through the air shafts. Unused to any physical activity since the fire, he moved slowly and we took frequent breaks. Plus he babied the arm with the sutures. At this rate, it would take us hours to reach Sector D4.

Despite my impatience, we arrived at the edge of the Sector.

Locked wire mesh air filters blocked the duct that led into the Travas apartments. I had encountered them before when sweeping for the active link so it didn't take me long to unlock them.

I left Logan behind so I could scout for a computer. Looking for an apartment with only a couple Travas living there, I also wanted one close to where Logan waited. I found a small one-bedroom apartment with three male Travas. They played cards on the table right below the air vent. It was almost perfect.

I grabbed the stun gun from my belt and flipped the safety off. Easing open the vent, I aimed at the farthest man and pulled the trigger. As the loud sizzle slap filled the room, the pulse of energy hit him in the torso and he jerked. The chair toppled backward. Before he hit the floor, I had stunned the second man.

The third spotted me. He jumped to his feet and dashed toward the washroom. I dropped to the table, aimed and caught him before he reached the door. Stunners overloaded a body's nervous system. When directly hit with a pulse, a person lost all feeling in his body and couldn't move for a couple hours or more, depending on the intensity. If hit on the arms or legs, then it just deadened that extremity. I had been hit below the waist and it had numbed both my legs and hip area.

I hurried back to Logan and led him to the apartment. Logan ignored the three men and aimed straight for the computer, loading Domotor's disk into it. With nothing to do, I straightened the cards and moved the guys into more comfortable positions.

The couch looked inviting, so I sat on the end, tucking my legs up under me. It had been only fifteen hours since I last slept, but the pace had been nonstop. I rested my head on the couch's arm.

A weight settled next to me and I startled awake. Logan slouched beside me.

"Well?"

"No luck. Everything's blocked."

"What about Domotor's isolated system?"

"I can retrieve data from it, but I can't get into the executable files. The ones that run the systems."

"What type of data?" I asked.

"Useless stuff like the population control stats, fuel data, hydroponic fertilizer mixtures and sheep feeding times."

"Useless to you, but not to those workers."

"True," Logan said.

Checking the time, I calculated how long we had until the Travas recovered. Hour sixty-five. They would get feeling back soon. And we had fifteen hours until Logan's escape was discovered.

"Let's get out of here."

"Do you want to see the Outsiders?" he asked.

I almost fell off the couch. "How?"

"One of the isolated systems is the Video Cameras pointed to Outside. I took a quick look to confirm my suspicions."

My brain stumbled over his words. I felt as if I was always the last person to know. "Just tell me, Logan."

"I studied the damage to the Transmission. Bad, but not five explosions worth. One did the job. So what were the other four trembles? I guessed the saboteurs used the blast at the Transmission to cover the Outsiders attaching to Inside."

"Attaching?"

"Yep. They have to line up and attach to Gateway in some way or risk being exposed to Outer Space." Logan returned to the computer.

I stood behind him as the screen turned black. Then the view changed and spots of dim daylights illuminated a bumpy rectangle made out of black metal...a bubble monster! I had forgotten all about them in the craziness of the past few weeks. Eight long arms hooked onto an otherwise smooth metal wall...Inside. At least, I had been correct in assuming the monsters were a conveyance. Small comfort.

Logan pointed to the arms. "When these clamped on, they caused those tremblers. I'm guessing they attached two at a time. See this?" He tapped on a spot on the belly of the monster. "That's their Gateway. Even though they're moving slow, they'll link theirs up with ours soon."

"How soon?"

"Depends on them. They have control of our computer. We're completely unprepared and nothing can stop them."

"Thanks for staying optimistic," I said.

Maybe we weren't as unprepared as Logan thought. I wondered if those bubble...ships in the top level could stop them. Would they have weapons or could we use those arms to pull the Outsiders off? No idea.

I helped Logan back into the shaft and followed, closing the vent behind us. With no closer options, I led him to Riley's storeroom.

The room had an abandoned feel to it. Or was that just my heart?

Logan plopped on the couch. Dust puffed and I sneezed.

"This is just temporary. Once we figure out our next move, I'll find you a better place to hide," I said.

"There is no next step. The Outsiders will come in. The end."

"Unacceptable. Try again."

He groaned and massaged his forehead. "I'd think better without these headaches."

"I can bring you painkillers."

"I know. I only get them when I've been straining to see too long." He sagged back against the cushions. "I could go back to my room. All my stuff is there, and I have a shower."

"And that solves our problem how?"

"At least it doesn't add to it."

We sat in silence. I felt useless with my limited computer knowledge. Besides knowing how to turn it on and off...

"Logan, what would happen if we turned the network off?"

"Nothing. You can't just switch it off. It's impossible." He straightened. "I see what you're getting at. Hmm..." Drumming his fingers on his chin, he got that distant mind-crunching look on his face. "We could disconnect each life system and operate them manually. Except..."

"What?"

"We don't know how to operate those systems manually."

"Aren't there instructions?"

"Even if we could access the computer, there aren't any instructions on the network. After the damage to the Transmission, I searched for them and found nothing. Which makes sense. If something happens to the network, you don't want your operating instructions lost as well."

"Would they be written down somewhere? Or on disks?"

"Ink on a wipe board would fade over time and I couldn't find any disks with the information. Unless they're packed away in one of those storage boxes in the Expanse."

His words triggered another memory. "What would these instructions look like?"

"Diagrams and schematics. Mostly visual step-by-step guides. Why?"

"Like some of the symbols that show up on your computer screen?"

"They would be similar."

The walls of the top level of Inside had been filled with diagrams. "Uh...Logan... How do you feel about heights?"

Logan didn't have a chance to answer because Lamont's voice squawked in my ear. "Trella, where are you?" A nervous tremble tainted her voice.

"Level four. What's wrong?"

"I have a medical emergency and need your help," she said with a slight quaver.

Warning signals rang in my head. "Who's sick?"

"Emek's appendix is about to burst."

Which would be a medical marvel since we removed his appendix weeks ago. "Is he stable?"

"No. He won't last *two* hours. I'm stunned by how fast his vitals turned critical. You have to hurry or we'll lose him."

Damn! "I'll be right there."

Logan raised his eyebrows, inviting me to explain. How do I tell him two people had forced my mother to call me so they could ambush me when I returned to the infirmary? He would insist on coming along and I couldn't risk him.

"I need to go help Lamont," I said instead. "Will you be okay here or do you want to return to your room?"

He considered and I almost screamed at him to think faster.

"I might as well go back. No sense tipping them off about me. It's just a straight shot over to my room, isn't it?" he asked.

"Yes. Head east, you're the very last vent." I scrambled up the ladder, but paused as a horrible thought struck me. What if my "rescue" ended badly? No one would know about the Expanse's ceiling.

"Logan, just listen." I explained about level eighteen at the top of the Expanse, describing the symbols on the walls and the Bubble Monsters. "If I disappear, get Anne-Jade and climb up to the near-invisible hatch. I left the safety line tied to the ladder and I doubt anyone's noticed."

"Wow, Trella. How long have you known about this?"

"A few weeks. I've been busy fetching *your* junk."

He smiled. "And you didn't inform the Committee?"

"Probably a bad decision at the time, but now I'm thrilled I kept it quiet."

"Me, too. How long should I wait?"

"Ten hours. That'll give me enough time to help Lamont and sleep. But if the Outsiders enter, don't wait. I'm assuming you can contact your sister?"

"Of course. I have this sweet little device—"

"Tell me later." I entered the air shaft. As I hurried over and down to the infirmary, I replayed Lamont's exact words in my mind. She managed to give me quite a bit of information. Two ambushers, armed with stun guns and they waited in the exam room.

I slowed as I reached the ducts over the infirmary. Looping over the patient area, surgery and exam room, I noted how the two men had positioned themselves on either side of the door to our suite. Lamont had been strapped down on the exam table. White medical tape covered her mouth, but she had the best view of the air vent.

Potential rescue scenarios raced through my mind. I could find Anne-Jade and a bunch of ISF officers. Except they were unarmed and these two not only had stunners, but the one on the right side carried a kill-zapper. Who else could I trust? Logan might have some gadget… Zippy!

Sliding over to the vent above my room, I lowered myself down and grabbed Zippy from my bed. I hefted him up and into the shaft without too much noise. Hopefully, they'd think the few thuds meant I had returned.

I tucked Zippy under my arm so he wouldn't rub against the metal shaft. Back at the exam room, I removed the cover with care. Lamont's eyes widened and she gestured at the men with her head. I nodded and put a finger to my lips before lowering Zippy just enough so he cleared the shaft. Flipping the switch, I hoped he would do his silent electronic pulse thing.

Once I pulled Zippy back, I swung through the vent and dropped to the floor. I had the element of surprise and a stun gun. In the second it took for them to react, I shot them both. The sizzle slaps rang, but they didn't fall down.

The man on the left pointed to his belt buckle. "Anti-stunners." He aimed his weapon at my chest.

I flinched but nothing happened. Good job, Zippy. Then I realized it was me against the two of them. I bolted toward the patient area. And I would have escaped, too.

Except one of them yelled, "Stop or we'll hurt Doctor Lamont."

Damn. I turned. The right side goon held a scalpel to Lamont's throat. Her angry eyes aimed a clear signal at me to keep running. They were probably bluffing, but I couldn't take that chance. Not with her life.

"Drop your weapon," Right Goon ordered.

An odd request considering I couldn't hurt them with it. I placed it on the floor and Left Goon picked it up. Before I could even say a word, Left Goon stunned me with my own gun. The sizzle slap hit me in the middle of my chest, knocking me back.

15

AS THE PULSE FROM THE STUN GUN TRAVELED THROUGH
my body, it left behind a stinging pain as if thousands of needles jabbed into me. The numbness followed, but it seemed slower. Eventually I couldn't move, or think clearly, or talk. Voices reached me, but their words were jumbled. My vision blurred and I was unable to focus on one person or thing. I'd never felt so helpless and uncaring at the same time.

Encased in something white, I sensed movement. I concentrated on the sounds around me. After a while, I heard the washers slosh and spin. Then the hum of the power plant dominated as the laundry noises faded.

The crunch and clink of the recycling plant grew louder and I smelled the hot, sweet scent of the glass kilns. The light changed to bluelights and all sounds were cut off.

The white material disappeared. The two goons talked and my view changed to a lower point. They fussed with things around me, then left.

Time passed until pain pricked my feet, then sizzled up my calves. Sensation returned with agonizing slowness. When the effects of the stun gun finally wore off, I felt relief that the fuzziness had lifted from my mind. It was quickly followed by panic.

I sat in a chair, but my wrists were clamped to the armrests with metal cuffs. A hard ring bit into my ankles, and I guessed they were cuffed to the chair's legs. My waist was strapped in, as well. The chair wouldn't move when I squirmed. I considered screaming for help, but the walls had been sprayed with insulating foam, which scared me more than being secured to a chair.

Taking deep breaths, I calmed my terrified thoughts and focused on the positives. I hadn't been recycled. I wasn't in the brig with Karla and Vinco. And Logan knew about Inside's top level. What else?

I glanced around in the dim bluelight. Shelves full of metal parts lined two of the walls and half of the wall with the door. A storage closet for maintenance was my first impression, but this chair didn't fit. And the work table filled with half completed gadgets meant this could be where the goons had built the anti-stunners.

I looked for air and heating vents, but didn't find any. That would explain why I didn't know about this room. It also meant the only way out of here was through the door. A gap under it let in daylights and air.

It didn't take a genius to guess Jacy had ordered my abduction. Although I was unclear on the *why*. Sloan obviously had informed him of my visit to the recycling plant, so Jacy knew I had tricked my tracer. Why would that goad him into doing this?

A couple of hours later I still didn't have any answers. Or food and water. My stomach grumbled. Finally, the door opened and my two goons and Jacy slipped inside the room, closed and then locked the door.

Clearly unhappy, Jacy studied me for a while.

I stared right back. "What's going on?" I demanded.

"You tell me. What have you been up to?" he asked.

"I helped lance a boil—that was gross. I stitched a patient's hand, I disinfected every surface of—"

"Stop playing around, Trella. You know what I mean."

Like I would tell him. "This isn't the right way to ask me, Jacy."

His scowl deepened. "I needed to get you away from the infirmary and Bubba Boom."

"And you couldn't have asked me to meet you somewhere else?"

"Would you have come?"

"No." A wave of pure exhaustion swept through me. "What do you want, Jacy?"

"I need to know what you and Logan have been doing for the last few weeks."

He knew about Logan. Not good. "Why would I tell you?"

"Because we're on the same side."

I made a show of looking at my restraints. "Is this how you treat all your cohorts or am I just that special?"

"I know Bubba Boom fed you a bunch of lies. I didn't realize what he was up to until too late. And I couldn't think of another way to make you listen to reason," Jacy said.

"So you attack me and tie me to a chair and I'm supposed to believe *you're* the voice of reason?"

"Yes."

I laughed at the pure ridiculousness of the situation. "Save your speech, Jacy. I saw you with Sloan and James Trava. I heard you plotting."

"Did you hear the entire conversation?"

"Doesn't matter."

"Yes, it does."

"Fine. I heard the last ten minutes or so."

"And Bubba Boom told you about the meeting, right?"

"Yes, but don't try to twist it back to him. You *were* with Sloan and Trava."

"For a good reason. We—"

"Jacy, I'm not going to believe anything you say. So there's no sense trying to convince me." As soon as the words left my mouth I realized my mistake. I had messed up any chance to pretend to believe him in order to get out of here. I could blame my lack of sleep or the side effects of being stunned, but sheer stupidity was the culprit.

"All right, Trella. We'll do this the hard way. You're usually pretty smart so I'm going to give you time alone to think about everything that has happened." Jacy conferred with his goons before leaving.

Right Goon crouched in front of me and rested his hands on my legs as if balancing himself. A sudden surge of fear flooded my body as I met his gaze. A hideous thought surfaced. Would Jacy's men resort to… Unable to even consider it, I shied away from that terrible scenario.

"I suggest you tell him what he wants to know," he said.

"Why?" I was proud my voice didn't shake.

"Because he's going to get our world back." He stood and left with the other man.

I remembered to breathe when they didn't immediately return. But the muscles in my legs still trembled from the goon's touch.

In order to pass the time and distract myself from my dry throat and empty stomach, I considered Jacy's argument. The meeting with the Captain and with the bomber had been pretty damning. What other evidence did I have?

Sloan. He pulled me from the duct and we started the riot.

Why? To empty the waste handling plant of workers so one of his buddies could plant that bomb.

But Bubba Boom disarmed the bomb…well…sort of. It didn't matter how it had been stopped, just that it did stop. And Sloan knew right where to find me in the air shaft. Or did he? My tool belt had clanged.

Jacy wanted to plant those mics above the Control Room and Anne-Jade's office. Which made sense if he was worried about what the Committee was up to. Except he was on the Committee so why would he need to bug those areas unless he was more concerned about the Controllers?

And the whole situation with the Transmission hadn't added up either. Everything I learned about Jacy had come from Bubba Boom. Then again, Jacy had cuffed me to a chair in a locked room. And time remained critical. What if the Outsiders came in?

Logic remained on Jacy's side if he told the truth, but I just couldn't trust him. As the time passed and I grew hungrier, thirstier and stiffer, my inclination to believe Jacy diminished with each minute.

When the door finally opened, I wished I could strangle him. He slipped in with Sloan and another goon. A visit with Sloan—now my week was complete.

He approached me warily, which, considering the circumstances would have made me laugh, but I glared at him.

"Did you think it through?" he asked.

"Yep."

"And?"

"I've decided I'd wrap my hands around your neck and crush your windpipe first."

"Not helping, Trella."

"That's the point."

He sighed. "I'd hoped my involvement with the Force of Sheep rebellion would have earned me some of your trust."

My gaze flicked to Sloan. "Why did he pull me from the shaft?"

"At first, I was just playing around," Sloan said. "I heard you up in the duct. I planned to let you go, but when I found out about those mics…I lost it. It was like the Pop Cops all over again."

"Captain Trava?" I asked Jacy.

"We need to get the Transmission fixed. He knew the right people and he knows the Controllers are not… They're…"

"Outsiders," I said.

"I should have known you'd already have that figured out. Who told you—Bubba Boom?"

I kept my mouth shut.

"James Trava is helping us. He knows what Inside can do. How fast we can travel, how to maneuver our world. It's probably too late, but something had to be done!" He pulled in a few breaths as if to calm down. "That's why I need to know what you've been up to. You could be compromising our efforts."

He had explained the two inconsistencies, but still. "I'm not."

"What about Logan?"

"You should know better than me. He's in protective custody by order of the Committee."

Jacy stepped toward me, balling his hands into tight fists. I feared he would strike me.

Instead, he uncurled his hands and tapped his fingers against his thighs. He looked at Sloan. "Last try?"

"Don't bother. She doesn't believe you, boss. We don't need her. She can stay in the Pit until we have the situation under control," Sloan said.

The Pit? That didn't sound good.

"I would, except we *do* need her. Go." Jacy cleared a spot off the work table and sat down.

"Is he bringing food and water?" I asked, trying to keep my voice steady.

"No. But if this doesn't work, I'll make sure you're fed."

"Nice of you," I said with a flat tone. "Since we're having this lovely chat, did someone rescue Doctor Lamont?"

"Yes. And Bubba Boom, Hank and a bunch of the maintenance workers have been searching for you ever since, causing us trouble. That's why it took so long to get back here."

"Too bad." Sarcasm laced my words. And when the silence lengthened, I asked about the Pit.

Before he could reply, the door opened. I braced for their "last try" by clamping my lips tight. But when Riley stood there with Sloan, a little yelp of surprise escaped me.

Riley turned on Jacy. "What's this?" He gestured toward me. "You said you were going to *talk* to her. Let her go. Now!"

Not what I had been expecting. Maybe Riley's anger was part of the ruse.

"She thinks we're the saboteurs," Jacy replied mildly. "How was I supposed to get her to sit down with me for a nice conversation?"

I noted the use of "we're." Nausea rose in my empty stomach.

"That's why I wanted to be the one to convince her," Riley said.

"You're needed elsewhere. We're running out of time." Jacy jumped to his feet. "This has been a total waste of precious time. Sloan, take her to the Pit. We'll manage without her. Riley, are the wires in place?"

"Not yet."

"Then go. Get it done. They're already attached to us. Sloan'll deal with Trella."

Riley didn't move. He met my gaze. "Did Logan find a way around the Outsiders?" he asked.

I might not trust Jacy, but despite Riley's belief, I did trust him. I should have trusted him with the bomb, and I should have tried to figure out what he'd been doing all these weeks. But my own hurt feelings had kept me away from him. Now though, if Riley thought Jacy's gang was doing the right thing, then I had no qualms. "No. Not yet. We think we have one last chance, but it would require a coordinated effort from a bunch of people."

Jacy and Riley exchanged a look.

"I have the manpower," Jacy said. "We can combine our efforts?"

That last bit sounded like a question. "I thought your sources dried up when you joined the Committee."

"Things have changed."

Riley knelt in front of me. "Will you help us, Trell?"

Looking into his eyes, seeing the concern on his face, I couldn't resist him. "Yes."

Free at last, I stood and rubbed feeling back into my muscles.

"What do you need from us?" Jacy asked me.

"We have to confirm that our plan can work first, and then we'll need a few workers we can trust from every system."

"Okay, I'll find you three for each. Is that enough?" Jacy asked.

"Yes."

He nodded and turned to leave.

"Jacy, you said you needed me. What do you want me to do?" I asked.

He glanced at Riley. "You might as well tell her everything. Then get back to those wires."

Riley gave him a mocking salute. "Aye-aye, Captain."

Jacy smiled and left the room.

"Can you tell me in the cafeteria?" I asked. "I'm starving."

"No," Sloan said. "You'll have to be rescued by maintenance. I'll go get everything set up and come back for you." He shot me a sour look before leaving.

"I have a feeling I'm not going to like this," I said.

"I don't like it at all, but it's our best chance," Riley said.

"Just start from the beginning." I sat on the table in the place Jacy had cleared. No way I would sit in *that* chair again.

"Here's the condensed version. Bubba Boom is working for the Outsiders. He built those bombs and attacked Logan. We don't know how he contacted them, and we don't know who else is helping him. We suspect Hank, but have no proof. Jacy and I are trying to bypass the Outsiders by building another computer network independent of the existing one. Then we'll switch controls over to the new network. But we can't do that if Bubba Boom is just going to hijack the new network. We need to know more."

I connected the logic. "You want me to get closer to Bubba Boom and find out how he is communicating with the Outsiders?"

"You've been hanging out with him so...yeah." He didn't look happy about it.

"He's supposedly helping me with finding the active link to the Outsiders. And searching for Sloan and company. But he doesn't know about Logan."

"That's good."

"Yeah. I guess he wanted to make sure I didn't join Jacy." Fooled me big time. Why was I so easily convinced? Perhaps because I had lost faith in my own judgment.

"He did save your life," Riley said.

"So did you. I'd never have washed off the chemical so fast."

He shrugged. "If you had trusted...never mind."

I grabbed his arms and forced him to look at me. "I *do* trust you. I would have told Jacy to go recycle himself if *you* hadn't come in here. I didn't trust *myself.* I now know I made a mistake by listening to Bubba Boom. A big...huge mistake and I paid dearly for it." I huffed. "That's why I didn't want to be in charge. What if I make another wrong decision?"

"Then we'll deal with it. I'd rather have you make a mistake then have Outsiders tell us what to do."

"Are you sure? I've made some doozies."

"I'm positive. Besides, you're not the only one to mess up. Jacy screwed up your recruitment, I've done and said things I regret and your mother has had a couple lapses in judgment. Hopefully, Bubba Boom and the Outsiders will make mistakes that we can take advantage of."

He made me feel better, but I didn't fully agree with him. "You shouldn't have anything to regret."

A sad smile touched his lips. "I regret my harsh words. I regret my anger. "

"You shouldn't. I needed to hear those words and to be woken up to Inside's problems. Although, I don't have a death wish!"

"I know. Just voicing my frustration. You'd dash off to the rescue, but couldn't see Inside needed more rescuing." His smile reached his eyes this time. "If I only knew to tell you to *not* get involved, it would have saved us a lot of trouble. Plus, Sheepy's been miserable these last few weeks."

Sloan returned. "The room's ready. Let's go," he said to me.

"What's going on now?"

"I'm gonna lock you in a maintenance closet, we'll tip off Bubba Boom to your location and he'll sweep in for the rescue," Sloan said.

"You can tell him Jacy didn't trust you and wanted you out of the way. Try to get…close to him. Convince him you're on his side." Riley's queasy expression said more than his words.

I stepped closer to him and lowered my voice. "If you could change one thing, what would it be?"

He pulled the sheep pendant from his pocket. A question filled his eyes. I held out my hand. Riley placed it in my palm and I curled my fingers around the necklace, pressing the metal into my skin.

The trip to the maintenance closet with Sloan was part of the ruse. After giving Riley time to return to his wires, Sloan grabbed my elbow and pulled me along a few corridors in level one. We passed a bunch of people who ignored us. I was supposed to look scared—not hard to do considering I was with Sloan.

He shoved me into the closet. Only two meters wide by two meters long, the closet's shelves had been filled with mechanical parts. Sloan closed the door and turned on the light. No vents.

Sloan pulled out a roll of tape. "Turn around."

"Excuse me?"

Spinning me around, he yanked my wrists behind my back and taped them together, rolling the tape a few centimeters up my arms. He pushed me down to the floor, and did the same to my ankles.

"It's gotta look real," he said, but a perverse little smile played on his lips.

Being small may be beneficial when climbing through the ducts, but it sucked big time against Jacy's oversized goons. I needed to get my stun gun back.

"Did Jacy tell you to do this?"

"No. I really don't like you. Figured this is a little payback for not trusting us scrubs enough that you had to place a microphone over our barracks."

He ripped off another section of tape and slapped it over my mouth. My head jerked back and a stinging pain radiated over my jaw. I didn't know how or when, but I silently vowed that I would retaliate in some way.

"I hope it takes your boyfriend a long time to find you." He clicked off the light and locked me in the dark.

16

AFTER I CONCOCTED A LIST OF CREATIVE WAYS TO
pay Sloan back, I squirmed into a more comfortable position. Sloan had my arms pinned too tight for me to bring
my hands forward.

Should I try to escape? From my brief glance of the parts
and supplies on the shelves, I figured I could find something
sharp enough to cut through the tape. If this were indeed a
real abduction, then I would try my best to get free.

Getting up on my feet was harder to do than I expected.
Once stable, I hopped over to the light switch. Or rather to
where I thought the switch was located. I bumped into the
door, then rubbed my cheek on the cold metal wall to find
the light. It was too high for my hands to reach, but I managed to flick the tab up with my shoulder.

I inspected the shelves, and discovered one positive aspect
of my imprisonment. Sloan had taped my wrists so that my
palms touched. If I found a sharp object, I could grab it with
my fingers and saw through. If he had turned my wrists the opposite way, I wouldn't be able to manipulate an item as well.

I also searched for sharp edges jutting from the shelves that

I could rub the tape against. The metal bins on the left side contained nuts, bolts, rivets and washers. Tubes, electrical connectors and rolls of wire filled the bins along the back wall. Finally on the right wall, I found a pile of nails. Long pointy nails.

Turning around, I tried to pick up a couple, but the bin was just high enough that even up on my unsteady tiptoes, I could touch it, but not get to the nails. Instead, I grabbed the bin and yanked.

I fell forward, landing on my knees. Nails rained down on my legs and bare feet. Sloan would regret his little payback, I promised. At least I had plenty of nails to use. And after a few awkward tries, I succeeded in keeping the nail in my hands long enough to poke it into the tape. When I added in being light-headed from lack of food and water, I realized a quick escape wouldn't be in my future.

Time ceased to have any meaning and by the time the doorknob twisted and the keypad beeped, I'd only ripped a little bit of the tape. I sagged to the floor in exhaustion.

The door flew open and Bubba Boom was next to me in a heartbeat. "Are you all right?"

I nodded. He pulled out his penknife, and cut through the tape on my wrists and ankles. I winced as he peeled it away from my skin.

He touched the one on my mouth. "Do you want to do it or should I?"

I pointed to him.

"On three?"

Again I nodded.

"One. Two." He ripped it off.

I yelped. My lips burned and tears stung my eyes. "No three?"

"Sorry. I thought that would be better."

A sticky residue from the tape coated my cheeks, wrists and ankles. "That's okay." I touched his arm. "Thanks."

He gave me a shy smile. "You certainly keep a guy hopping." Bubba Boom freed a few strands of my hair that had stuck to my cheek, and tucked them behind my ear. "Doctor Lamont's on the way."

"I'm fine. Just starving."

He took my right hand in his. Turning my wrist, he traced the tiny scar on my forearm. "We would have found you sooner if you hadn't taken the tracer out."

"We?"

"Hank and the others. And Doctor Lamont. We've all been searching for you."

"Did she rat me out about the tracer?"

"No, but we figured it out pretty quick." He grew serious. "Who locked you in here?"

"Sloan."

He nodded as if expecting that answer. "Who were the two guys who took you from the infirmary?"

"Jacy's goons. I don't know their names."

"Do you know why they grabbed you?"

"I think Jacy found out about my tracer. He wanted to know what I had been doing and I wouldn't tell him. It's obvious he's up to something and he thought I'd figure it out and cause trouble."

"So he made a preemptive strike," Bubba Boom said.

"Sounds like—"

"Trella!" Lamont rushed into the room. She dropped her medical bag and wrapped me in a tight hug. Her muscles trembled.

Stunned, I didn't move.

"I've been so worried!" She pulled away to look at me. "Are you all right? If they've hurt you, I'll dismember them without antiseptic and feed them to Chopper one tiny bit at a time."

Impressive. All I wished to do was slap Sloan a few times.

"Can you walk? I want to do a full scan right away." Lamont checked my pulse.

"I'm fine. Just really thirsty and hungry." I appealed to Bubba Boom. "Can you come with me to the cafeteria?"

But Lamont wouldn't take the hint. "I'll come along. You haven't eaten in at least twenty-six hours. You'll need to be careful about what you put into your stomach."

"Twenty-six hours? Are you sure?" That seemed too long. I wondered if Logan had been successful and what was going on with the Outsiders.

"Oh yes. I felt every one of them." Lamont thumped her chest. "You were stunned and, since you're small, it probably knocked you out for ten to twelve hours."

Funny, I didn't remember being unconscious. I'd been stunned before and hadn't blacked out.

Bubba Boom helped me stand. The room spun for a moment and my knees considered buckling. He put his arm around my shoulders, steadying me before we headed to the cafeteria.

Our ragtag group caused quite the stir in the dining room. At this point, I didn't care. Lamont fetched me a tray of food. Then everything blurred together as if a part of me had already fallen asleep. Gulping water, eating, returning to the infirmary and being tucked into bed by Bubba Boom combined into one long dream.

Before leaving, he kissed my forehead. I slid my hand into my pocket and clutched my pendant as I slipped into a deeper sleep.

★ ★ ★

When I woke, I took a long, scalding hot shower. Lamont descended on me as soon as I finished, ordering me to eat a large bowl of her special soup. I needed to visit Logan, but she wouldn't let me leave until I agreed to a full physical.

I stifled the desire to argue and remind her of her promise not to mother me. Her medical request bordered on over-protectiveness. However, it had been nice to know people had been upset by my abduction and had been looking for me. Before I had gotten involved in the search for Gateway, I could have died in the pipes and only Cog would have cared.

"Aside from some bruising, a couple strained muscles and slight dehydration, you're in good health," Lamont said.

I jumped down from the examination table glad to be done.

"Do you really need to leave so soon?" she asked. "You should rest and rehydrate."

"There's too much going on right now. I'll rest later," I said.

I debated if I should climb into the shafts or not. Almost everyone in Inside knew about the tracer. Deciding not to risk being seen in the wrong place by the wrong people, I returned to my room.

Lamont trailed after me. "Trella, wait."

I turned. She hovered in the doorway, uncertain and vulnerable. Not Doctor Lamont, but Kiana Garrard. Interesting how she morphed from one to the other. At least I had some warning that this wasn't medical.

"You understood my clues, right? You knew there were two armed men waiting to ambush you."

"Yes. That's why I dropped in from the ceiling and tried to stun them." I still needed to get my gun back from Jacy.

"Why did you come? You could have saved yourself twenty-six hours of suffering. You had to know they wouldn't hurt me, and yet you came anyway and ended up turning yourself over to them."

Ah. A good question. Did I have a good answer? Was it because she was my mother? Or because she was an excellent doctor? Or because I was the reason she had been targeted in the first place? How about all of the above?

Riley's comment from the maintenance closet replayed in my mind. "It's what I do. I guess you could say it's my role or job. Rushing to the rescue, and doing what I can so others don't suffer." I spread my hands, trying to find the right words. "I don't really think about it, I just react and hope for the best." I shrugged. "Worked so far."

"You shouldn't have risked yourself for me, Trella."

"A moment of weakness." I smiled. "A mistake even. Everyone is entitled to make a few mistakes."

Logan slept on the couch. His arm covered his eyes and one foot dangled off the edge. I dropped down. The light thud woke him. Before I could say a word, he hopped up and embraced me.

"Trella! You're here," he said with glee.

"Even though I'm not as smart as you, I do know where I am."

"I feared the worst. No one could find you. Anne-Jade had all her ISF officers searching."

"I wasn't in any real danger. And I'm sorry to have kept you in suspense, but no one had time to stop by here." I explained about Jacy and Riley's plans to build a separate network. "Riley's stringing wires as we speak."

"Ooh. I like! Why didn't I think of that?" He bounced on his toes as his gaze turned inward.

"Because it's been me, you and Anne-Jade, while Jacy has recruited a bunch of people."

"True."

"What about your idea?"

He stopped bouncing. "When you said I should climb the Expanse, you didn't explain there wasn't a ladder."

"The ladder starts about seventy-five meters up, but there are lots of things to hold onto."

"That's assuming I have the strength to hang on and pull myself up the Wall. I don't know how you did it, but I didn't make it past twenty meters before my legs and arms turned to mush."

"What about Anne-Jade?"

"She was too busy, and I thought it would be less suspicious for one person to be up there. Besides, I doubt she would have climbed much farther." He plopped back onto the couch. "Is there another way up there?"

I considered. "I could rig a pulley to the end of the ladder and hoist you up."

Logan bent over and pulled a wipe board out from under the couch. "You'll need more than one wheel in order to lift my weight." He wrote a list of supplies on the board and drew a little diagram of how to hook them together. "This should work as long as the pulley is securely attached to the ladder."

I studied his diagram. It didn't appear to be too complicated. Hank could put this together in no time. Except Hank wouldn't like us exploring in the Expanse. I had a difficult time believing Hank was behind all the sabotage. He was Cog's right-hand man and good friend. Perhaps he wasn't involved. And perhaps I was kidding myself.

Why did I have no trouble accepting Jacy's involvement with the Outsiders? No answer. My head spun and I sat next to Logan. The trip to his room had taken me twice as long as normal. I had to keep stopping to catch my breath.

"Are you all right?" Logan asked.

"Just a little dizzy."

"Me, too. I'm not sure if I'm sick, but I keep having these dizzy spells."

That seemed odd. Lamont had also commented on feeling light-headed. "Since when?"

"A few hours after you rushed off to help the doctor. Do you think something's wrong with the air plant?"

"Could be. Last I heard, it was working even though not all the air filter bays have been repaired." A strange thought floated to the surface of my mind. "Logan, do you know what's going on with the Outsiders?"

He gestured to the computer. "I managed to get into a few subsystems. It's frustrating as hell, like putting my toe in the water, but not being able to jump in!"

"And?"

"Oh. Their vehicle is still attached, but I think no one has opened Gateway yet. I don't understand why they haven't."

"Maybe our air isn't right for them? Maybe the people who want them to come in have to adjust it slowly or risk hurting us?"

"Pure speculation. Maybe they're waiting for us to be told about them. Can you imagine if they just showed up? Massive panic."

"Then why aren't their cohorts spreading the word?"

"Maybe they plan to sneak in? Get a sense of the situation first?"

Too many unknowns at this point, guessing would be a

waste of our limited time. "You're right. It's all conjuncture. We need more data."

"That's my girl." Logan slapped me on the back. "Spoken like a true Tech No!"

Unfortunately, in order to get more data, I would have to get closer to Bubba Boom. I'd rather be getting reacquainted with Riley. I checked the power plant's control room on level four, the air plant and maintenance in Sector B2, but couldn't find Bubba. He might be sleeping. I didn't even know what barrack he lived in. Actually, I knew very little about him.

While climbing around level four, I had placed the wipe board with the pulley diagram in Riley's bedroom, hoping he could make one and pass it to Jacy. Since I'd run out of places to look for Bubba Boom, I returned to the infirmary to help Lamont.

People filled the patient area. Lamont moved among them, handing out cups of water and white pills. Hair stuck out from her braid and she moved as if walking through a thick stew.

"What's going on?" I asked her.

"Headaches, dizziness and nausea," she said. "And a few patients have minor bumps and bruises from passing out. Everyone's blaming the air plant."

When I had poked my head into the plant, the air filtering machinery appeared to be working. However, a number of maintenance workers had been repairing one of the air scrubbers. "How can I help?"

"Can you wrap Jenna's sprained ankle? She twisted it when she stumbled down the stairs."

"Sure." I grabbed a roll of bandages and crossed to the girl with a bag of ice on her ankle.

We worked for a few hours as a steady stream of people from level three came in. My energy dropped faster than normal. And a couple times, I needed to stop and catch my breath. I worried that the Outsiders might just be slowly killing us all, which added to the low-simmering panic in the pit of my stomach. At any moment, it felt as if the terror would erupt into a full boil.

Bubba Boom arrived. He appeared upset, and I asked him if he was feeling sick.

He glanced around the full room. "No. I heard you were *all over* Inside, looking for me."

One of the maintenance workers must have spotted me. I rubbed my eyes. It was getting harder to sneak around Inside when everyone recognized me.

"Did I hear wrong?" he demanded, but somehow I sensed he already knew the answer.

"No. I wanted to ask you about Jacy and Sloan. And the air plant."

"Did you consider the danger? It's not safe for you to be running around without a couple bodyguards. Do you want Jacy to grab you again?"

Ah. The reason for his anger. "No. I just—"

"Let's go for a walk."

We headed west toward the common area in Quad A3. The hallway was empty and the few people in the area sat listlessly on the couches and armchairs. Stranger than the emptiness was the quiet. So used to the constant babble of voices, I felt as if every word I said could be heard by everyone.

We sat on a couch in the corner. I willed myself not to sit as far away from him as possible, but still left a half meter between us.

"Jacy's goons caught me in the infirmary so I'm not—"

"You are now. Since you returned, we've had people in there to protect you."

"I didn't see anyone."

His anger deflated a bit. "You're not supposed to."

"Oh."

"Can you at least understand why I would be upset?"

"Yes. I'm sorry."

"You're lucky word didn't get back to Jacy. Must be all these headaches."

"Are you getting them, too?" I asked.

"No. Not yet, anyway."

"You're one of the few who isn't sick," I said. "Is the air plant malfunctioning?"

"No."

"How can you be sure? Everyone's been complaining."

Bubba Boom studied me as if trying to decide what to tell me. "Did Sloan or Jacy say anything to you about the network?"

"No. All they wanted was information."

"About what?"

"What I've been doing these past few weeks."

"What exactly have you been doing when everyone *thought* you were in the infirmary?" he asked. "You still haven't told me how you know so much."

Damn. I decided to stick to the truth as much as possible. "I've been searching for Logan."

"And?"

"I haven't found him yet."

He relaxed a bit more. "The information?"

"I've been spending a lot of time in the air ducts, so I've overheard quite a bit."

He considered. "Trella, I need to know who you believe. Me or Jacy?"

"You, of course! Jacy—"

"Was part of your rebellion. You were friends."

Interesting word choice. Your rebellion. I acted confused.

"Not since you told me about him and Sloan and the Captain. Not since he locked me in a storage closet, leaving me to die of thirst because he's too much of a coward to finish me off. Where are he and Sloan anyway? Shouldn't the ISF arrest them?"

"The ISF won't touch Jacy. Plus Anne-Jade has enough problems right now. We plan to deal with them." He took my left hand in his. "They both *will* suffer for hurting you."

"We?"

He drew in a breath and let it all out at once. "Me, Hank, our core crew and…the Outsiders."

I jerked as if surprised. "Outsiders? Who are—"

"They're from the Outside and they're angry about your rebellion. They have taken over the network, not Jacy."

"They're mad at me?" No need to fake the tremor of fear in my voice.

"No. Not at you." He rushed to assure me. "They're unhappy that our society has gotten out of control. Soon they will come Inside and fix everything!" His eyes glowed with conviction.

"Really? They're coming inside?" I pretended to be stunned. Then I leaned closer as if suddenly enthusiastic. "Will they repair the air and power plant?"

"Yes, and put our society back in order. No Committee, no ISF, no scrubs or uppers, they're going to fix it all."

"How?"

"By returning our society to its original configuration."

"Original as in Pop Cops?"

"No. As in the Outsiders once again being our Controllers, making the rules, enforcing the rules and the rest of you can return to work. I'll be one of their chosen liaisons."

Sounded like the Pop Cops, but I knew better than to argue with him. "When are they coming?" I asked instead.

"Soon. We have to prepare for them. And that's where you come in."

"Me?"

"Yes. You're a natural leader, Trella. You united everyone to fight the Pop Cops. They told us to convince you of their benevolence. They want you to get everyone excited about them. That's why Jacy wanted you out of the way. He knows about the Outsiders and is trying to prevent them from coming inside."

"Oh." A twist I hadn't been expecting. "Did they contact you?"

"Not me. Hank. He's believed that the Controllers live Outside and have been instructing us on how to live better lives. Though his beliefs were shaken a bit when you found Gateway and it lead to Outer Space and not to them. He's been searching the computers since your rebellion. He never gave up faith that they existed.

"All that nonsense about the Controllers being operating parameters and fail-safes was just that. Nonsense. When you think about it, there had to be a higher authority than the Captain and Admirals. The Travas followed the Controllers' rules, and we should have as well. A mistake that Hank and I are going to fix. And now you can help us." He leaned toward me. "We're not going to let Jacy win. We're going to have an ordered society again, but this time you and I and Hank and all our supporters are going to be the leaders."

Bubba Boom closed the gap between us. He wrapped his arms around my back and drew me in for a kiss.

For a second, I froze. Then, remembering my mission, I returned the kiss. It wasn't the same as when I had kissed Riley. Riley's zipped through my body, leaving a trail of fire in its wake. Bubba Boom's made me nervous. I wouldn't be able to do more than kiss him, and I hoped I wouldn't have to.

When he broke off, he pulled me tight to his chest. "Unlike Hank, you understand," he whispered in my ear. "Understand what it's like to be at the mercy of another. To suffer and be forced to make a choice between your friends."

"Are you talking about Vinco and the Pop Cops?"

"Yes. He wouldn't stop until I told him who the Tech Nos were, but I kept Anne-Jade and Logan's names to myself, giving him the others. Every time I close my eyes to sleep, I see all their faces. Your mother understands as well."

I hadn't thought of it that way. Karla had threatened to recycle her husband and daughter if she didn't cooperate. She had named friends in order to protect them…me. And then we were taken from her anyway. She had lost everyone.

Bubba Boom released me. "That's why we need Controllers. They won't torture or trick people."

"Do you know why they wish to come in?"

Again his face shone with a fervent glow. "We're their lost children. We have run away and made a mess of things. They've been trying to catch up to us, but Inside is faster than they are. But not anymore. We've stopped accelerating so they could join us."

That's why the Transmission had been targeted twice. "Then we better prepare everyone for their arrival." I tried to sound like an avid believer.

His smile encompassed his whole face. "I knew you were smart. Hank said you'd be impossible to convince, but the logic is hard to ignore." He stood. "Come on, we have lots to do."

I hurried to keep pace with him as he headed back toward the infirmary. When we arrived in the crowded patient area, he said, "Go and get your things. I'll talk to the doctor."

"Why?"

"You can't stay here. It's too dangerous. We have an extra room for you and you'll be protected at all times."

Which also meant *watched* at all times. Not much I could do without blowing my cover. I collected my meager possessions. When I returned, Bubba Boom was talking to Lamont.

My mother met my gaze with a question in her eyes. I got the impression all I needed to do was signal her in some fashion and she would prevent him from taking me from the infirmary. Half tempted to see what she would do, I almost nodded in encouragement. But the need to find out all I could stopped me. Instead, I kept my expression neutral.

"Trella, can I have a word in private?" she asked.

"Uh. Sure." I turned to Bubba Boom. "Be right back."

Lamont led me to her office and shut the door. She motioned toward the chair and I perched on the edge. Remembering how Domotor and Bubba Boom both avoided talking to me in the infirmary, I guessed Lamont's office probably had a hidden microphone somewhere inside.

"I understand he rescued you and saved your life, but don't you think you should wait a few weeks before staying with him?" she asked.

"That sounds like a mother's question and not a doctor's concern," I said.

She stiffened as pain flashed in her eyes. "You had a rough week. You're not fully recuperated."

"I'll be fine. In fact, I can rest better surrounded by Bubba Boom and his colleagues. There's no way Jacy can get to me there." Unable to leave her without a better explanation, I took a wipe board and marker from her desk and wrote, I*t's not what you think. This is part of a plan.*

"Oh. Well…then…I just wanted to make sure you considered your health. You'll come back if your headaches get worse?"

"Yes." I erased the words from the board and wrote, *Thanks*.

Bubba Boom led me up to level five. Although it had been completed before the first explosion, the Committee hadn't had time to decide who should move in. Bluelights lit the hallways and our footsteps echoed. The layout of the new level matched all the others so when he stopped in front of a set of double doors, I knew we were close to Quad A5.

He turned to me and took both my hands. "This is the new headquarters for Inside. All the system controls are now here." Letting my left hand go, he knocked on the door.

A thin hidden panel opened and eyes peered at us before the doors hissed apart. Bubba Boom didn't hesitate. He strode in like he owned the place, towing me along like a prized possession.

The area resembled the main Control Room in Quad G4, but it wasn't finished. Computers and half completed manned stations sprouted exposed wires. Desks and diagrams were drawn on the walls. Lots of general activity and buzz of voices that ceased the moment we entered.

My heart paused as I glanced around. A feeling that I had just made the biggest mistake in my entire life overwhelmed me.

I expected to recognize a bunch of the maintenance crew. I also knew a few uppers and a couple scrubs.

I expected to see Hank. And expected he would be the hardest one to convince of my newfound faith. Hank jumped to his feet and barreled toward us clearly upset. No surprise there.

I didn't count on Karla Trava sitting with a group of uppers around a small conference table. But as much as her presence upset and surprised me, she wasn't the reason my heart tore a hole in my chest, fleeing for its life.

Two...beings wearing strange white reflective suits stood near a bank of computers. They had round silver metal heads with black tubes that ran from their chests to small tanks on their backs.

The Outsiders had come in.

17

EVEN THOUGH THEY WERE SHAPED LIKE US—TWO legs, two arms, hands, torso and, I guessed, a head—I backed away from the Outsiders. Bubba Boom stopped me. "It's okay, Trella, they're just wearing protective suits. They look just like us, and these two men are here to help us get ready for the others."

Men? Their silver heads reflected like a mirror. Hank's broad shape alone covered half of the one's on the left.

"Are you out of your mind?" Hank asked Bubba Boom. "Why did you bring *her* here?"

"She understands. I was right about her."

Hank snorted. "You're a fool."

It was time for me to convince Hank. I forced my gaze away from the strange Outsiders and met his. "He isn't a fool. *I'm* the foolish one. I thought once we gained control of Inside, my job was done. A mistake I plan to fix. I'm here to do it right this time. To get us back on track."

Hank stared at me as if he could read my thoughts. I suppressed the urge to squirm under his intense scrutiny. "Cogon told me you didn't believe in the Controllers. And you never stopped to consider our beliefs before you carelessly announced they didn't exist." He stepped closer to me. "The Controllers are just system safeguards and directives from our ancestors, you and Logan said. Do you know how upsetting that was?"

He didn't wait for my reply. "Do you even understand that when you told the scrubs Outside was not the paradise they believed in for thousands of weeks, but some airless void, you destroyed their hope of ever reaching a better place?"

"I do now."

"Too late! The damage's been done. I never gave up hope. I kept searching for them. I knew they wouldn't abandon us." He swept his hand out. "And here they are. Just like us. On a journey through Outer Space to find a home. And now I don't have to play nice with the Committee or you."

I glanced at Bubba Boom. "If everyone believes the Controllers are our leaders, then why did you say you needed me?"

"Because there are many like you who don't believe. And who trust your word," Bubba Boom said.

"But all you need to do is show them proof." I gestured toward the Outsiders. They moved closer. Their gait awkward. And so did Karla Trava. Oh joy. Two nightmares within easy reach.

"We don't want to spark a panic. They accepted the Committee because you endorsed them, so they'll accept the Outsiders as our Controllers as well."

Such confidence that I didn't deserve. Hank had been right about me. I hadn't considered the ramifications of my discoveries. But I did know taking out the Pop Cops had been a good thing.

"Why is Karla here?" I asked Bubba Boom.

"The Travas have been cooperating with the Controllers

long before your rebellion. She helped us when they contacted us."

"Did the Travas know they're from Outside?" I asked.

"No," Karla said. "We believed they were intelligent beings living inside the computer network. The reality is far more logical."

"How did you get out of the brig?"

Bubba Boom answered. "Anne-Jade. All this time Logan's been under our...protection, not the Committee's. We have control of the life systems as well. Anne-Jade won't risk her brother's life. She cares too much to refuse us."

"I think Trella does, too," Hank said. "And I'm not convinced of her change in heart either."

Bubba Boom pulled me close as if to protect me. "She was taken by Jacy. Sloan tried to kill her and she understands."

"Understands what, exactly?" Hank asked.

"I understand that we need something to unite us," I said. And this I believed one hundred percent. Except my thinking skewed to uniting us as Insiders and not as servants to the Outsiders. "And I believe the Controllers will help and not hurt us."

Hank turned to Karla. "What do you think?"

"I think you should recycle her right away," she said. "She will ruin all your plans. She should *never* be trusted."

Bubba Boom's grip on my hand tightened. "I trust her. And Cogon loved her like a sister."

"And look how that worked out for him," Karla said.

Hank chewed on his lip. "I'll let the Controllers decide. Come with me."

It was a good thing my heart had already run away, otherwise it would have exploded in my chest from the sudden surge of terror.

Bubba Boom pried my hand from his. "It'll be okay. Just

tell them the truth." He nudged me toward Hank and the Outsiders.

They waited for me to join them. I followed them into another room. When the door hissed shut, I couldn't breathe in the thin air. Gasping, I felt as if I suffocated. Panicking, I glanced around.

The room was a standard conference area with table and chairs. But big silver tanks lined the far wall and metal boxes had been stacked in the corner. Metal plates covered the air and heating vents.

Hank gestured to a chair. Once I sat, he showed me the small tank near the chair's legs and the oxygen mask. Understanding cut through the dizziness and I covered my nose and mouth with the mask, filling my lungs with thick air.

The Outsiders fiddled with clamps around their necks. A popping noise followed a whoosh and they removed their round silver helmets.

They did resemble us. Short brown hair, brown eyes, a nose, mouth and ears. But their skin had an unhealthy yellowish cast, almost like jaundice. And their expressions were far from friendly.

The Outsider on the right crinkled his nose as if he smelled something rotten. "This is sheep leader?" He spoke with a thick accent. He struggled to pronounce each word.

Hank pulled his mask away from his face. "Yes. This is Trella Garrard."

"She look…"

"Insignificant," the other Outsider said.

"She is not. She caused much trouble for our world, but her actions enabled us to contact you."

As if I didn't feel bad enough.

Hank introduced the Outsiders. "This is Ponife." The Outsider on the right inclined his head. "And Fosord."

"What is problem?" Ponife asked Hank.

Hank explained in concise sentences how they needed me yet they doubted my sincerity. The two Outsiders conferred in a strange dialect. I could understand every fourth or fifth word.

Ponife stood and went to the stack of metal boxes. He removed the top one and set it on the floor, then rummaged in the second one. He returned with a thin silver loop, walking toward me.

"Stand, Trella Garrard," he ordered.

I glanced at Hank.

"If you truly believe, you'll do as they say," Hank said.

Escape would be difficult, considering the blocked vents, and the roomful of people between me and freedom. I rose. Ponife touched a small metal X to the loop and it opened, breaking into two half circles hinged together.

He held the broken loop out and approached me, aiming for my neck. I decided I had learned more than enough, and ducked. Running for the door, I hoped the element of surprise would be on my side when I raced through the new control room.

It wasn't. The door refused to slide open. Hank tackled me to the ground. Despite my struggles, Hank kept me pinned, and Ponife snapped the loop around my neck. It felt big at first, but the metal warmed against my skin and…softened then tightened. Hank released me and I dove for the oxygen mask, convinced I was being choked to death.

After a few deep breaths, I realized my windpipe had not been compressed. I tried to hook a finger under the loop, but it was skin tight.

"I knew you were lying. Did Jacy send you to spy on us?" Hank asked.

"No. I panicked." I pointed to Ponife. "He scared me." I tugged on the loop. It didn't budge. "What is this thing?"

"A command collar," Ponife said. "You will…listen to us."

"But she can't be trusted," Hank said.

"No matter. She is…attached to us. We know where she go."

"She will listen or…" Fosord, who hadn't moved during the whole incident, motioned to his colleague.

Ponife twisted the metal X with his fingers. Sharp needles of pain stabbed into my neck and traveled down my spine. Unrelenting pulses of fire coursed through my body. I collapsed to the ground, shrieking. Vinco's knife had been a caress in comparison to this anguish.

The pain stopped as quickly as it had arrived. My relief was almost as intense as the pain. Hank pressed the mask to my mouth as I gasped. Shudders overwhelmed my muscles as sweat pooled. If I had to guess how it felt to be kill-zapped, I'd imagine that torment came pretty damn close.

Hank straightened. "Impressive. Do you have more of those command collars?"

"Yes," Ponife said. "We find them to be…useful for… solving problems."

"Can I?" Hank wanted to take the X.

"No. Only Controllers can…correct problems."

"What else can it do?" he asked.

Ponife pulled on one of the ends. Numbness spread down my body, deadening all feeling below my neck. I could only move my head.

"She is…stopped," Ponife said. He flipped it around and tugged another side.

Feeling returned with a sudden flush of heat. My body tingled like I had just been kissed by Riley. It intensified as pure pleasure raced along my skin as if invisible hands stroked my body. To me, this was more humiliating than the pain.

"She is...rewarded. That is all." He righted the X.

The tingling stopped, and I had control of my body. For now.

"Plus you know where she is, right? It works like a tracer?" Hank asked.

Ponife dug into the pocket of his suit. The white material creased like fabric, but crinkled like very thin metal. He pulled out a small box that resembled a hand-puter the Pop Cops had used. He opened it, displaying a miniature screen. Inserting the X into the opposite side, he pushed a few buttons. Then he showed Hank the screen.

"That's a map of level five," he said. "What are those numbers on the side?"

"Her vitals. To know if she tells untruths," Ponife said.

Just when I thought my situation couldn't get any worse, he proved me wrong.

"Can we interrogate her now?" Hank asked.

"No. She is...terrorized. You must wait until her vitals return to normal."

"How long?"

"Depends on her."

Hank yanked me off the floor and hustled me from the conference room. He pushed me toward Bubba Boom. I fell into his arms.

"What happened?" Bubba Boom asked, supporting me.

"She tricked you, boy. She's spying for Jacy," Hank said. He tossed a long thin box at Bubba Boom who caught it in midair. "Take her to the lockup. When she settles down, we're going to have a nice long chat." He returned to his post.

Bubba Boom looked at me with a pained expression, but he followed orders, half carrying me from the control room. Right before the doors closed, I spotted Karla Trava watching me with a smug smile.

I tried to explain to Bubba Boom. "It's a misunderstanding. I got scared and—"

"Hank said you're spying for Jacy."

"You believe Hank over me?" I asked.

"Yes." Then he didn't say another word.

He kept a bruising grip on my upper arm. I was really sick of being manhandled all the time. We arrived in what would be Sector D5, which should contain apartments. Except the normally open hallways had barred double doors. Bubba Boom aimed that long box at the first set. He pushed a button and a click rang.

"What's this place?" I asked as he opened the gate.

"Anne-Jade had wanted more cells because of all the Travas. The Committee agreed to convert this Sector into a brig." Bubba Boom pointed his box to the first door on the right. It clicked open. This door was solid except for a panel about eye-level. "You're our first guest." He shoved me inside.

Daylights switched on as the door banged. I shot to my feet, but it was too late. There were no handles or anything on my side of the locked door. The cell was two meters wide by three meters long. A mat covered the floor near the back wall. Solid bars covered the vents. Nothing else here but a toilet.

Trapped, I experienced a sudden premonition that being kill-zapped and fed to Chomper would be a kindness in comparison to my future.

* * *

As I lay on the mat in my cell, I tugged and pulled at the loop around my neck, but it refused to budge. I doubted even Logan could remove it. Not that I could go anywhere.

There was only one thing I could do. I slid my hand into my pocket and removed Riley's sheep pendant. Dangling it over my face, I considered my next move. Should I trigger the beacon? It would probably alert Hank. And without working computers, would Riley even know I had signaled for his help?

What if he tried to rescue me and was caught? I couldn't risk him. Jacy needed him. But did they know Hank had been using level five as his own personal headquarters? Did they know two Outsiders had come in? Too many questions and no answers. My emotions flipped from terrified to worried and back again.

One thing I did know. I trusted Riley. He was smart and wouldn't be as easy to catch as I had been. At least that was the reason I clung to in desperation as I pressed the sheep, sending the signal.

I waited for Hank to arrive and confiscate my pendant, but as the hours passed, I slowly relaxed. Eventually, I lost track of the time. It seemed so long ago when Bubba Boom had arrived in the infirmary around hour eight of week number 147,026. Would the Outsiders repair the Transmission and resume our journey?

The click of the lock startled me from my musings. I shoved my pendant back into my pocket as Hank and one of the Outsiders—I couldn't tell with his helmet on—entered my tiny cell. I noted Bubba Boom's absence. The door closed behind them. Ice-cold fear spread inside me. This would be painful.

Hank questioned me and Ponife played with the metal X. The interrogation went something like this:

Hank—"What is Jacy up to?"

Me—"I don't know."

Ponife (with a mechanical sounding voice)—"An untruth." He twisted the X.

I screamed in pain.

Hank—"What is Jacy up to?"

Me—"I don't know."

Ponife twisted the X.

I screamed.

And so on until I lost count. Eventually, I broke and confirmed I had been spying for Jacy, and he had been attempting to bypass the Outsiders' hold on our network. At least I retained some dignity and hadn't said how they planned to circumvent the controls to all our life systems. Although right now I wished he hadn't shared that with me. Not when my muscles vibrated from the repeated bouts of agony and my clothes reeked of fear. Not when I lay curled tight in a ball, wishing for a quick trip to Chomper.

Hank seemed happy with my confession and left, but Ponife remained. My terror doubled. He popped his helmet off. Terror tripled. Ponife knelt next to me. Terror headed off the scale.

"Do not...fear," he said, panting with the effort. "Your air is...thick. We will not harm...world. We desire...to reclaim what is ours."

"What is yours?" I asked.

"This ship."

That was the last thing I expected. "Are you sure?"

"Yes. Your...ancestors stole it. Exiled us."

I noted his use of the word *exile*. Of course, it could have a wide range or meanings. "How do you know? As you said, our air is thicker than yours."

"We have…records. We had to…ration air so long…we are used to it. The air mixture is easy to alter. We'll find a… common setting. Good for all."

"Why are you telling me this?"

"You are leader," Ponife said.

I touched the collar. "Not a good one."

"Work with us. You will have…chance to repair damage."

I doubted it would be that easy. "Why did they exile you?"

His demeanor changed in an instant. Wrong question.

"Impertinent child." Ponife twisted the X.

When I came to my senses, Ponife was gone. In his place was a tray of food and a glass of water. My throat burned so I gulped down the water. Then I attacked the food. Only after I had consumed most of it did I consider the danger. I shrugged. They didn't need poison or drugs. A couple more sessions with the collar and I would do anything for them.

I considered Ponife's comments, trying to list reasons for banishing a person. It would also depend if the Insiders at the time knew about the extra space or not. We hadn't recycled the Travas, but if we didn't know about the Expanse I was sure we'd have had to in order to make room for all of us. Maybe instead of recycling the trouble makers, our ancestors put them into a Bubble Monster and sent them on their way. Was that better or worse than being recycled? Given the choice, I would rather take my chances in Outer Space in a Bubble than be Chomper's dinner.

Eventually, I fell into an exhausted sleep.

★ ★ ★

A rasping sound woke me. Disorientated, I blinked in the daylights as the shushing grew louder. Deep down, I recognized the noise, but my brain hadn't quite connected it.

After a few more seconds, I jumped to my feet. Climbing up to the air vent, I peered inside. Zippy had come!

I rattled the bars over the vent, but they wouldn't budge. Riley would guess I was stuck. Otherwise, I would have escaped by now. I searched with my fingers and found a cloth bag tied to Zippy. Good boy.

Pulling the bag through the bars, I carried my treasure back to the mat. Funny how the smallest things became so important when you've been reduced to utter helplessness.

I upended the bag. A microphone and receiver tumbled out along with a diamond wire. Inserting the receiver in my earlobe, I turned on the mic.

"Anyone listening?" I asked, trying not to sound pathetic, but strain shook my words, giving me away.

"Trella!" Riley's relieved voice reached me.

I collapsed back onto the mat. This was the first thing to go my way in a long time.

"What's wrong?" he asked.

Worried about Hank detecting the transmission, I explained about the new control room and the Outsiders as fast as I could.

After I finished, Riley asked me a few questions. Then he said, "Get out of there, and meet me at—"

"I can't. They have a...tracer on me."

"Can you cut it out? I could send a scalpel."

"No. It's around my neck." I gave him a basic rundown on all the wonders of the command collar.

He responded with an extended period of silence.

Unable to endure another minute, I said, "Don't be upset. I tried to run away, but Hank—"

"Trell, I'm not mad—well, not at you. I'm going to throttle both Hank and Bubba Boom and feed them to Chomper myself." He paused. "I'm thinking of a way for you to escape. You could use Zippy's short range EMP to disable it."

"I thought that only worked on weapons."

"Logan had to limit what the pulse could affect because of all the sensitive equipment and computers back when you ambushed the main Control Room. But you're far away from anything vital right now. Actually, if Zippy was stronger and if we had our network in place, he could have taken out Hank's new control room."

"How do I switch him over?" I asked.

Riley told me how to remove the safety filter.

"How can I tell if it works on the collar?"

"You escape, hide and wait. If it's operating, they'll find you pretty quick. But the pulse will ruin your microphone and receiver. If they don't come after you, meet me in our storeroom."

"Sounds like a plan. Thanks for the help." Before Riley could switch off, I said, "If this doesn't work, I just want to tell you that…" I closed my eyes. Why was this so hard? "That…I was an idiot to keep my distance from you. That I didn't realize how much I love you until I lost you."

"You'll get free, Trella." Riley's voice sounded tight. "You've survived worse than this. And this time you have more motivation."

"More motivation?"

"Yes. I'm not going to respond to your comment through a microphone. You'll have to hear it from me in person."

★ ★ ★

After Riley clicked off, I used the diamond wire to saw through the bars over the air vent. I hoped Ponife didn't check my vitals because my accelerated heart rate would alert him. Once I had enough space to wiggle through, I pulled Zippy from the shaft and removed the safety filter.

With nothing else to lose, I flipped the switch on Zippy. My receiver whined and popped, but the little cleaning troll remained silent. Logan had given Zippy a special protective coat so his inner electronics weren't zapped as well. I shoved the cleaning troll back into the duct, and climbed in after him.

In case Zippy's pulse hadn't disabled my collar, I didn't want to hide in any of my favorite spots. Instead, I worked my way up to the top of level ten, which was the bottom of the Expanse. Finding a space between two storage containers, I settled in to wait.

At first, every single noise jolted me. Eventually, I grew used to the sounds of the Expanse looming over me. After I felt like enough time had passed—if my collar worked, they would have found me by now—I descended to level four and headed toward our storeroom.

The glow of bluelights shone through the vent, indicating no one was in the room. Disappointed, I aimed my feet at the ladder and climbed down. The clock on the wall read hour forty-seven. I sank onto the couch. Thirty-nine hours had passed since I left the infirmary with Bubba Boom.

The horror, pain and fear had taken a toll on me. My head throbbed from the thin air. Exhausted, I curled up on the couch with Zippy, but I wished for Riley and Sheepy.

Chaotic dreams swirled. Outsiders chased me. Daylight

reflected off their silver helmets, blinding me. Then a wall of people blocked my escape route. Jacy led the group and I ran to him. Instead of protecting me, he grabbed my arm and dragged me back toward the Outsiders. He handed me over to Ponife in exchange for the metal X. As Jacy laughed and turned away, Ponife's white gloves stroked my skin.

I woke with a cry and with cold hands on my shoulders. My nightmare had turned into reality. I was caught.

18

FLAILING AND KICKING THE OUTSIDER, I FOUGHT WITH
all my strength. I would rather be sent to Chomper than be
under Ponife's control again.

It took me a couple of seconds to realize he wasn't fighting
back. And finally, his soothing tone and caring words reached
me. I stopped struggling and embraced Riley.

"I didn't mean to scare you," he said. He sat on the edge
of the couch. "I just couldn't wait until you woke up."

"Not your fault, I was having a nightmare," I said, clinging
to him, soaking in his warmth and enjoying the feel of his
arms around me.

After a few minutes, Riley pulled back to look at me. A
smile quirked and he smoothed a few strands of my hair from
my face. My braid had fallen out hours ago and I was sure
rats would have no trouble making a nest in my hair.

"How did you cut the collar off?" he asked.

"I didn't." Confused, I touched my throat. The collar remained in place. My fingernails clinked on its hard surface.

Riley squinted. He ran his fingers along my neck. When
he found the collar he explored the surface and tried to

tug it. "No seams. It doesn't feel like metal. The color is amazing."

"Why?"

"It blends in. It matches your skin. Didn't you know?"

"No mirrors in my cell."

He gasped with mock horror. "So cruel! How did you ever survive?"

I laughed and it felt good. It had been such a long time since a happy feeling has touched me that I wanted to prolong it. I cut off whatever Riley planned to say next by drawing him in for a long kiss that left us both breathless. Deciding that conversation was overrated, I claimed his lips again and yanked him down so he lay next to me on the couch.

My fingers unbuttoned his shirt, I snaked my hands along his chest and around to his back. I would have ripped it off, but he pulled away.

"As much as I would love to continue," he panted, "we don't have any time to spare."

"We might not get another chance," I said.

"If we don't get moving, we're guaranteed not to get any more chances."

"That bad?"

"Yep. We need weeks to finish installing a second network. Which we won't get now that the Outsiders are already inside. We're hoping your and Logan's idea has a quicker turnaround time?"

"I'm not sure. We'll have to ask Logan."

"We'll need to regain control of the air plant first," Riley said. "Without that, we're sunk."

"I'll get Logan and take him up to the top of the Expanse."

"The top?"

Describing level eighteen to Riley, I filled him in.

"Why didn't you tell me this before?"

"I really don't know. Just after I discovered it all this trouble started between us. At the time, I felt overwhelmed, scared and uncertain. Almost like I do now except for the uncertain part." To prove my point, I kissed him again, letting my hands slide all the way down his back.

Riley sat up and grabbed my wrists. "Your timing sucks. You know that, don't you?"

"I hate to waste this opportunity."

"We'll get another one. I promise."

"You can't promise. Not this time. I've seen the Outsiders. I've been…" I closed my eyes as memories of pain rolled through me.

Riley cupped my face with his hands, getting my attention. "Sounds like the Outsiders are too hard to beat. You can't fight them. So you can stay here while Jacy, Logan, Anne-Jade and I make a token attempt to thwart them."

"I know what you're doing."

"Me?" He tried to appear innocent.

"You're telling me I can't fight so I'll get angry and prove you wrong."

"Did it work?" he asked.

I huffed with amusement. "A little."

"How about if I add on guilt? Reminding you that Sheepy wouldn't be happy if the Outsiders replaced the Pop Cops and his rebellion was all for nothing."

Guilt was a factor. Not for Sheepy, but over Cogon. He would hate this. I'd like to turn back the clock and start again from when we beat the Travas. That was impossible, but I remembered a phrase that kept me focused during the bad times. Maximum damage. This time I would impart maximum damage for Cogon.

"I can see that little evil gleam in your eyes. You're back!" he said.

Riley's broad smile shot through me and I couldn't resist kissing him again. But this time, I pulled away so we could discuss plans.

"Did you have time to make that pulley system?" I asked him.

"One of Jacy's men put it together." He reached under the couch and pulled it out. "We didn't know how thick the rope would be, so we guessed, erring on a bigger size."

I spun the wheels, examining the device. "What's this lever?"

"The brakes in case you accidently let go. We don't want Logan smashed flat."

"Good idea."

When we finished coordinating our plans, Riley rummaged through the drawers of the desk, returning with a small pair of bolt cutters and a jar.

He tossed the jar to me. "Sheep oil."

I peered at it in suspicion. "Did you have this before?" Riley had cut off a metal cuff from my wrist during our Force of Sheep rebellion, but he had claimed not to have the oil which was supposed to help with the pain.

"I can't recall." He batted his dark eyelashes at me.

"Look who has the evil gleam now." I grumbled as I spread the oil around my neck, trying to get it under the control collar. "Okay."

Riley thought the back of my neck would be the best place to cut it off. I held my hair up. The cold touch of the metal sent shivers down my spine. At first, I didn't feel anything, but when he grunted with effort, a sharp pain stabbed into my throat. I cried out and he stopped.

"What's the matter? I didn't pinch your skin."

"It hurt."

"It doesn't look like I even dented the damn thing," he said. "I'm going to need bigger cutters."

A sudden and very unpleasant thought occurred to me. "Could it still be active?"

Riley examined Zippy. "He's working fine. Do you have the receiver and microphone I sent?"

I pulled them from my pocket and also removed my sheep pendant. He took all the devices over to his desk. I peered over his shoulder as he tested each one.

"They're all broken." He then put the tester's two prongs on my collar as he stared at the display. "No reading either. It's busted."

Relief surged through me.

"I'll have to have Logan help me make another pendant for you." Riley swept the items into the recycle bin.

I retrieved the pendant.

"But it can't send a signal anymore."

"Doesn't matter. It's still precious to me." I looped it around my neck then tried to distract Riley with a passionate goodbye kiss, but he wouldn't let me procrastinate anymore.

Since we really couldn't delay any longer, I climbed the ladder with reluctance and entered the air ducts again.

The trip to Logan's room didn't take long. When I arrived, I peered down to check for his keepers. At first the significance of the mess below didn't register in my mind. Logan was never tidy, but this seemed extreme even for him.

The couch had been turned on its side. Computer parts and metallic gadgets littered the floor. The white stuffing from the ruined cushions had settled over everything like a coating of dust.

But no sign of Logan.

★ ★ ★

Logan was gone. After the shock wore off, I considered where he might be. If he had decided to "escape" from his room, Riley would have known about it because Logan would have sought him and Jacy out. But what if he couldn't?

I glanced down at the door. No wires hung from the locks, which meant Logan hadn't escaped. Anne-Jade could have opened it from the outside. Again, Riley would know unless she was unable to tell him. But why would the room be in such disarray?

The final and most likely scenario entailed Hank bringing Logan up to the brig on level five. It was a logical move. Logan's knowledge and abilities made him a dangerous enemy. And from the mess, it appeared as if one of his keepers had discovered his stash of gadgets.

Just in case Anne-Jade knew where her brother had gone, I searched for her on level four. She was slumped in her chair in the ISF office in Quad A4, staring at nothing that I could see. No one else worked at the other desks. An odd silence filled the room.

Not wanting to scare her, I called her name before jumping down from the vent. Anne-Jade waved me over half-heartedly. Utter defeat looked at me through her eyes. I almost stepped back as my heart lurched in my chest.

"Did something happen to Logan?" I asked.

"Not yet."

Unsure if I should be relieved or not, I asked, "What do you mean by that?"

"Come on, Trell. You don't need me to explain it."

"Did Hank take him?"

She straightened and for a brief second the old Anne-Jade frowned at me. "How did you know Hank's involved?"

"He tried to recruit me to his cause."

She slouched back. "You should have signed up. They're in charge now, you'd have saved yourself a lot of trouble." A wry smile twisted. "Sorry. I forgot who I was talking to. Trouble is exactly what you crave. I just want peace."

Anger flared. I banged a fist on her desk. "I wanted peace, too. And you *know* what happened while I sat around mooning over our state of affairs. I don't crave trouble. It's just one of those unfortunate side effects when I finally decided to take action." I leaned in close to her—almost nose to nose. "If Hank has Logan, then I know exactly where he's being held. Are you going to sit around moping or are you going to help me?"

"It's too late."

"That's such a load of crap. It's never too late."

A spark of ire flashed. "What more proof do you need? My brother's dead body? Would that convince you it's too late?"

"No. Not Logan's. Not Riley's. Not mine or yours. They haven't won, Anne-Jade. They just think they did. Which gives us the advantage."

She laughed. "You're insane."

"That's certainly debatable. But give me another chance."

"Another chance to do what?"

"Prove to you it isn't too late."

She snagged her lower lip with her teeth and chewed. "I don't have any resources. They took everything."

"Everything?"

She nodded.

"You mean you don't have a few loyal lieutenants who would take a risk for you?"

"Well…"

260 MARIA V. SNYDER

I sensed a small victory. "And you didn't keep a few weapons hidden away just in case?"

"I might have."

"Might? When will you know?"

Anne-Jade huffed in annoyance. "All right. I'll make you a deal. If you rescue Logan and get him to a safe location, I'll help you."

"I accept." I shook her hand, sealing the deal.

I turned on my mic and hailed Riley, informing him of Logan's disappearance and my plans to rescue him. He had given me another microphone and receiver. They worked on a specific frequency so it was very difficult for Hank and the Outsiders to pick it up.

"Do you have the diamond wire?" he asked.

"Yes."

"Do you need backup?" His voice held a nervous edge.

"I'll take Zippy."

"I'd be happier if you took a dozen armed men and women along."

"And I'd be happier if the Outsiders decided to leave us alone."

"Point. Be careful…please."

"I will."

The problem with using a diamond wire to aid in my escape became apparent right away. Wires ringed the bars covering the air vent to Logan's cell. Wires that I assumed would set off a loud alarm if I sawed through them.

I hadn't called attention to myself just in case Logan had company. It was interesting how fast my ability to crawl through the shafts without making noise had returned. Either that or just the amount of time I'd been spending traveling through them had sharpened my skills.

Logan sprawled on his back on the thin mat. His cell was a mirror image of mine. I called his name when I was certain he was alone. He jerked and scrambled to his feet.

"Trella, don't touch the—"

"Bars, I know. I can see the wires."

He slouched against the wall and rubbed his face. "I think I'm stuck for good this time," he said in a tired voice.

He didn't appear to be injured, but I knew what the Outsiders were capable of. "What happened?"

"My keepers made a surprise visit," he said. "I didn't have time to hide all my toys. They were strewn all over. I guess I shouldn't have been so relaxed about them. Another mistake caused by overconfidence."

"Another?"

He waved a hand. His right one still covered his eyes. "The whole Outsider fiasco could have been avoided."

"How?"

"If I had kept track of all communications, I would have spotted Hank's link to the Outsiders."

"Why didn't you?" I asked.

"Privacy. I didn't want to spy on the Committee members or others."

"Exactly, Logan. You didn't want to be like the Travas and Pop Cops, monitoring all our activities. You're not to blame."

"I'm not helping, either," he said. Clearly miserable, he massaged his temples.

"Did you meet the Outsiders?" I asked.

He straightened, dropping his hands. "They're here?"

"Only a couple. I've met them both."

"You? When?"

"Long story. I'll tell you later. First, we need to bust you out of here."

"How? The heating vent has the same trip wires. All you have to do is touch them and they'll set off the alarm."

"How?" I asked.

"There's a weak electrical current going through the wires. If you touch it with your finger, you'll block the current and that sets it off." He began to pace. "But if you touch it with both hands, the current will travel through you and back to the wire. I could cut the bars... No. Won't work. You'd be stuck holding the wires. No way for you to move once the bars and wires are cut. Unless we made a connection with a separate wire and some metal clamps, which we don't have. Plus we would need one bypass for each bar, unless the wire is continuous."

I traced the wire. It wrapped around all five bars before continuing down the air shaft.

"We still don't have the clamps and wires," Logan said when I described it to him.

"I have Zippy and my tool belt."

It was as if I had told him his computer access had returned. He stood under the vent and explained in an excited tone what I needed to do to bypass the current. I performed surgery on Zippy, removing wires and various parts, following his instructions.

Well aware that the Outsiders or Hank could come in at any time, we hurried. But it still took time to rig the bypass, cut the bars and pull Logan into the shaft with me.

"Will it hold?" I asked, pointing to the loop of Zippy's wire.

"It should. Unless a cleaning troll comes by and rips it off."

"Let's go." I put a finger to my lips. "Keep quiet until we get there."

"Where are we going?"

"To the roof."

Logan's rescue had gone smoothly. That worried me as I guided Logan to the top of level ten. My safety rope remained in place—another good sign. I had the pulley hooked onto my belt and I found a few extra kilograms to attach as well.

Before climbing up the Wall of the Expanse, I said, "Even with the pulley, I'm not strong enough to hoist you all the way to the top. So I'm going to use myself as a counterweight. As I sink down, you should rise up. Once you're at the top, grab onto the ladder and climb up a few rungs. I'll join you as soon as I can."

It had been five weeks since I had scaled the forty-five meters to the bottom rung of the ladder. Five hectic, muscle-bruising, energy-sapping weeks. And I felt every single one of them as I pulled myself from handhold to handhold.

Sweating, panting and nauseous, I finally reached the last rung. I clung to it as cramps and spasms plagued my body. It seemed like I lost another week while waiting to recover.

I secured the pulley to the rung, and threaded the rope through the wheels, dropping the end down to Logan. Vibrations traveled up the fibers as he tied it to his safety harness.

My plan worked—not exactly as I had hoped since I had taken on too much weight and fell faster than expected, but without any dire injuries. Returning to the top was a test of my endurance; I almost gave up around thirty meters, but pushed on.

We didn't encounter any new problems during the rest of the trip to the ceiling. I opened the near-invisible hatch and collapsed on the floor of level seventeen.

The daylights snapped on and Logan yelled in surprise over the sudden appearance of the Bubble Monster and his kid brother.

"Transport vehicles like the Outsiders used," I said to calm him.

"Oh."

"Ignore them, look at the walls." I didn't have the energy to play tour guide so he explored on his own.

From his cries of glee, moans of delight and pure ecstatic woots, I knew he understood the symbols and diagrams on the walls.

When I recovered, I found him tracing an array of…glyphs. His mouth hung open and his finger moved along the raised metal with reverence.

"Did you find out how to work the air plant manually?" I asked.

"Huh?"

I snapped my fingers in his face. "Air plant. Outsiders. Remember?"

"Yes, but…" His gaze returned to the wall. "These markings… They're incredible. They're our history! They're blueprints for our whole world! I'm sure there are schematics for the whole network. Our ancestors or the builders put this here in case we lost the computers, or forgot why we're here. It's… It's…" He stroked the wall again.

"Focus, Logan. Will it help us?"

"Oh yes." He shuffled along the wall, exclaiming over various symbols.

"So you found the data for the air plant?"

"No."

I yanked on his ear until I had his full attention. "Logan, we need to reclaim the air plant. We don't have much time. You can drool over all this later. How can I help?"

He described what the schematics of the air plant would look like. I searched the south and then west walls, while he continued with the east. He moved faster than me and had looped around the room, reaching the north wall before me.

The series of beeps alerted me. I would never forget that sound. Running as fast as possible, I still couldn't reach him before he finished entering the code.

"It's just like—oof!"

I tackled him to the ground.

"What's wrong?" he asked. The squeal of metal filled the room. "Oh."

Logan had opened the large door on the north wall. It was big enough to fit the huge transport vehicle. That same vehicle that could probably fly through Outer Space. Which meant that Outer Space must be waiting on the other side of the door.

The noise rattled my teeth and vibrated in my bones. Not wasting a second, I dragged Logan over to one of the legs of the transport.

"Hang on," I said, bracing for the absence of air, the skin freezing cold and the floating sensation.

The door finished moving with a bang. Daylights clicked on beyond the entrance, revealing an empty room with walls covered with more symbols.

Logan cocked his head. "Why are we clinging for dear life?"

"I thought Outer Space was on the other side. That door reminded me of when Cogon and I had opened Gateway."

"Sorry. I guess I should have told you."

"Told me what?"

"This door leads to a spaceport." He walked into the room.

I followed him. The area was much larger than I had first thought. It appeared to be as long as two Sectors, but only one Sector wide. Three doors at equidistant intervals were on each of the two long sides, including the open one. And one door at the end.

He gestured to the doors. "There are seven bays that contain two transport vehicles. The Scout and the bigger Cargo vehicle. They can come out here, then the doors all close and..." He pointed at the ceiling. A huge hatch occupied the center. "Fly out to Outer Space."

"How do you know all that?"

"I read it on the wall."

"Why didn't you tell me before?"

"I thought you saw something."

I drew in a deep calming breath. "Let's keep looking for the air plant information."

Keeping Logan focused, I hustled him along the port. We searched the next two bays, but didn't find anything until we opened the third bay. Then he cried out with more excitement than the last ten times. He had found the information on how to manually run the plant.

I gave him a spare receiver and microphone, letting him explain it to Riley. Then we decided he should remain up here to explore and learn everything he could. I would tie a bucket to the rope so I could use the pulley and send up supplies, food and water.

"How are you going to get into the air plant?" Logan asked. "Hank's people are there."

"Anne-Jade has to make good on a promise."

"But she doesn't have any weapons or manpower, and you don't have Zippy."

"We'll work it out."

"Good luck. You're going to need it."

★ ★ ★

Anne-Jade had hidden a few stunners, and she also had a number of anti-stunners for our force. To tell the truth, it wasn't much of a force. Word had already spread throughout Inside that the Outsiders were coming to reclaim control over us. While many worried, more seemed grateful, claiming the Outsiders would solve all of Inside's problems. Hank and Bubba Boom hadn't needed me to be their prophet after all.

At hour sixty, week 146,026, Anne-Jade led a group that contained three of her lieutenants, ten of Jacy's goons, Sloan and Riley. I scouted ahead, crawling through the ducts over the air plant, counting how many maintenance workers—seven—and reporting their locations back to Anne-Jade.

It was a beautiful raid. Anne-Jade and her lieutenants charged into the plant and stunned most of the maintenance workers before they knew what hit them. A couple of Hank's men fought back, swinging large wrenches. The supervisor pulled his stunner and disabled a few of Jacy's goons before Anne-Jade shot him.

By the time I jumped down from the air shaft, the fight was over. We had taken the plant.

"We have the air plant. What's next?" Anne-Jade asked.

"We disconnect the computer and work the controls the old-fashioned way."

"Old-fashioned?" she asked.

"Manually."

"You can do that?"

"Not me. Riley." I pointed. He and Sloan had unscrewed the main console's covering. They bent over the jumble of wires and circuits with rubber-handled pliers. "Logan's talking him through it right now."

Anne-Jade acted a bit strange. She kept glancing at the

entrance where two of her lieutenants guarded the door. And she kept tugging the collar of her uniform as if it chafed her skin.

"Logan sounded in his glory when I talked to him earlier," Anne-Jade said.

"He's been exploring and learning all about the history of Inside and how it works. It's only a matter of time until we get back control of our life systems, and send the Outsiders away."

"I wish I'd known your plans before you rescued Logan," Anne-Jade said.

"We've been sort of making them up on the fly. Why?"

Anne-Jade touched her neck. "When they had him in the brig on level five, the Outsiders threatened to put a command collar on him. You know he would have been a mess. He doesn't do well with pain."

"What are you trying to tell me?" I asked, even though I had my suspicions and they weren't pleasant.

"I'm wearing the collar meant for him. I agreed to—"

"Work for us," a familiar voice said.

I turned. Hank, Bubba Boom and Ponife stood in the doorway.

19

ANNE-JADE AIMED HER STUNNER AT RILEY. HE DIDN'T
have an anti-stunner. I yelled a warning to him as I knocked
her arm aside, causing her to miss. Riley ducked behind the
console.

She cursed and pointed the gun at me. Now I knew why
I didn't get an anti-stunner as well. "Sorry, Trella. I really
am. I guess I lost faith in the Force of Sheep."

Hank's people ran into the plant, shouting at Jacy's goons
to surrender. They were armed with kill-zappers.

Hank, Bubba Boom and Ponife drew closer to us. I glanced
around. All the members of our force—except Anne-Jade's
men—knelt on the floor with their hands behind their
heads.

I met Riley's gaze. He inclined his head toward the air
console. A tendril of smoke rose from it.

Lowering my voice, I said to her, "We know how to disable the collar."

She covered her surprise as Hank and his smug entourage
reached us. Ponife wore the standard off-duty clothes of an
upper, but there was no hiding his sickly-colored skin.

The smoke thickened and puffed from the console.

Riley shouted, "Fire," and dove to the floor as a bright light flashed.

I followed his example. A microsecond later a boom shook the room. A wave of energy knocked anyone on their feet to the ground. Riley and a few others bolted toward the door during the ensuing confusion. I was close behind them when a sharp pain ringed my neck, knocking me flat. We hadn't disabled my collar after all. And now, Hank and the Outsiders knew our plans to bypass the computer. Knew about the instructions on the walls of the port.

They had let me escape and allowed Logan to be rescued. A ruse to discover Jacy and Riley's strategy. It had worked. I'd been a fool.

Awareness crept back. Shapes coalesced from my haze of agony and sharpened into Hank and Ponife. Their words reached me, but failed to make sense inside my head until I concentrated. My memory returned. I had been taken to another cell on level 5—this one without any vents—and questioned. Repeatedly.

"Her vitals off the scale. Her heart will not…tolerate more at this time," Ponife said. "Another…session will stop it."

Hank hovered over me. "Do you understand him? One more blast and you'll die."

I nodded.

"Last chance, Trella. Where are Riley and Jacy?"

"Level one." My words were just audible.

Hank leaned close. "Where on level one?"

"Sector…"

He cocked his head to the side to hear me better.

"Sector…" I wrapped my hands around his throat and squeezed with all my strength.

Ponife twisted the metal X and my body numbed from my neck down. The up side—no more pain. The down—Hank removed my hands.

"Damn, she's stubborn," Hank said, rubbing his throat.

"We can threaten to harm her friend... Anne-Jade wears a collar," Ponife said.

"I don't think they're friends anymore. But..." He considered. "We can find someone she does care about. Release her."

Feeling returned in a sudden rush. I gasped as pins and needles attacked my skin. But the pain was a small distraction compared to the self-satisfied gleam in Hank's eyes.

"You can tell us where your boyfriend is hiding, or Bubba Boom will invite your mother up here for a little visit."

An impotent fury burned in the pit of my stomach. I bit my lip. "Level one, Sector H1."

"That wasn't so bad now, was it?" Hank's condescending tone grated on my nerves. He lumbered to his feet and moved toward the door.

"Why didn't the EMP disable the collar?" I asked Ponife before he could follow Hank.

"It is protected," he said.

I ran my fingers over it. "What's it made of?"

"Living metal. An ingenious piece of technology we have perfected."

After they had secured the cell's door, I lay on the mat and wondered how long it would be until they figured out I had sent them to the waste-handling plant. Not to any hiding places. I didn't know Riley's or Jacy's location.

Then it occurred to me that if my collar had been working all along, Ponife knew all the places I'd been. Hank hadn't asked about the Expanse or the port. Which might mean

Ponife had kept that information from him. An interesting possibility that I may be able to use to my advantage.

Ponife returned hours later with Fosord, the other Outsider. No Hank. I pushed up to my elbow and regarded them. They both wore uppers' clothes and solemn expressions. Ponife held the metal X in his right hand.

Fosord gestured to me. "Come."

No real choice, I gained my feet and followed Fosord. Ponife stayed behind me as we navigated the brig on level five. The closed doors with the red light glowing near the lock meant the cell was occupied. I stopped counting after ten—too depressing.

At one door, Fosord stopped and slid back the metal panel.

"Look," he said.

Dread rose like bile in my throat. I swallowed it down. Peering into the cell, I saw Jacy. Bruises covered his face and he tugged at something invisible around his neck—probably a collar. Fosord shut the panel before I could say anything.

He did the same thing at the next cell. I refused to move, but his gaze slid behind me.

"Trella," Ponife warned.

Bracing for another shock, I glanced inside. Logan sat on the mat with his head buried in his hands. We moved to the next cell. Riley lay on a mat as if asleep, but he could have been unconscious. Blood dripped from a large gash across his forehead and temple. My legs refused to hold me up and I sank to the ground. Fosord closed the panel.

Ponife crouched next to me. "See? We have all your friends. You will cooperate now."

"You don't need me," I said. "Unless you have injured?"

"No. Come."

Once again wedged between the Outsiders, we left the brig and walked through level five toward Quad A5. The hallways were filled with Outsiders. I shouldn't have been surprised. Many of them still wore their white suits and helmets.

"They're getting used to the air," Ponife said.

We climbed up to the top of the half-completed level ten. I stopped in amazement. Bright daylights filled the Expanse, reflecting off the ceiling. And the Outsiders had attached a lift to the west Wall, explaining the smooth groove and tracks I had noticed on one of my early explorations.

An odd thought occurred to me. It seemed we've been stumbling around in the dark for thousands of weeks, while these Outsiders had no trouble making everything work for them. Maybe our ancestors had stolen this ship from them.

I turned to Ponife. "Why didn't you try to talk to us? We probably could have worked out an agreement between us."

"We do not want to be…a part of your world. We want our ship back."

His answer confused me. "You want to be in charge, right? And make the rules?"

Ponife attempted to smile. I shuddered at the creepy effort and hoped he wouldn't do it again. "No. We want our ship back and you…gone."

Oh. No. "As in *gone* gone?"

"Like your ancestors had done to us." He gestured to the ceiling. "Put you in transports with little food and supplies and send you all out to die in space."

My emotions flipped from horrified to terrified and back. "Why did they—"

"It does not matter why!" Fosord shouted, grabbing my shirt and slamming me into the Wall. "No crime deserves such punishment. Your people are...savages. You kill your own and crush them into...pulp."

I thought it best not to argue with him.

He released me. "Tell her," he said to Ponife.

"You will help us find everyone," he said. "Hank says you know all the hiding places. We want *everyone* gone."

Even overwhelmed with the information, I still couldn't help asking, "Even Hank?"

"Yes. Everyone," Fosord snapped.

Ponife glared at him. Fosord wasn't supposed to tell me that. Good to know they can make mistakes.

"Does Hank know?" I asked.

"No. And you will not tell him," Ponife said. He held up the X. "Understand?"

"Yes." I just needed a little time alone with Ponife and his X. For him to forget to keep his distance from me. Just one lapse in judgment.

Fosord led us onto the lift. It rose up the Wall. Hanging next to it in the bright daylights was my safety rope. We reached the ladder and the pulley remained in place.

"You are certainly resourceful...for a savage," Fosord said to me.

A section of the ceiling had been removed. The lift shot through the gap and stopped level with the floor. Outsiders milled around the Bubble...er...transport vehicles.

"We are preparing them for your...journey," Ponife explained.

"Will we know how to operate them?"

"Yes. Several of your people are quite...able," Fosord said.

"When are we leaving?"

"As soon as the Transmission is repaired. We will not make the same mistake and let you catch us." Ponife gestured to the bays. "Hank says you did not know this place, or Outer Space existed until recently?" He seemed amused.

"We had a bit of trouble about fifteen thousand weeks ago."

Ponife and Fosord exchanged a glance. Interesting.

"What trouble?" Ponife asked.

"Another rebellion. According to the records, saboteurs deleted a bunch of computer files. The Trava family defeated them and took over control of Inside to avoid any more issues. We thought the sabotage was a ruse by the Trava family to justify their takeover, but…" I shrugged. "Maybe it had happened. We thought the Controllers were a fabrication as well."

Another look passed between the Outsiders.

"There is some truth. We controlled all Inside's mechanical and life systems." Ponife thumped his chest. "While the nine families bred like rabbits and took care of all the soft jobs…" He cast about as if looking for the right words. "Soft like growing and cooking food, cleaning clothing and raising children. The Trava family were the saboteurs. They wanted more." His speech had winded him even though, of the two, he had seemed to adjust to our air faster.

I mulled over his story. Fosord mentioned a crime when he had been upset, which didn't match this explanation at all.

When he regained his breath, I asked, "Why are you working with Karla Trava then?"

"She offered her help," Fosord answered instead.

"But you can't trust her."

"She doesn't know. The Trava family created a new history and deleted all records of the old. After enough time passed and the following generations grew up learning this false history, no one questioned it," Ponife said.

Yet they had. Stories of Gateway had persisted. The

Controllers had transformed into mythical beings. Beings the Travas listened to. As Logan had explained, the Controllers were Inside's operating parameters, fail-safes and the keeper of directives set by the builders. If I believed Logan—which I did—then when the Travas took over, they naturally accessed the Controller files to learn how to run our world.

So who were the Outsiders?

"Why are you telling me this?" I asked.

"Once all your people are on the ships, you can tell the others why they have been exiled," Ponife said.

"Really? Sounds like you're feeling guilty." The comment sailed from my mouth without censure. Big mistake.

Their expressions hardened.

"We do not tolerate insolence." Ponife played with the X, bending the one leg back and forth.

The first wave of pain brought me to my knees. The second jolt forced me to the floor and the third seized my muscles and wouldn't let go. Each one lasted longer than the last until they all blurred together.

I woke back in my cell. As I lay on the mat, I reviewed everything Ponife had told me. Besides being touchy over the reason for their exile, all I had was their version of the events fifteen thousand weeks ago. I tried to think of a way to counter their plans, but failed to come up with a brilliant strategy.

Time passed and I wasn't any closer to a solution. I marked the hours by the arrival of food and water. The meals were delivered on trays slid through the panel into my cell. If Hank would believe me, I'd tell him he was going to be exiled with the rest of us. But Hank never came to my cell without Ponife.

The metallic scrape of my panel opening woke me from

a light doze. A hand held the end of the tray. I recognized the thick callused fingers and an idea popped into my head. I removed the meal and seized his wrist, yanking his arm inside my cell.

The element of surprise would only net me a few seconds. "Listen, please," I said before Bubba Boom could break free. "One minute."

He stopped. "Thirty seconds," Bubba Boom said.

"You once told me the Controllers wouldn't torture or trick people. But I've been tortured and tricked."

"You lied and were spying for Jacy," he said.

"So? When the Committee was in charge, we didn't torture or trick the Travas. We treated them well. Anne-Jade wouldn't even resort to strong-arm methods to get them to help us repair the Transmission. And we had no plans to recycle the Travas either."

"The Controllers won't kill anyone. You're trying to confuse me."

"No, I'm not. Think about it, Bubba Boom. I'm at Ponife's mercy. He's forcing my cooperation. Just like the Pop Cops did to you long ago."

Silence. I pressed my advantage. "You also told me we're their children who have run away. Do you even know *why* we ran?" I released his arm.

Bubba Boom drew it back and closed the panel. I hoped he would think about what I had said, but I had no idea if I had reached him or not.

A few meals later, my panel slid open. No tray came through, but Bubba Boom peered at me from the other side.

"The Transmission is repaired," he said.

No time left. No idea how to stop the Outsiders. No hope

of rescue. Anyone who had the resources or determination had been captured.

"Did they tell you what's next?" I asked.

"Yes." He waited.

"Are they still planning to send everyone out into Outer Space?" I asked.

"How do you know?"

"Ponife told me."

"Did he tell you that those who aided the Controllers will be allowed to stay?"

"No. Fosord said everyone."

"You're lying."

"I wish I were."

Bubba Boom shut the panel.

The next time my door opened, Ponife rushed in. His agitation was clear. I braced for pain, but he yanked me to my feet and dragged me from the cell. It was the first time he had touched me. He was surprisingly strong. Unfortunately, he didn't have the X in his hand.

He hurried me to a room in Sector E5. Five Outsiders lay on a row of beds. Blood drooled from their mouths and they were all curled on their sides as if in agony. Bubba Boom, Hank and a few others hovered nearby, but they looked panicked.

I didn't wait for orders. Running to the closest Outsider, I felt her pulse. It raced and her skin felt clammy. She shook as a spasm seized her muscles. I opened her eyes. The whites were stained red.

"They had acclimated and were doing fine," Ponife said.

"We need to get them to Doctor Lamont, now." I shouted to Hank and Bubba Boom to help me carry them. The beds didn't have wheels.

They jerked, but remained frozen in place.

"Hurry! They're dying," I said.

Ponife said, "We will bring the doctor—"

"No. She'll need access to her medicines and equipment." I pulled the slight female Outsider upright and managed to get her weight over my shoulders.

Bubba Boom followed my example and swept one of the Outsiders up in his arms. Without waiting to see if the others followed, I bolted for the lift between Quad A5 and Sector B5.

We carried them down to the infirmary.

Lamont pushed a gurney over to me. "What's wrong?"

I rattled off what I had learned as I laid the Outsider on it. Without hesitation, Lamont took control, shouting orders and checking vitals. I filled syringes and fetched instruments.

Bubba Boom and Hank helped as well. Ponife and the two others who had carried the Outsiders stood to the side, keeping out of the way until Lamont ordered them to bring canisters of the Outsider's air mixture down from level five.

We worked for hours and saved three of them. The other two never recovered. I closed their eyes, arranged their arms and covered them with a sheet. When I looked up I met Bubba Boom's gaze. He had been watching me.

"I'm sorry," Lamont said to Ponife. "We did everything we could. They were just too far gone. Do you need me to prep them to be recycled?"

"No. We send our dead out into Outer Space." Ponife didn't act too upset. "Come, Trella, we must return."

"No." Lamont stepped in his way. "I need her help."

"I will send you plenty of helpers."

"She knows what to do. You saw for yourself. I don't have the time to train another."

He hesitated.

"Where do you think she'll go that you *can't* find her?" Lamont asked.

"Do not leave the infirmary," Ponife said to me.

Hank, Bubba Boom and the other maintenance men followed Ponife. Before he left, Bubba Boom once again met my gaze. He gave me a slight nod. Hope touched my heart for the first time in weeks.

Lamont grilled me as soon as the men were out of hearing range. She already knew quite a bit about the Outsiders and the command collar. Riley had explained much of it to her before he had disappeared. Her questions focused on me.

And after I assured her I was at least healthy, she asked, "Okay what's the plan?"

"I've no idea. I don't even know what week this is."

"It's week 147,027, hour fourteen."

"Thanks."

"And you don't have to worry about being overheard. Riley found the microphones planted in the infirmary and removed them."

"It doesn't matter. I've got nothing. Everyone's been arrested. Level five is filled with Outsiders and everyone thinks they're the long lost Controllers who are going to make life better."

"Thinks?"

I explained our soon-to-be change in location.

"Then we need to stop them."

I laughed, but the sound lacked mirth. "How?"

"You tell me." She stared at me as if daring me.

"I told you—"

"Nothing, I know. Let's see if we can change that. Did you know that even with all this insanity, I've been testing people and telling them their family bloodlines?"

I had forgotten all about that. "But I didn't send anyone to you. And you can't—"

"I *couldn't* leave level three, but that was before. Once everyone knew I had the tracer, I removed it."

"How many—"

"About half have been tested. I've been busy."

"I see."

"And I know something else that'll help you." She had a smug smile.

"What?"

"The Outsiders need us. Otherwise they won't survive very long."

"How?" Now it was my turn to challenge her.

"All those weeks living in that transport vehicle has affected their heath."

"So? They'll be in here. Nice and safe."

"Won't help."

"All right, Mother. Spit it out."

She faltered for a bit and I realized what I had just called her. Oh well. Nothing I could do about it now.

"Well?" I prodded.

"They need us because they're sterile."

20

"STERILE? AS IN UNABLE TO HAVE CHILDREN STERILE?"
I asked.

"Yep," Lamont said.

"All of them?"

"That's harder to determine. Two of these three are and so was one of the two that died. From what I've been able to observe, the younger generation—those under twenty-five hundred weeks old or so are all sterile, but the older Outsiders aren't. It's just a matter of time before no one is able to have children."

"What caused their sterility?"

"Long-term exposure to the radiation in Outer Space. When you discovered Outer Space, I found a few files about the adverse health effects of being Outside. Inside's Walls have a lead lining to protect us from this radiation, but the article mentioned these things called…meteoroids that could hit us hard enough to make a hole, letting in radiation."

Yet more things we didn't know about. Lovely. If the Outsiders had indeed been in charge of running Inside, they had to know.

"They're planning to evacuate our entire population," I said.

"You might be able to use this information to your advantage. Plus, if you tell all the Insiders about the Outsiders' plans, I'm sure you'll have plenty of volunteers to help."

"The Insiders see them as our saviors. They won't help me. I'm the one who caused all this trouble in the first place."

"Then educate them. Recruit them. You can do it."

"The collar—"

"I've heard. Come back to the exam room, I want to take a look."

No arguing with the doctor, I sat on the examination table as she used various diagnostic tools to inspect the collar.

I explained how we had thought the device broken before the air plant raid. "Ponife called it living metal."

"It's quite amazing," she said. "As far as I can tell, it's connected to your body's electrical system and using it to power itself."

"I have an electrical current inside me?" I asked.

"Yes. A body produces a small electrical charge."

"Any way to turn off the current?"

"Yes. When you die, but that's *not* an option."

I considered. "Why? In a controlled situation, you could stop my heart and—"

"Absolutely not." She shot me her fiercest frown. Impressive. "Besides," she said, "it might not work. The collar is also linked to your nervous system, which is why it causes such intense agony." Her voice softened. "You have some nerve damage. Did they…"

"Yeah, but don't worry. I can handle it." I lied to my mother, and I half expected the collar to zap me. "Would my nervous system shut down if I died?"

"Not an option, Trella. You'll have to find a way to get that X from Ponife."

"He won't come close enough. And most of the time he has a couple of the maintenance guys with him."

"You'll have to wait for the right opportunity."

Easy for her to say.

Ponife visited the recovering Outsiders at hour twenty four. Bubba Boom and Egan accompanied him. I felt much better. Almost optimistic, even. Amazing what a long shower and eight hours of sleep on a real bed could do.

Lamont and I answered his questions about his colleagues' health. Then Ponife dismissed Lamont. Shooting me a significant look, she headed to her office.

"We have started to load the first transport ship," he said. "In six hours all the residents of level four will be on board."

I did a quick mental calculation. "The ships can fit over two thousand people?" I asked.

"They are designed for one thousand. They were intended to ferry people down to a planet's surface and not to live on." Bitterness laced his tone. "We have eight ships and your population is currently at 22,509 people."

This calculation was a bit harder. "You're going to put a little over twenty-eight hundred people on one ship?"

"You are fast. Seven ships will have 2,813 and the eight will have 2,809," he said.

I glanced at Bubba Boom. Did he catch that? Ponife had counted everyone. Bubba Boom wouldn't meet my gaze. Instead, he told Ponife he needed to speak with the doctor and went into the back.

"But that's too many." I tried.

"Not your concern. We are going to need you to do a

sweep of each level and in all the ducts as boarding progresses," he said. "No one is to be left behind."

They were trusting me with an important task. Too important. There had to be a catch. "What if I miss someone?"

"We plan to fumigate before we move in. Anyone still here will die from the poison. Try not to miss anyone. We do not wish to dispose of too many corpses."

Lovely. "Do you need me now?" I asked.

"We will start in two hours." He gestured to my clothes. I had changed from my climbing suit to my medical clothes. "Make sure you are ready and the doctor has a suitable assistant."

"Okay."

Bubba Boom returned and, without looking at me, followed Ponife from the infirmary. Curious, I searched for Lamont. She was in the surgery, organizing supplies.

"What did Bubba Boom want?" I asked.

"He asked a bunch of strange questions."

"Like what?"

"Questions I really couldn't answer. Like how much food and water would two thousand people need to survive. I told him to ask Riley's brother, Blake. He works in the kitchen and should know."

Blake! I had forgotten about him and Riley's dad. And if I thought harder, I could name a number of others who would support me. Unless they had been arrested? Too bad I couldn't go anywhere.

"Bubba Boom also asked for... Trella, you have that gleam in your eyes. What are you thinking?"

"How are your persuasive skills?"

I had two hours, but we had six until the first transport left. Lamont ran around Inside, recruiting the people I named.

They trickled in at first, Jacob, Blake, Emek, Rat and even Sloan came, although he didn't look happy to see me. Then Domotor rolled into the infirmary, followed by the remaining free members of the Force of Sheep—Takia Qadim and Hana Mineko. Breana Narelle had already been evacuated. Kadar and Ivie arrived along with Wera and Cain—Sloan's friends. And the last person to arrive was Captain James Trava.

They had come, but they sat or stood in little peer groups or alone as if they couldn't trust each other. That would be the first thing I'd fix.

"Stop it," I said to them. "Stop thinking about being a scrub or an upper. About being a Trava or an Ashon. We're all *Insiders*. And we've been boarded by hostile Outsiders who are going to take our world and kick us out unless we stop them."

I waited as their protests about not having weapons or access to the computer network dwindled.

"Doesn't matter," I said. "We'll work around it."

"How?" Sloan demanded.

"We have weapons. Blake, how many knives do you have in the kitchen?"

"Dozens," he said. "And we have meat cleavers and some nasty serrated blades."

"Can you gather them all and hide them in Quad A1?" I asked. It was a common area and would be the last level to be evacuated. His resemblance to Riley made it hard for me to look at him for too long.

"Hide them where?" he asked.

"The ducts should work. Can you do it now?"

"Sure," he said.

I then turned to the stink bombers. "Kadar and Ivie, how many bombs can you make?"

"Depends on how much time we have, and how big of a

blast you need," Ivie answered. Dirt stained her overalls and she had a smudge on her cheek. She was a pretty girl with long golden brown hair twisted into an oversized bun.

"I need distractions that won't injure people or damage equipment. Something like a stunner, but more widespread. You'll have about five hours," I said.

"One an hour."

"When you're done, bring them to Quad A1 and someone will tell you what to do with them."

"What are you planning?" she asked.

I wasn't sure, but it wouldn't be good for morale for me to confess this. "A coordinated attack from all sides."

"What about the air plant?" Domotor asked. "If we resist, the Outsiders will fill the air with poison."

"We can disconnect the poison gas canisters," James Trava said.

"What's he even doing here?" Domotor asked me. "The Travas are *cooperating* with the Outsiders."

James answered before I could. "I'm an *Insider.* I don't want them taking *our* ship. Some Travas are helping, but the rest are being loaded onto the transports with everyone else."

"Trella, you aren't going to trust him, are you?" Domotor asked.

Jacy and Riley had trusted him. That was good enough for me. "Do you know where the gas canisters are and how to disable them?" I asked the Captain.

"Yes, I do. But I'll need a few helpers."

Wera and Cain volunteered without hesitation. The three of them rushed off.

In order for us to be effective, we needed more Insiders. Many of them won't believe unless…unless they see it for themselves! "Domotor, can you put together a working computer that isn't tainted by the Outsiders?"

"If I had the right supplies," he said with a surly tone, still annoyed.

I turned to Emek and Rat. "Can you fetch for Domotor?"

"Yes," Emek said.

"Jacob, can you rig the electricity for the computer?"

"As long as there's juice nearby," he said.

"Where do you—Quad A1, right?" Domotor asked. He stroked his narrow chin with his long fingers.

"Yep. Call it our headquarters." Then I had another idea. "Any way to make the monitor bigger? So a lot of Insiders can see it at the same time?"

"We have a projector," Emek said.

"A projector?" I asked.

"It's old tech. It has a light and lenses." When he realized we didn't understand, he said, "Basically, it takes a small picture and makes it bigger. You can aim it at a wall."

"I'll take a look at it," Domotor said. "Couldn't hurt."

They left. Emek pushed Domotor's wheelchair, Rat wrote down supplies on a wipe board and Jacob added items.

Sloan, Takia, Hana and Lamont remained. They waited for their orders. I squelched a moment of doubt. This wasn't the time for second thoughts.

"Takia and Hana, I'm going to need you to be evacuated with the others."

The women were alarmed and unhappy until I explained why. "I'll have to find them first, so if you can hide in one of the rooms in Sector F4 that would be perfect."

They agreed and went to get into position.

I drew in a deep breath. Sloan and Lamont remained. Since I'd been collared, I needed an admiral to bring this whole attack together. Who to trust? My mother, who betrayed us during the last rebellion or the man who started the riot and slapped me?

Deciding I needed both, I addressed Sloan. "You're in charge of getting recruits. You'll need to bring them to Quad A1 and convince them about the Outsiders. Then you'll be needed to lead teams up to level five."

He laughed. "And then I'll grow a metal skin so I'm invincible. See? I can be ridiculous, too."

I stared at him until he frowned. "Why are you here, Sloan?"

"Guilt. I failed to protect Jacy and the Outsiders got him."

"Leading those teams will save him," I said.

"Are you sure?"

"Yes."

"I don't know how I'll be able to convince everyone about the Outsiders."

"If Domotor and Emek get the computer and projector working, *you* won't have to."

Sloan straightened his shoulders. "We'll need to coordinate. Do you have any microphones?"

"No. Mine busted ages ago."

He pulled out a couple sets from his tool belt. "For you and the Doc. I'll make sure the others get them as well."

I couldn't wear mine yet so I slid them into my pocket. "Thanks."

"If you manage this thing, I might change my opinion about you," Sloan said.

"Just when I thought there wasn't a reason to stop the Outsiders, you go and provide me one." For a moment I almost forgot the pain he'd caused me. For a moment.

He gave me a sly grin. "After that crack, I can't like you… ever."

"Fine with me. Then I won't feel guilty when I slap you later."

"If we survive to later, I'll give you a free shot."

"There it is! That's all the motivation I need."

After Sloan left, I discussed Lamont's job with her. "You have a legitimate reason to be on level five. You need to check on their health, see if others might be on the verge of having a seizure. Plus you need to discuss their fertility problems and see if it's widespread."

"And incapacitate as many Outsiders as possible when the attack starts?" she asked.

"Unless it goes against your doctor's creed?"

"I'll be a doctor up until that moment, then I'll change jobs for the duration."

Curious. "To which job?"

"A mother."

"Fighting Outsiders isn't in that job description."

She laughed. "It is when the child is you. No one hurts *my* little girl and gets away with it."

Bubba Boom and Ponife arrived right at hour twenty-six. I had just finished changing into my blue climbing suit, and adding a few special items to my tool belt.

Ponife gestured to the belt. "Why do you need that?"

"Since you destroyed the air plant, there are a number of air filters blocking the ducts. I need my tools to get through them. Unless you want me to climb down and bypass all of them. It would take up more time." I shrugged.

"No. Bubba Boom, make sure she does not have any weapons in there."

Damn. I unhooked my belt and gave it to him.

He inspected the various pockets. Handing it back to me, he said, "Looks good to me."

I hooked it around my waist, suppressing a relieved grin. He knew exactly what a few of my special gadgets did, yet he'd kept quiet. An excellent sign.

The Outsiders had the stairway blocked so no one could go to the upper level. I'd assumed they guarded the other stairs and the lift as well. I hoped Takia and Hana had found a way to bypass them.

As we climbed to level four and walked down the deserted corridors, I asked Ponife how they managed to convince everyone to leave.

"A trick," he said. "We asked them to come along on a… tour of the great Expanse. To see their world beyond the white metal walls. To go inside the vehicle to see the Outside."

"It's an effective trick." I tried to meet Bubba Boom's gaze. He ignored me.

"Fosord's idea. We also avoid them begging to bring personal belongings along. There is no space for frivolous things."

"Are food and water included as frivolous things?" I asked.

"No. But there won't be enough. However, our ancestors did not have enough either and they survived."

"How?"

"Survival was the reward for the bravest, the smartest and the strongest. All the others died quickly."

He avoided answering my question, but from his comment, I could guess it hadn't been pretty.

All the living quarters had been emptied by now. The Outsiders corralled those they found in Sector H4 and the few holdouts in the main Control Room. I started my sweep in Sector F4. Ponife and Bubba Boom stayed close, but couldn't be with me the entire time.

I spotted Takia and Hana in one of the apartments and the

tightness in my throat eased. Takia slouched on the couch while Hana paced. I caught a snippet of their conversation as I passed above them.

"...sure this is a good idea?" Hana asked.

"Doesn't matter," Takia said. "This is our *only* idea."

Hurrying to the room where they had kept Logan, I dropped from the vent and searched for those little Video Cameras. None in the living room. I glanced at the clock. Ponife would grow suspicious if I took too much time. I checked the washroom and the bedroom. Nothing.

My whole plan hinged on finding them. I never claimed it was a stellar plan. It was the best I could devise in two hours. These thoughts weren't helping. I stood in the center of the room and put myself in Logan's place. Where would he hide his most prized device? His most fragile device. His smallest creation.

I returned to the bedroom and picked up his pillow. Stripped of its case, it had been tossed into a corner. Examining the edges, I found new loose thread. I ripped the seam open and dug inside the pillow. Four video cameras were nestled in the stuffing.

I tucked them into my tool belt and raced to where Takia and Hana waited. They both jumped in surprise when I swung down between them. I gave two cameras to each woman.

"If you can, place two of these on the wall of the port without calling attention to yourself. Aim them at the transport ship." I showed them how to activate them. Holding my receiver to my ear and the microphone up to my mouth, I hailed Sloan and recited the frequencies to him.

"What about the other two?" Takia asked.

"Place them inside the ship at locations where we would see what it's like." Their confused expression didn't reassure me. I tried again. "Think of it this way. If you wanted to show an Outsider what's it like in here, you would place one of these in the dining room. It's crowded and noisy and busy there. Understand?"

"Yes," Hana said.

"Ready?" I asked them.

They shared a look and nodded. I escorted them from the room and found Ponife and Bubba Boom. Ponife clutched my X in a tight fist, but he relaxed as soon as he saw the women. He called for an escort and soon one of Hank's men arrived to take them up to the port.

As I searched the remaining rooms, I checked in with my team, receiving progress reports. Not too bad so far. Domotor's curt reply indicated Logan's computer expertise would be helpful. I told him to ask Sloan if he knew of anyone. Jacy had probably recruited an expert once Logan disappeared.

At one point Bubba Boom and I lagged behind Ponife. He touched my shoulder, stopping me as Ponife disappeared around a corner.

Leaning in close, he asked, "Is it a coincidence Hana and Takia had been missed by the Outsiders?"

I studied his expression. Trustworthy or not? Based on his actions this last week, I decided to trust him. "No."

"You have a plan?"

"Yes."

"It won't work," he said.

"Why not?"

"You don't know enough about them."

"Then tell me."

"There's too much." He jerked back as Ponife peered around the comer.

"What is problem?"

"I'm dizzy. The air is too thin up here," I said, placing my hand on the wall as if to steady myself.

"It will be thinner in the transport," Ponife said. "You will get used to it. Unless…"

"Unless I'm not brave? Or do I need to be smart and strong as well?"

"No. Unless we decide to keep you."

It felt as creepy as it sounded. "Keep me?"

"On this ship. We will need…" He glanced at Bubba Boom. "Workers."

"You mean like scrubs?" I asked.

"Yes."

"Why did you change your mind?"

Annoyed, he removed the X from a pocket. I had asked one question too many. Encouraged by my conversation with Bubba Boom, I rushed Ponife, hoping to surprise him.

I grabbed his wrist just as he twisted the X. The pain rolled through me. I clung to his hand for a moment longer, before dropping to the floor. Even with the deafening sound of my heart slamming in my chest, I heard Bubba Boom's boots as he ran past me.

"You're enjoying this. You're a sick bastard, Ponife," Bubba Boom said.

A thud followed a yelp. The pain stopped. Once I recovered, I glanced up. Ponife sprawled on the floor next to me. Bubba Boom crouched over him. He had my X.

We locked gazes. For a second, I thought he'd keep it, but he handed it to me.

"How do I—?"

"I'll show you later. Put it in a safe place for now," he said.

I tucked it into my tool belt. "Thanks. How did you knock him out?"

He showed me the used syringe. "The doctor was very

helpful with finding a way to free you. I just needed to find the proper motivation. It was a difficult decision."

"Why did you help me?"

"When I saw how you and Doctor Lamont tried so hard to save their people and treated them not as an enemy, but as a person in need, I knew you were right. They'd planned to send *all* of us out to die."

"Now what?"

"You're the boss. You tell me."

"Can we rescue Logan, Anne-Jade, Jacy and Riley?"

He flinched a bit when I said Riley's name. "Not Jacy. He's been collared and Fosord holds his key. Anne-Jade isn't in the brig. She's been helping us…them. It'll be dangerous to free the other two. Why do you need them?"

"Logan for his computer expertise and Riley for his knife fighting skills."

"Knives, huh?"

"All we have besides a few noise makers. Should we look for something else?"

"No, they might work."

"Might isn't a reassuring word."

"A sharp blade can cut the hoses on the Controllers' air masks, making it hard for them to breathe. That is, if you can get close enough. So might is the best I can do."

According to Bubba Boom, Lamont had filled the syringe with one of her narcotics. I estimated Ponife would sleep for another three hours.

Bubba Boom "escorted" me to my cell on level five. The main entrance to the brig was now guarded by two armed men. He joked with the guards, but when the guy on the left turned to open the gate, Bubba Boom moved.

Punching the man on the right, he then took the guard's stun gun and shot them both.

"So much for being subtle," I said as he unlocked the gate.

"No turning back now." Bubba Boom dragged them one at a time to an empty cell and locked them inside.

We released Logan first. He rushed out and hugged me. "If I live through this, I'm having a spacious suite built just for me. I never want to be locked in a small room again!"

Riley stayed calmer than Logan. He kept his guard up as he eyed Bubba Boom. The gash over his left eye and temple had scabbed over, but black and blue bruises colored the left side of his face. His shirt was torn and bloody. I wanted to make sure he had no other injuries, but settled for a quick hug instead.

"Are you sure we can trust him?" he asked me.

"Yes."

He relaxed a bit. "Then let's go."

I stayed next to Bubba Boom and Riley. Logan followed us as we headed to the exit.

Unfortunately, Hank had beat us there.

At first Hank was confused as to why no one guarded the gate. And why Bubba Boom had three prisoners with him. Bubba Boom didn't say a word, just waited for Hank to catch up.

When Hank put it all together, I feared for Bubba Boom's life. Murderous rage filled Hank's face as he drew his weapon—a kill-zapper.

He stepped close to Bubba Boom and said with a voice of steel, "You're a traitor. You're no son of mine."

Hank shoved the nozzle of his weapon toward Bubba Boom's chest. I yelled and squeezed between the kill-zapper and Bubba Boom. Pushing Bubba Boom back with my hips, I leaned forward as Hank pulled the trigger.

21

THE KILL-ZAPPER'S NOZZLE BURNED MY SKIN AS CUR-
rent slammed into me. My muscles twitched with the pulses
of power, but the pain seemed minor in comparison to the
collar's. I remained standing as Riley and Bubba Boom ran
past me. They tackled Hank and wrestled the kill-zapper
from his hands.

By the time Bubba Boom stunned Hank, the tremors in
my arms and legs had ceased. Riley scooped me up in his
arms intent on rushing me to Lamont.

I wriggled from his grasp. "I'm fine."

But Riley wouldn't let go of my arms. He stared at me a
bit wild-eyed. "The kill-zapper made contact. Your shirt is
burnt."

Glancing down, I saw the scorched fabric. I pulled the
material away. My skin underneath the black mark was red
and blistering.

"My heart's beating. Besides the burn, I don't feel any
pain," I said.

"Maybe it didn't have enough time to do any damage,"
Logan said.

Bubba Boom shook his head. "It has a very high amperage so it only takes a fraction of a second. The command collar saved you. It has a surge protector so an EMP can't damage it. Ironic, isn't it."

"You're still wearing it?" Riley asked.

"Don't worry." I showed him the metal X. "It'll soon be gone. Although..." I touched its smooth surface. "Maybe I'll wait until *after* we've taken back our ship."

"It might neutralize the stunner's blast as well," Bubba Boom said. He dragged Hank to an empty cell and then he relocked the gate to the brig.

"How do we get down to level one?" I asked Bubba Boom.

"The lift. It isn't guarded on this level, just the other four," he said.

"And what happens when the doors open on level one?" Riley asked.

Bubba Boom handed Riley one of the stunners he had taken from the guards. He offered the other to Logan.

"No thanks," Logan said. "That's not my thing."

As we descended to Quad A1, I asked Bubba Boom about Hank's comment.

"Yeah, he's my father," he said. "Hank kept track of his four children and made sure we were all assigned as maintenance scrubs. I didn't know until all this started." He met my gaze. Sadness filled his eyes. "I also learned Cogon was my half-brother. Cog believed in the Controllers, but he wouldn't have believed their lies for as long as I have."

"By helping us, you've made up for your mistakes," I said, hoping that when all was said and done, I could say the same thing.

The guards outside the lift on level one had already been incapacitated. Quad A1 teamed with people. Groups of them sat together. Wary, suspicious, angry and uncertain, they glanced at the buzz of activity around Domotor. Murmurings of resentment increased as they noticed my arrival.

Riley went to search for his father and brother, and Logan sprinted toward Domotor. He understood what they had been trying to do in an instant and immediately took charge.

"How long?" I asked.

"Give me a few minutes to sort this out, and then I'll give you an estimate," Logan said.

Sloan sidled over to me. "Where's Jacy?"

"I'm sorry we couldn't rescue him. He has…" How to explain? Not many people knew about the command collars. "A tracer on him that we can't remove without hurting him."

He scowled and jabbed a finger at Bubba Boom. "But you could bring *him* along?"

"Without him, I wouldn't have been able to free Logan and Riley."

"How do you know they don't have tracers?" Sloan asked.

"Only a few have them," Bubba Boom answered.

"And you trust him?" Sloan asked me.

"With her life," Bubba Boom said, pointing to the burned patch on my shirt. He turned to me with a puzzled expression. "Why did you? You didn't know the kill-zapper wouldn't work."

"You saved me from the fire. Consider us even," I said.

"No. You didn't hesitate. There was no moment of consideration."

He was right. "As I told my mother a while ago, it's what I do," I said.

Sloan snapped his fingers. "Almost forgot. The Doc's been trying to reach you."

When I pulled out my receiver and microphone, I laughed even though it sounded a bit like hysteria. Blackened and half-melted, the devices would never work again.

"What happened to them?" Sloan asked, marveling over the ruined pieces.

"Kill-zapped. Do you have more?"

Sloan stared at me a moment. "Not if you keep frying them." But he dug into one of his pockets and handed me two more sets. "One for Riley."

Inserting the receiver into my earlobe, I clipped the mic on, hailing my mother. The relief in her voice came through, but she remained professional, reporting that she was in position and would await our signal.

Logan estimated he would have the computer working in fifteen minutes. It was week 147,027, hour twenty-eight. Time for my speech.

I stood on a table as Sloan used a loud and high-pitched whistle to get everyone's attention. Quiet descended and they focused on me with various expressions—all unhappy. I sought the little group of smiling faces and took courage from Riley and his family.

"Thank you for being willing to listen to me. Scrubs and uppers coming together is vital now. But I first want to apologize for turning your lives upside down and then abandoning you. For letting a Committee make important decisions without your input. For dismissing your beliefs in the Controllers and life Outside.

"But these people who have entered our world are *not* the Controllers. They're Outsiders and they plan to exile us. Send us into Outer Space to die."

Voices rose, yelling I was crazy or deluded. Others reminded everyone I had gotten them all into this mess. Sloan used his whistle to settle them down again.

"I understand why you won't believe me." I glanced at Logan; he gave me a thumbs up. "Even if you can't trust me, at least you can trust your own eyes."

The lights dimmed and a large bright rectangle lit up the north wall. Images appeared. First of the transport ship clinging to our world, then of the port. Outsiders hustled people into the belly of the transports and then the scene switched to inside the ships. Every image was crammed with people. Scared and frightened people.

The buzz rose again, but it had a more muted, uncertain sound.

"These are live images of what the Outsiders are doing," I said. "They pretended to be the Controllers so they could get into our ship. They're people from our world who had been exiled for crimes against us, and are now planning to exile all of us Insiders."

Sloan joined me on the table. "She's right," he said over the din. "We're trying to stop them, but we need your help. Trella freed us from the Pop Cops. She can free us from the Outsiders."

A man stood up and asked, "How can we trust her? The Committee and Mop Cops were just as bad as the Travas and Pop Cops."

"This time I promise not to let a Committee make the decisions. *You...*" I swept an arm out. "*You* are going to make them." I waited until the ruckus died down. "You will vote for your leaders."

Then the image on the screen showed two Outsiders dragging Anne-Jade toward the transport vehicle. She fought and broke free for a second before the Outsider on the right tackled her to the ground. I glanced at Logan. He stared at the screen with his mouth gaping open in horror.

I turned back in time to see the other Outsider twisting a metal X.

"NO!" Logan screamed.

Everyone watching gasped as Anne-Jade bucked and shook in obvious agony. The Outsider kept zapping her over and over until she lay still. Her lifeless gaze stared at nothing.

Logan screamed again and bolted for the door. Sloan and Bubba Boom chased him down. Chaos erupted as fear and outrage rolled through the assembled. Numb with shock and horror, I couldn't move. Anne-Jade was my friend.

A third Outsider came into view. It was Fosord. He pointed at Anne-Jade's body and then pointed directly at the camera. Instant silence followed his gesture.

Fosord reached to the side. When his hands reappeared, he held a wipe board. Three words had been written on the board: *Surrender or die.*

My grief for Anne-Jade would have to wait until later. I shoved it deep down and took advantage of the stunned silence. "They're scared of us," I said. "We need to act *now* before they do."

"Before they can poison our air?" one man called.

"Before we die of thirst?" a woman asked.

"No to both. We have a team at the air plant. And we'll either win or lose by the time water becomes an issue." I conferred with Sloan.

"I'll need two groups of twenty each to secure the stairways," he said. "I'll lead one team."

"And I'll lead the other," Riley called.

I wanted to say no, but as I told Bubba Boom, Riley knew how to fight. The teams formed quickly and I took heart from the eager helpers.

Sloan, Riley and Bubba Boom grouped together and I joined them.

"...suits then the stunners won't work unless they have their helmets off. In that case, aim for their heads," Bubba Boom said.

"Once we have the stairways, we can send bigger teams to advance up through the levels, securing each," Sloan said.

"How big?" I asked.

Sloan looked at Bubba Boom.

"Hank has at least two hundred maintenance people, plus four dozen Travas and five hundred Outsiders. Watch out for the armed Outsiders. They have this weapon that looks like a black metal tube, but it spits out round disks with razor sharp edges. It'll slice through skin and bone," Bubba Boom said.

"What do we do if we encounter armed Insiders working for the Outsiders?" Riley asked.

"Incapacitate, but don't harm," I said, handing him the communication set from Sloan.

"How?" Riley asked. "We only have two stunners and a handful of knives."

"We need more weapons," Sloan said.

I spotted Ivie and Kadar hovering by the door and gestured for them to join us.

Kadar carried a laundry sack. He handed it to me. "Five stun bombs. Yank the pin out and roll it toward your target. You'll have about four seconds before it goes off. It should affect anyone within a six-meter radius from the bomb."

"They'll help, but still not enough," Sloan said.

"We'll make more as long as we can," Ivie said.

"Thanks," I said. In the meantime, we still needed weapons. I asked Bubba Boom if the ISF's weapons were still locked in the safe.

"Hank removed a bunch for his men and the Outsiders,

but the last time I saw there were a few left. But he changed the code for the lock."

I glanced at Logan. He huddled on the floor next to Domotor. Kneeling next to him, I hugged him close for a moment. Then I explained my need.

"Can you help?" I asked him.

He wiped his eyes. "On one condition."

I waited.

"That I get to kill-zap Fosord."

"I thought that wasn't your thing," I said.

"It is now."

"No. We're not killers. Anne-Jade wouldn't approve and you know it. You can stun him, how's that?"

"Can I at least kick him a couple times?" Logan sounded like a petulant child.

"Yes."

"All right. I'm in." He went in search of a few supplies, calling to Emek and Rat to fetch items.

The Captain's voice startled me. He called through the receiver. Sloan cupped his ear.

"...have us pinned down," Captain Trava said. "We disconnected the gas, but we won't last long."

"Hold on. We're on our way," Sloan said.

"Go up the Quad I stairs. Don't worry about securing the stairwell. Take two bombs, both stunners and go help the Captain," I said, digging into the laundry bag. The bombs had been built inside clear glass balls. A metal pin had been stuck through a small hole.

I gave two to Sloan and one to Riley. They both looked surprised.

"If we don't have the air plant, we're done," I explained. "I'll take Logan, two bombs and we'll retrieve the weapons from the safe."

"How are you going to bring all of them down here?" Riley asked.

I thought fast. "Laundry chute. Make sure you have bins half full of towels to cushion their fall waiting below. And put together another team plus the follow-up teams. Once you have weapons, go up and secure all the levels. We'll all meet in level five at Hank's control room."

"Yes, sir." Riley snapped a salute.

Sloan laughed then rushed off with his team to help the Captain. I helped Riley organize his team as I waited for Logan.

When Logan returned he had a small cleaning troll tucked under his arm.

"Zippy?" I asked, hoping somehow he found his way home.

"No. Still on level five," Logan said. "This is his…younger brother, Zippy Too."

Bubba Boom boosted Logan into the air duct, but before I climbed in after him, I grabbed Riley's hand. "Be careful."

"Shouldn't I be telling you that?" He pointed to the burn mark on my chest. Riley slid his hands around my back, pulling me close. "Since you tried and failed to electrocute yourself, does this mean you're done jumping in harm's way?"

"I doubt it. In fact, I need to give you…" I dug in my tool belt.

"Your heart?"

"Pretty close." I handed him the metal X. "Keep it safe for me."

"A dangerous move. I could use this to keep you out of trouble."

"But you won't."

"Why not?"

"Because you're one of the good guys. You'll do what it takes to neutralize the Outsiders even if that endangers me."

He grumbled. "Great. Go me."

"There are perks to being a good guy," I said, smiling.

"Ohhh…do tell?"

"Well, after all is said and done, the good guy gets the girl."

"And then what happens?"

"Whatever he desires," I whispered in his ear.

He jerked back in utter surprise.

After I had scrambled into the duct, Riley shouted to me, "Promise?"

I poked my head out. "Yes." No need to add, "if we were both alive."

Climbing up to level four through the air ducts would be difficult so I led Logan to the near-invisible hatch on level one and entered the Gap between levels. One thing Hank had time to repair was the ladder attached to the Wall. It now spanned the entire four levels. I just hoped Hank forgot about it. Getting to the ladder remained tricky. I balanced on the thin I-beam that attached the level to the Wall. Without looking down, I crossed to the ladder.

Logan opted to crawl over and I worried he would fall. He reached it, but not without cursing. We climbed to level four and entered the air shafts. Quad A4 appeared to be deserted, but I wasn't going to trust my eyes.

Removing the vent without making a sound, I poked Zippy Too into the room. A red light glowed on his head.

"Motion sensors," Logan whispered.

I flipped the white switch on the troll's body and the light turned green. Lowering him to the ground, I followed. Then Logan climbed from the shaft. He headed toward the safe and removed a small device from his pocket. While he opened the heavy safe, I reprogrammed the lock on the main door.

So far so good. One problem remained—bypassing the weight sensor on the floor of the safe. Logan worked on the sensor and I counted at least thirty stunners and six kill-zappers inside.

"It's off," he said.

"Get back into the duct, I'll hand you weapons. There's a laundry chute about two meters east," I said.

He grumbled about all the climbing, but he scaled the wall like a pro. I handed him two at a time, waited while Logan dropped them down the chute and returned for two more.

Working together, we managed to empty the safe. We also managed to alert the Outsiders. The door's lock beeped. I glanced at the clock. It had taken us two hours to complete our task.

"Go," I said to Logan. "Get back to level one."

"How?"

"Laundry chute. Wait thirty seconds after you send the last weapons. I'll let them know you're coming." I closed the vent and signaled Riley.

More beeps emanated from the door, then pounding and, finally the buzz of a cutter.

"And when can we expect you?" Riley asked.

"I'll meet you on level five."

"You better," he grumped.

I removed the vent from the heating duct as the door flew open. By the time five people rushed into the room aiming their weapons at me, I had the stun bomb in hand. I recognized Phelen, one of Hank's supervisors.

"Don't move," Phelen said.

Counting on my collar's protection, I yanked the pin on Ivie and Kadar's stun bomb and rolled it toward the group. They all glanced down, but nothing happened. A dud. Damn.

"Made you look," I said.

"Ha. Ha." Phelen deadpanned. He gestured to the door with his stunner. "Let's—"

A bright flash cut him off. I dove for the heating vent as a wave of energy exploded from the bomb. The glass shards pelted the walls as the men grunted. When quiet returned, I peeked out from the duct. Lying on the floor, Phelen and his team remained motionless. A few sported cuts from the glass.

I checked to make sure the gashes weren't too deep and they all had strong pulses. Then I removed all their weapons and anything else that looked interesting, like Phelen's communication device.

Back in the air shaft, I signaled Riley, warning him of incoming and sent my loot down to the laundry room. I kept one stunner. "Any damage?" I asked him.

"One really annoyed Tech No, but otherwise all came through fine. How many did you neutralize?"

"Only five."

"Better than getting caught. What are you planning now?"

Good question. "I'll spy around level five. See what we're up against."

"Be careful. We're starting our ascent. Bubba Boom is leading the Quad I team, and I have the Quad A stairs."

I ghosted through the air shafts on level five for the next hour. No one guarded the brig. It was my first clue of something strange. Groups of Hank's supporters raced through the hallways, but I didn't see any Outsiders. And Lamont failed to answer my hail.

Sloan reported success in the air plant.

Riley and Bubba Boom encountered only a token resistance as they secured each level.

The fight to reach Hank's control room in Quad A5 lasted a mere five minutes. We met up outside the double doors. They opened without trouble.

The control room appeared the same. Banks of computers. Half completed consoles leaking wires. And Hank, sitting in the big captain's chair in the center. He was alone.

22

"RIGHT ON TIME," HANK SAID.

"For what?" I asked.

"Nothing. Absolutely nothing. All thanks to you," he said.

Riley and Bubba Boom flanked Hank, but he was unarmed. All his supporters had been stunned, but a threat still hung in the air.

"Okay, I'll bite. What are you talking about?" I asked.

"The Controllers have made some changes to their plans. They've acknowledged their growing sterility so they're going to keep that transport full of people alive to breed with. That's the good news."

"And the bad?"

"They're going to clean house." Hank swept his arm out, indicating all the people standing in the control room. "They're going to kill us all."

"How?" Riley asked. "We have the air plant."

"They're going to hide in those transport ships and turn the power plant off," Hank said.

No power meant no electricity, no heat and no pumps to

move the air around. It would be a slow death. So much for not wanting to dispose of corpses.

"How?" I gestured to the computers. "They don't have control of the network."

"They don't need all this for control," Hank said. "There's an antenna on the Outside. That's what they used to hijack our network." He explained how the Outsiders could communicate with the network without wires.

"Maybe Logan can bypass the power plant controls," I said. I signaled and asked him to join us.

"Logan's one sharp fellow," Hank said. "The Controllers are well aware of his knowledge and don't plan to wait for us to save ourselves."

"Why are you telling us all this?" I asked.

"I'm in the same position you're in. Since I couldn't handle one small problem," he glared at me, "I was left behind. Ponife couldn't handle you either, but that didn't seem to matter to him." He continued to stare at me. "You know, Karla was right. I should have kill-zapped you long ago. Before Ponife put that damn collar on you." Hank mimed shooting me with his finger and thumb.

"Where is Karla?"

"Up with the Controllers. Along with your mother and Jacy."

Worry mixed with relief. Lamont would be safe with the Outsiders. They would need her expertise if they planned to repopulate.

"What did you mean by the Controllers don't plan for us to save ourselves?" Riley asked.

"They're not playing around this time. They're going to open up Gateway and all our air will blow out into Outer Space. I'm guessing it'll take us four to six minutes to die of asphyxiation."

"You don't seem upset," I said.

"Well...when your saviors turn out to be thugs from the past and you've been nothing but a fool, endangering the entire population of Inside, then dying seems insignificant in comparison."

I understood the feeling.

"How do we stop them?" Riley asked.

"You can't. Not in time," Hank said. "They're already up in the port."

"And even if the lift is working, we could only get a few people up there at a time. Easy pickings." I considered. "What about their transport? Is it still attached to Gateway?"

"No. They flew it up to the port," Hank said. "All they left is a couple of their space suits and a bunch of empty gas cylinders."

"Space suits? Can you survive in Outer Space wearing one?" I asked.

"Yes, but that would only save four or five people and not for long. As you said, easy pickings," Hank said.

He was right. Except I hadn't been thinking along those lines. "Can you install a sheet of metal over Gateway?"

"It'll still leak air," Hank said.

"But it'll give us some more time." I glanced at the people who had volunteered to fight. Not many had the arm strength to climb up the Expanse. "And I have an idea. I'll need those suits, a few volunteers, safety harnesses and some magnets. Can you help us, Hank?"

His considered for a moment, keeping his gaze locked on mine. "Ponife underestimated you. Hell, we all underestimated you. Yes, I'll help."

Riley, Sloan and Bubba Boom all volunteered right away. By the time Hank had collected the other supplies we needed, Logan had joined us.

"Logan, do you remember seeing the symbols about the port?" I asked.

"Sure. I read a bunch of them when I was up there. Until the Outsiders came for me."

I explained my plan to him. "Will it work?"

"It should, but I'd better come along to make sure," Logan said.

"It's suicide," Riley said.

"Do you have any better ideas?" I asked.

"No."

"Then let's move."

Hank shouted orders and we dressed in the Outsiders' suits. Captain Trava rushed up from the air plant with the gas cylinders now full of our air. We hurried to Gateway before the Outsiders could open it. The code to open it hadn't changed from when Cog and I had used it—our first lucky break.

The outer door swung open. Squeezing into the inner room, which wasn't designed for five people in space suits, I gave the signal. Hank and his crew closed the door and would seal it with a sheet of metal. Once he finished with that, he had another job to do.

As the room emptied of air, I explained to the others what to expect and not to panic, trying not to let my own fear taint my voice. Of all my adventures, this was the scariest so far. To keep from floating away, we were all harnessed to magnets which clung to the side wall.

I felt light as the door to Outer Space swung open. My stomach rolled as if I fell from a great height. Various exclamations and curses reached me through my receiver.

Funny thing about Outer Space, I couldn't hear the door as it opened but I could hear Logan's voice inside my helmet. He thought he was going to get sick.

"If you puke, try not to cover the glass on your helmet," was Sloan's advice to him.

The magnets keeping us attached could be turned off by squeezing the handle. I released one magnet and moved it, then the other, working my way to Outside.

The nothingness didn't seem so empty this time. Pricks of light dotted the blackness. I ignored the beauty behind me and climbed slowly up the side of Inside. The others followed.

"Don't let go," I said again. "One magnet on the metal at all times."

"Yes, mother," Logan said.

The climb was easy because we were weightless, but difficult due to our cumbersome suits and magnets. I marveled over the audacity of this attempt, at what—or rather, where—we were. On the outside of Inside. In Outer Space. It was humbling, thrilling and terrifying at the same time.

When we finally reached the top of Inside, we all took a moment to drink in the amazing sight of Outer Space and to catch our breaths.

"Okay, Logan. Do your thing," I said.

While Logan hunted for the antenna and the override controls, I signaled Lamont. "If you can, it's time to start acting like my mother."

The plan was to disable the antenna and then access the override controls for the port's big bay doors. Once it was activated, the air would empty in the main hangar. From the Video Cameras, we knew the transport full of Insiders remained in the side bay with a dozen Outsiders guarding it.

We hoped the transport of Outsiders was in the hangar. By opening the hangar doors, the bay doors would seal shut, protecting our ship and trapping the rest of the Outsiders in their ship.

Lots of hopes and speculations, but anything was better than waiting around to die.

"It's a go," Logan said.

The doors widened. Our second lucky break—the transport was in the hangar. Figures moved behind that strange black metal, which Hank had called metalastic, a combination of metal and something named Plastic, making the vehicle lighter than if it had been made entirely of metal, but just as strong. It also let in the radiation Lamont had talked about, which was why it was only supposed to be used as a temporary transport.

We climbed down into the hangar before the doors closed. Since we had a limited amount of air in our tanks, we couldn't keep the hangar doors open. Bubba Boom unhooked his welding gun from his tool belt. Air began filling the hangar. It would take some time before we could remove our helmets.

As Bubba Boom headed toward the transport ship's access hatch, the Outsiders figured out what we planned to do—melt the metalastic so they couldn't open the hatch and escape their ship.

A long thin tube on the underside of the ship swiveled and pointed at Bubba Boom. I yelled for him to duck as the tube spat out bright disks. Our luck had run out.

"Get in close," Riley yelled.

Everyone scrambled to get underneath the ship, hoping the gun had a limited turning radius. Bubba Boom remained flat on the ground. Two more guns spun as if searching for targets. Sloan pulled a wrench from his belt and attacked the one gun. Riley grabbed the other, hanging from it with both hands. And I shoved the handle of a screwdriver into the opening of the last one.

Riley's gun jerked back and forth, shaking him like a toy. Mine belched. The screwdriver shot out and dented the far wall. Only Sloan had success.

"Take out the rest," I called to Sloan as Riley flew off his. "Before they..."

Too late. The hatch opened. Cold horror froze the sweat on my skin as one then four then seven suited and armed Outsiders poured from the ship. I checked the air pressure gauge that hung on my belt. There still wasn't enough air for us to shed the space suits. It would have given us a small advantage.

I pulled my knife. The others followed my example except Bubba Boom. He hadn't moved, but I didn't have time to worry about him right now.

The Outsiders fanned out, trying to surround us. They held those long tubes Bubba Boom had warned us about.

"Get behind something," Riley called.

I ducked behind one of the transport's legs, feeling too big for the first time in my life. Sloan finished bashing the last gun, but it was four against twelve.

"Trella, I admire your tenacity," Ponife said. His voice echoed from a speaker inside the collar of the helmet. "However, it is time to stop. Surrender and I will allow your cohorts to join the other survivors."

"No," Riley said.

"It would be unwise to trust them," Logan said.

"Thanks for the advice, Logan. Tell me something I didn't know," I snapped. Putting my knife on the floor, I glanced around, searching for a way to escape. "This *stinks,* but I don't think we have a choice. Too bad we didn't get to the hatch in *time.*"

I walked to the hatch and almost laughed when six Outsiders followed me. Tenacious I may be, and stubborn and maybe even a bit reckless, but I never would consider myself dangerous enough to need six escorts.

We entered the ship. The room was similar to Gateway with another door and a control panel. As the hatch closed behind us, I hoped Riley and the others had gotten my hint. One of the Outsiders punched a few buttons. I repeated the sequence aloud.

Ponife chuckled drily. "Your friends are in custody. No one is left to help you."

This was the second time he had claimed I was alone and helpless. It didn't go as he had expected the first time; you'd think he'd learn by now. Or I would. Fear still pulsed through my body.

After a hissing noise vibrated through my suit, the other door opened and we were in an area that resembled a changing room, with empty suits hanging on hooks and shelves full of helmets and gloves.

"Keep your helmet on," Ponife ordered. "We have no plans to kill you."

"I feel so *much* better," I said.

They removed their helmets.

Ponife had perfected his superior expression. "You should be happy. Your mother and friends will all be members of our new combined community."

"Is she here?" I asked.

"No. She is with the others. Only you will stay with us until our world below is…cleaned."

"Cleaned? Why don't you call it what it is? It's genocide."

"Because that would be technically inaccurate."

"That shouldn't bother you since you've gotten a bunch of stuff wrong already."

"Trivial issues, causing only minor delays."

"I'm glad you can put a positive spin on what I'd call stupid mistakes."

Ponife took the bait. "For example…?"

"You assumed that knife was my only weapon." I pulled the last bomb from my pocket and yanked the pin out.

Rolling it along the floor, I dodged a few Outsiders until one aimed his gun at me and pulled the trigger. One disk clipped my right shoulder, slicing through the suit, my skin and muscles. Fire burned as I lost the use of my right arm in an instant. The air inside my suit leaked through the rip with a high-pitched whistle.

When nothing more happened—damn, a real dud this time—Ponife asked, "Is that it? Do you have anything else?" He yanked me to my feet and took off my tool belt. He strode to one of the cabinets and rummaged. Returning, he slapped a white patch over the hole in my suit.

Pain from the slap mixed with amazement. "Why did you save me?" I asked him.

"I told you before—"

"No plans to kill me. But you said 'we' and he…" I pointed with my left hand to the one who still clutched his gun. "He didn't hesitate. Are you sure *your* plans match the others'? Because that particular idea is another mistake." I wasn't being suicidal, really. My will to live throbbed in my heart; I was just hoping to sow a little dissension among the Outsiders.

They glanced at each other until Ponife growled at them to stop. Then an ear-aching alarm sounded. Surprised, their focus shifted to the hatch. I was the only person to see the glass ball flash.

Once again, I flattened my body to the floor. Glass shards pelted my right side as a wave of energy rolled me over to my back. I stared at the ceiling, silently thanking Ivie and Kadar.

"Trella, quit napping while we do all the work." Logan's voice filled my helmet.

Riley's face blocked my view. "Are you hurt?" he asked.

"Nothing Lamont can't fix," I said, groaning as I ambled to my feet. Ponife and the other Outsiders had been stunned by the bomb. "How did you two get in here?"

Logan gestured to Riley. "His knife. Sloan's wrench. Bubba Boom's surprise recovery. And my genius." Then he muttered, "And your help with the code."

"Can you repeat that last part?" I asked.

"Later," Riley said. "We need to leave before the rest of the Outsiders come to investigate."

We made it through the hatch. Bubba Boom waited nearby with his blow torch. His face was peppered with cuts and a cracked helmet rested by his feet.

"Disk deflected off my helmet," Bubba Boom explained. "I passed out from lack of oxygen. I woke when there was enough air, but decided to stay down until the odds looked a little better."

As Bubba Boom sealed the hatch, we removed our suits. Riley helped me with mine.

He inspected the cut on my shoulder. "I see bone. Do you know where your mother is?"

"On the other ship."

We all glanced at the bay door. Two possibilities waited on the other side. One—Outsiders controlled the ship. Two—Hank and his people had managed to free our Insiders.

Logan examined the panel next to the door. "When should I open it?"

Riley handed me a gun he had taken from the fallen Outsiders and then armed himself with two. I held the unfamiliar weapon in my left hand. Sloan also held one and his wrench rested on his shoulder. Bubba Boom finished sealing the hatch and joined us. Riley gave him one of his guns, then pulled his knife from his belt.

"On three," Riley said. "One."

Logan pressed a few keys.

"Two," Sloan said.

More beeps followed. Logan's hand hovered above the glowing red button.

"Two and a half," Bubba Boom said.

A nervous chuckle rolled through us.

"Three," I said.

23

LOGAN PUNCHED THE BUTTON. THE DOOR SLID OPEN.
Chaos greeted us. We clutched our weapons and peered into
the crowd of screaming people. I searched for Outsiders, but
only Insiders poured from the hatch of the ship.

My brain finally sorted through the overwhelming scene.
The screams were happy cries and the Insiders were hugging
and celebrating. I spotted Hank leaning against a far wall. We
crossed to him, dodging a few overly excited people.

"Looks like my idea to widen the lift worked," I said to
him.

"Your idea was crap, Trella," he said. "I could only send
up a few people at a time."

"How did you take out the guards?"

"I didn't." He gestured to the Insiders. "They did it before
we reached them."

"How?"

Riley clapped me on my good shoulder. "You taught them
how to stand up for themselves."

"I don't think so," Hank said. He poked a finger toward
one woman, standing off to the side by herself. "Rumor has

it the Doctor knocked out all the Outsiders inside the ship, then rallied and organized everyone else to attack the guards in the bay. The Outsiders didn't stand a chance." He glared at me, but it didn't reach his eyes. "Now I know who *you* inherited your pain in the assness from."

I smiled. "I'll take that as a compliment."

Riley and Logan accompanied me as I went to congratulate my mother. Sloan went searching for Jacy and Bubba Boom stayed with Hank.

My mother's eyes lit up when she spotted us. She wrapped her arms around me, but pulled back when I hissed in pain. Then there was no talking to her as she transformed into doctor mode, tsking over the deep cut and insisting on getting me to the infirmary without delay.

Wishing to remain and find out more details, I grumped at her. "I'd rather have you mother me."

"Then you're in luck since I can do both. Get moving or I'll make you stay in the infirmary long after you're recovered."

"Yes, Mother."

The cleanup took longer this time than when the Force of Sheep had won. Even though the Insiders had all rallied against the Outsiders, resentment still lingered between them. A few of us—me, Hank, Emek, Jacy and Domotor—sat together and decided how to proceed. Yes, we included Hank. He always wanted the best for Inside and he had good insights into what changes the people craved after the Pop Cops were gone.

We kept the family names and soon everyone Inside had a family. Then we asked everyone to sign up for a job. Except this time, there wouldn't be scrubs cleaning and uppers working the controls. If a person wished to work in the air plant, he would learn *every* aspect of the plant and his job would rotate from computer controller to changing filters to hauling cleaning trolls around from shaft to shaft then back to being a controller.

For the jobs no one wanted—like cleaning out the waste pipes—every single person of Inside would take a four-hour shift, which, when you considered we had a population of 22,500 and some, that meant I would have to do my four hours every nine hundred weeks. Doable.

Levels five to ten would be completed first and then everyone would be able to move out of the barracks at the same time.

As for the Outsiders, they would be invited to join us, to choose jobs and vote. For those who declined our offer, they would be given a room in the brig. We realized the danger in letting someone like Ponife have freedom in our world, but agreed not to limit or incarcerate someone with a difference in opinion. Actions and not words would land an Insider in trouble. Jacy volunteered to head the ISF for now.

Soon after I had recovered, I joined Logan, Riley, Bubba Boom, Hank and a handful of others in saying goodbye to Anne-Jade. We lined the hallway up to Chomper's lair and paid tribute to a hero. Logan wished for her to be recycled and not sent out into Outer Space.

"She will always be with us," he said.

By week 147,033, we had completed the work schedule for everyone and repaired all the damage to the machinery and computer. At hour zero of week 147,034 we held elections for Admiral, Vice Admiral, Captain and for the Commander of the ISF. Logan had rigged Video Cameras with sound so every Insider could hear the candidates' plans for our future. I had campaigned for either one of the Admiral positions.

The other Admiral candidates were Domotor, Riley's father Jacob, Emek and Takia. Logan, James Trava and Bubba Boom ran for the Captain's position. Jacy and Sloan campaigned for Commander.

Riley brought the early election results to me at hour twenty. They would be announced to everyone at hour twenty-five. I was helping Lamont in the infirmary, but he wanted to tell me them in private. We retreated to my room and he closed the door.

He sat on the edge of my bed with me. Impish delight lit his blue eyes. "Remember your promise?"

I pretended to be confused. "Which one? I just promised everyone to keep our world safe and sane. Did they vote for me?"

"I'll tell you *after* you keep your promise to me."

"Well…" I tapped my lips with a finger as if I considered his words. "I could just wait five hours—"

He cut me off with a deep passionate kiss.

When he broke it off, I said, "Waiting really isn't my thing." And I drew him close for another kiss.

Before we could go any further, Riley pulled away. "I have something for you." He stood on the bed and opened the air vent. Reaching in, he grunted and pulled out a small cleaning troll.

"Zippy?" I asked.

"Yep. Logan fixed him." Riley set Zippy in my lap then took both my hands in his. "You made a commitment to the people of Inside and I'm proud of you."

I sensed he had more to say so I kept quiet.

He squeezed my hands as if suddenly nervous. Then he took a breath and said, "I'd like you to make a commitment to me as well. Will you be my mate?"

Before the Outsiders came, I would have been too scared to say yes. Good thing this was after. "Yes."

It was too awkward to kiss with Zippy in my lap, but Riley stopped me from moving him.

"Open Zippy," he said.

"He opens?"

Riley pointed to a button on the top. I pressed it and a panel opened. Tucked inside Zippy was Sheepy. With a cry of delight, I pulled the little stuffed sheep out. Tied around his neck was a pendant. It was the symbol for Inside—a square with a capital I in the middle, but on the opposite side was a sheep.

"Does it—"

"Yes. If you push on the sheep, it will send out a distress signal."

"I hope I won't have to use it."

"I'm sure Jacy will make certain that Emek and you are properly guarded, but, knowing you and considering you'll have to work with Captain James, I won't be surprised if you get into trouble."

"Jacy? Me and Emek? What are you talking about?"

"Sorry, I can't divulge election results until hour twenty-five." He smirked.

I considered. "Was I voted Admiral or Vice Admiral?"

"Does it matter?"

The Vice Admiral's position had a little less stress, but otherwise... "No."

"Good, because right now you should concentrate on fulfilling your promise to your mate."

I added the new pendant to my other one. "Are we official now?"

Riley put Zippy and Sheepy on the floor then pushed me back onto the bed as he lay beside me. "Yes. It's official.

And since I'm one of the good guys, I can have whatever I desire."

"And what do you desire?"

"To have my way with you."

And he did. Except I think I had my way with him. Either way we were together and that was all that mattered.

★ ★ ★ ★ ★

Acknowledgments

I CAN HARDLY BELIEVE THIS IS BOOK NUMBER EIGHT.
When I wrote my acknowledgments for my first book, *Poison Study*, I included every single person who helped me just in case that book might be my last. But due to a combination of a great editor, an excellent agent, loyal readers, my Book Commandos and the continuing support of my family, I'm on number eight.

Eight books that continue to appeal to my readers because of the efforts of Mary-Theresa Hussey, Elizabeth Mazer, Bob Mecoy, Kim J. Howe and the amazingly brilliant support staff at Harlequin. Eight books with gorgeous covers thanks to the incredible talent of the art department's artists, photographers and designers.

Eight books that are recognized by the public due to the hard work of the marketing and publicity departments.

Eight books my loyal Book Commandos continue to recommend to everyone they know and to strangers searching for a good book.

Eight books that would not have been written without the love, support and patience of my husband, Rodney, and my children, Luke and Jenna.

Thank you all!

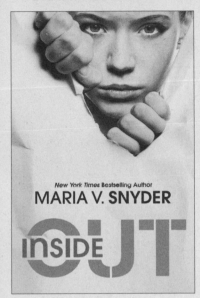
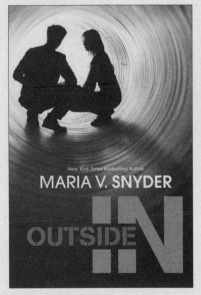

JULIE KAGAWA

THE IRON FEY

Book 1

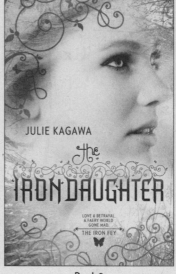

Book 2

www.EnterTheFaeryWorld.com

HTIRONFEY3BKTR.I